PUBLIC ANATOMY

A NOVEL

A. SCOTT PEARSON

Oceanview Publishing
LONGBOAT KEY, FLORIDA

ISBN: 978-1-60809-009-9

Published in the United States of America by Oceanview Publishing,
Longboat Key, Florida
www.oceanviewpub.com

2 4 6 8 10 9 7 5 3 1

PRINTED IN THE UNITED STATES OF AMERICA

PUBLIC ANATOMY

Also by A. Scott Pearson
Rupture

FOR ROBIN

PUBLIC ANATOMY

Title Page, First Edition, Vesalius, Andreas.
De Humani Corporis Fabrica Libri Septem.
Basel: Johannes Oporinus, 1543.

CHAPTER ONE

Minutes from completing another successful operation, Dr. Liza French made the final cut. In an operating room designed specifically for her, she'd performed the entire procedure without touching the patient, a distinct advantage, in her mind, for any gynecologist. Surgical gloves weren't needed because her hands did not touch a drop of blood. Never one to conform, Dr. French wasn't even wearing shoes. From the start, she had slipped off her sling-back, open-toed, two-inch heels and scooted them aside.

Barefoot in her own operating room, she knew the only way to improve on this procedure would be to perform it from the living room of her Victorian mansion, Rachmaninoff crashing in the background, an iced vanilla latte for the finale.

All in due time, she thought. *Just finish this case.*

Five yards of glistening tile floor separated her from her patient. She sat within a stainless steel console in a corner of the operating room and stared at a video screen. Delicate movements of her fingertips were transferred robotically to instruments that her chief resident had inserted an hour earlier through tiny incisions in the patient's lower abdomen. A single flicker of Dr. French's thumb generated precise movements on the screen, magnified exponentially. Robotic surgery—a computer-driven, three-dimensional, precision-controlled operation performed from a million-dollar console detached from the patient.

The console was comparable in many ways to a flight simulator for pilots with Dr. Liza French and her team on the final approach. The circulating nurse stationed herself in front of a computer documenting the time of procedure, title of the operation, and personnel involved. By this point, the patient's anesthesia was mostly controlled by autopilot and both the anesthesiologist and anesthetist were bored with watching the video screens and listening to the monotonous beep-beep-beep of the monitors.

Liza glanced at the operating table. Her scrub nurse stood with gloved hands folded and resting gently on the drape, a sure sign that things were going well. Just a few more bands of scar tissue and the patient's diseased uterus would be out. Everyone was relieved.

Liza's bare feet worked the foot pedals at the base of the robotic console. She liked the feel of her toes on the controls. Skin to metal. She had tried it in stocking feet—high heels definitely didn't work—but even nylon diminished the sensation of touch. *I don't like anything between me and what I want to feel.* She smiled devilishly, her face hidden deep in the high-priced instrument.

At the patient's side, chief resident Thomas Greenway was scrubbed, as was medical student Cate Canavan. Thomas was responsible for maintaining the exact position of the instruments that traversed the patient's abdomen. The student's job was to hold the steel camera instrument at the start of the operation while the robotic instruments were inserted through the patient's abdominal wall and then at the end of the procedure while the instruments were being removed. Cate had been instructed by Dr. French in how to hold the camera steady while it was not secured by the robotic arms. This had been accomplished, and a lens on the tip of the camera transmitted the image of the uterus to the screen.

With the two nurses and two-person anesthesia crew, seven medical personnel occupied Liza's operating room, a typical number for this type of operation. But this was no typical operating room.

Another nonmedical team milled about carrying shoulder-mounted cameras hooked to portable video screens. As video computer technotypes, the team was somewhat less accustomed to hospital scrubs and the need for a sterile environment. The Internet film company, SurgCast, had dispatched a dozen of its best personnel to film Dr. French and her surgical robot, an operation for which the week's premier viewing spot was reserved.

Surgical Webcasting. Log on to your computer and watch real operations live from the OR. Cardiac surgery, obesity surgery, even breast augmentation.

Bigger, better, faster.

The ultimate reality show.

Only part of the production centered on viewing an operation. Real-time communication through viewers' e-mails offered the hot marketing tool. Prospective patients could "call in" their questions, experience an exchange of information, and soon have an appointment with the surgeon on their computer screen for a visit preliminary to their own surgery. For what was basically an hour-long commercial, Gates Memorial Hospital was more than happy to contract with SurgCast.

The patient, of course, was unaware of all this at the moment. A fifty-three-year-old dental hygienist, she was so appreciative of having been selected from the three-month waiting list for robotic hysterectomy, she would have consented to almost anything. Asleep, flat on an operating table fifteen feet from her surgeon, she was completely covered by a surgical drape except for a two-foot-square patch of abdominal skin. Black, pencil-thin robotic arms, each covered with its own sterile drape and aimed at her abdomen, pierced her skin and reached deep into her pelvis to grasp her uterus.

Now, images of her dangling organ were broadcast live for anyone with an online computer connection to see. The doctors, the nurses, and certainly the patient were carefully selected for these online dramas. The operating team even had scripts to follow. But a film crew cannot control for unexpected scenes.

As chief of OB/GYN at Memphis's busiest hospital, Dr. French had performed over two hundred hysterectomies. Only the last twenty had been accomplished robotically. She was especially relieved that of all those twenty, this one was going the most smoothly. After one botched operation six months before, her Program of Robotic Surgery, the first of its kind in the Southeast, was on probation, the detail of every subsequent operation under harsh scrutiny.

The revenue from her program alone had helped lift the hospital's bottom line from the red to a healthy surplus. The administrators of

Gates Memorial Hospital were eager to get Dr. French's lucrative robotic program up and running again. Each operation after the one disaster had been a complete success. This operation, the first since the probation was lifted, had to be successful for her program to continue.

So far, so good.

Throughout the procedure, Liza narrated each step for SurgCast's audience. She described the robotic instrument, how it worked, and how robotic surgery was so much better for the patient than traditional surgery performed through a gaping incision. She described how this patient suffered from a diseased uterus, the bleeding and pain, and how much better she would feel after the operation.

During this final portion of the operation, Liza looked up from her console, curious to see if the video cameras still focused on her. Glad to see one camera seeking a full facial shot, she winked over her mask and gave a quick head shake so her silver loop earrings would jangle and flash. The camera panned down, lingering ever so briefly at her waistline, and continued to the floor. Liza glanced at the monitor to see her naked feet.

"This is an important part of the robotic controls," she said. "With the foot pedal, I can manipulate two instruments at once."

She had anticipated that the cameraman might want to show this portion of the apparatus, so she'd prepared for it with a pre-op pedicure from her favorite salon. Her toenails were painted a glossy brown with a little yellow smiley face on each nail. She checked the monitor and wiggled her toes, the little faces performing a wavy dance.

Dr. French's narration, along with her camera-friendly intraoperative flair, created a logjam of viewer e-mails. The company's advertising specialist estimated the number of communications-per-episode to be up by 50 percent, a veritable windfall for the company. At first, the film crew kept up with each question received at "command central," a techno-modified work bench with a computer in the corner of the operating room. From this vantage point the whole filming process was controlled, from camera angles to audio control to an open phone line connected to company headquarters, where external image transmission was continuously monitored.

Most of the questions came from interested patients.

Should I have a hysterectomy?

Does the robot procedure cost more?

How do I make an appointment?

After screening for appropriate content, chief resident Greenway read each e-mailed question aloud for all viewers to hear. For a moment, the film crew focused on him. At six foot three, his athletic build and tanned face were attractive features for the camera, even though mostly hidden by surgical garb. The resident answered the questions as best he could, with additional color commentary added by Liza French. Each unanswered e-mail was catalogued and archived for a later individual response.

The release of tension toward the procedure's completion let a bit of frivolity seep into the room, and the rigid e-mail screening process relaxed.

"We have time for one more e-mail," Greenway announced, and he read the last question verbatim.

"My wife wants to have this operation and I was wondering if it changes the way, you know, how we make love."

After a moment's hesitation, the resident finished the message.

"She was the one who told me to ask the doctors."

Except for a few muffled laughs, the room fell quiet, then gave way to audio-detectable snickering.

Poised and waiting for the next prompt, SurgCast's crew hoped to move forward from this entertaining but awkward moment.

Dr. French brought the focus back to the operation at hand.

"The final step before closure will be removal of the already detached uterus itself."

She directed the chief resident to clamp the dangling organ and remove it. Then she returned to the viewer's e-mailed concern.

"I appreciate your question. Your wife will be the same woman she was before. I hope that's what you want."

After that last comment, Greenway shot her a wide-eyed glare.

Liza shrugged, temporarily pulled down her mask, and mouthed back, "Well?"

To complete the operation, Greenway began to remove the robotic instruments from the patient's abdomen.

During the distraction, Cate, the medical student, began watching her mentors instead of the telescopic camera she was holding. She accidentally banged the resident's uterine clamp with her instrument.

Cate quickly readjusted the camera. The resident readjusted his clamp, their rapid movements brushing against the sterile drapes.

Liza twisted inside the console to see what was happening at the operating table. Her bare foot slipped off the pedal. When she looked back at her screen, a pulsating geyser of arterial blood covered the field.

"What the hell?"

The SurgCast crew kept filming. A precipitous decline of the monitor's tone indicated the patient's heart rate was plummeting.

The anesthesiologist, quiet the entire procedure, announced, "I'm losing her pressure up here."

Cate scrambled to reposition the camera, again. But the lens was submerged in a sea of blood.

With no visualization of the abdominal cavity, Liza stared, paralyzed, at red waves splashing her screen.

"She's bleeding out," Greenway yelled. "We have to open her."

Nurses scrambled to get blood for transfusion.

The last words the online viewers heard were Dr. French's. "Cut the damn cameras."

She dashed to the operating table and watched her resident grab the scalpel, cut a long skin incision, and turn an elective, highly publicized operation into a last-ditch effort to save the woman's life.

Throughout the nation and around the world, each viewer's computer screen faded from red to black.

CHAPTER TWO

"Dr. Branch?"

Silence.

"Dr. Eli Branch? Are you in here?"

Eli Branch squinted at a bright column of light filtering around a large figure in the doorway.

"You-hoooooo, Dr. Branch."

The call room was big enough for only a bed and a nightstand. The bed was a gurney he had rolled in from one of the exam rooms. He just hoped the sheets had been changed since the last patient. Before sneaking away from the nurse's desk for a few minutes of sleep, Branch had cranked the thermostat way down. In contrast to the sizzling one hundred degree temps that had plagued the River City for over a week, the sheets, dirty or not, were now icy cold.

The heat wave, combined with a sixty-year record drought, tested the civility of Memphis citizens, their dispositions often frazzled on the best of days. Adding more burn to the heat, the city's sanitation workers decided to strike, leaving heaps of festering garbage along the curb of every apartment complex, residential community, and restaurant across the city. Hot, dry, and putrid were not the top three descriptors that the Chamber of Commerce would have chosen to advertise the metropolitan center of the Mid-South. More than forty years ago, the city had witnessed the tragic climax of its first sanitation workers strike: an assassination on the balcony of the Lorraine Hotel that sent the nation into turmoil. At the moment, Eli wished to ignore all this, as well as the nurse at the door, but as sure as the rain would stay away, she would not.

"Don't think I can't see you under those covers."

She shifted in the doorway, and the slender column of light switched from one side of her to the other.

A digital clock on the nightstand read 2:34 a.m. Five hours to go in his twelve-hour shift. Branch was accustomed to waking up for surgical emergencies at Gates Memorial—gunshot wounds, a perforated bowel —but since his scalpel-induced hand injury just a few weeks ago, he had been forced to take ER call in this small community hospital in White-haven, just south of the downtown medical center. It provided his only income.

Middle of the night, he thought. *No telling what this could be.* Something serious like a myocardial infarction, or fleeting like gas pains. Or suicidal ideations, a middle-of-the-night death wish. He could only hope it was something surgical, like a deep, nasty laceration.

"Don't make me come tickle you out the bed."

This brought him bolt upright.

"Yes, I'm here," he told the nurse.

"Sorry to wake you, doc, but we've got a walk-in."

Eli was fully awake now. He flipped on the bedside lamp and checked his pager. No calls missed.

"I don't use pagers. Easier to come knock on your door."

"What is it?"

"Male, early sixties, says the top of his head is crawling."

Eli ran a hand through his hair. "What?" *Top of his head crawling?*

The nurse stepped back and let the door start to close. "I don't know, doc. Probably some nut case."

"Okay, be right there."

She left, and Eli rubbed his face and stood. A month ago he was the new hotshot recruit at the University of the Mid-South Medical Center. An academic surgeon poised to rise to the top. Now, he was the doctor of choice for nocturnal crazies that roamed south Memphis.

Branch pulled a white coat over his wrinkled scrubs and threaded his splinted hand through the sleeve. Squinting under bright fluorescent lights, he approached the examination area. Outside curtain three, the charge nurse handed him a clipboard. He read the name.

Norman Felts.

"Do we know him?"

"Norman? He's here at least once a week."

Eli scanned the sheet and found a list of psychiatric meds. "Once a week?"

"Yeah, but we don't call him Norman."

Playing her game, Eli asked. "What do we call him?"

"He's known to the staff here as Tobogganhead."

Eli gave her an odd look. "Toboggan? As in wool cap?"

"You'll see."

He brushed the curtain back to see Norman sitting on the gurney, legs dangling, a blue stocking cap pulled low over his ears. The day before, the temperature had topped out at one hundred and three degrees. Today's prediction was a Memphis cool front, dropping to ninety-nine. Eli couldn't imagine anyone wearing a wool toboggan.

Eli extended his hand. "I'm Dr. Branch."

"He is?" Norman looked at the nurse. "And handsome too." Rather than shake Eli's hand, Norman ran his fingers across Eli's palm, as though reading the lines.

"Just tell him what's wrong, Norman," the nurse said.

"I'm getting to that, Janice." He said her name loudly, then looked Eli up and down. "He's new, isn't he?"

"Yes, this is my first night here," Eli said, hoping to speed up the process. "Why don't you tell me—"

Norman interrupted. "What kind of doctor is he?"

Confused by Norman's odd questions in third person, Eli noticed that Janice was thoroughly amused. She leaned forward with both hands on the bed, a stethoscope dangling from her shoulders like a necklace framing full-chested blue scrubs.

"You're lucky, Norman. Dr. Branch is a surgeon."

Norman spoke directly to Eli. "A surgeon. Oh my. I need a surgeon, yes I do. You do specialize in surgery of the neuroconnective tissue, don't you?"

Janice covered a silent laugh with her hand.

Eli looked at his patient. It was middle of the night, the place was quiet, deserted practically, yet Norman was somewhat charming in an odd sort of way.

"Yes. In fact, I'm a neuroconnective specialist."

"Well goody," Norman said, "because it feels like the top of my head is crawling off."

"Let me take a look," Eli said, reaching to remove the wool cap with his right hand. He held his left close to his side in a splint.

Norman pulled back. "What's wrong with your hand?"

Eli raised his arm and examined the splint as though for the first time. The scar down his forearm peeked through the support, the flesh still red and angry. He'd wondered how patients would react to his injury. Now he knew. Eli decided there was no reason to hide the truth.

"I was on the wrong end of a knife fight." He noticed that the nurse perked up, listening intently.

"A knife fight? Like in a bar?"

"No, not exactly. In the operating room. A scalpel, actually."

Norman thought about this. "So that's why you're here, taking ER call," he said. "You can't operate anymore."

Eli nodded. "Severed most of the tendons." He raised his hand and watched a flicker movement of his fingertips. "With rehab, I'm getting a little back."

Norman grimaced. "I'm sorry, doc."

Eli squeezed Norman's knee, then reached to remove his cap. "Let's take care of you, shall we?"

But Norman pulled away again.

Eli looked to Janice for assistance.

"He's never let us take it off before," she said.

Norman confirmed this. "I never take my cap off in public."

Eli's first impulse was to say, *How the hell do you expect me to help you?* He hesitated, calculated his words. "You're going to have to trust me." Eli reached for Norman's toboggan.

The edge of the cap was stuck as though sealed to his forehead. When Eli broke the seal, a tiny white flake, like a piece of skin, fell out and stuck to the bed sheet. Janice stepped back.

But rather than stick there, the white flake began to move, then wiggled to a crawl along the linen's surface.

"It's a maggot!" Janice's voice held both clinical objectivity and a touch of horror.

Eli peeled the cap back and slung it to the corner, a shower of white larvae following in its wake.

A heaped up landscape of ulcerated skin and crevices covered the top of Norman's head and bored down to the bone of his skull, each pocket teaming with maggots.

"I need my cap back," Norman said, as though unaware of the brood living with him.

"We'll give it back to you," Eli said, "after we clean you up a bit."

Norman volunteered more information. "I haven't shampooed in a while."

"Yes," Eli confirmed. "I know."

Janice continued to stare at the man's head. She couldn't seem to turn away.

Eli had encountered maggots once before. He knew some compromised patients, the sick, the homeless, the demented, were prey to the insects, especially in the midst of a hot summer. As a medical student, ten years earlier, Eli had treated a diabetic patient a full month after she scalded her insensate foot in bath water. The wound had not healed and maggots had burrowed a crevice between her toes.

"Will you have to operate?" Norman asked, hopeful.

Eli considered the options. Hundreds of maggots had taken residence in Norman's scalp. Too many to remove, one by one. Most of them happily burrowed in little maggot caves. He would need to blast them out, somehow.

"Yes, we *will* need to operate." Eli inspected the man's head again. "Using a very special piece of equipment." He turned to his nurse. "Janice, in the staff bathroom, on the bottom shelf, I noticed a WaterPik machine. Could you get that for me?"

"What?" Janice did not move but she did avert her eyes from Norman's head. "You can't be serious."

"Yes," Eli said, confidently, as though he had requested a state-of-the-art surgical instrument.

A minute later, Janice returned. Her eyebrows drawn in skepticism, she showed him the WaterPik, the unit in one hand, the pencil-sized applicator in the other.

"I had forgotten we had this. Is this what you want?"

"Perfect," Eli said. He took the small machine and Janice plugged it into a wall socket.

Norman's sagging posture grew erect.

Eli gave a test spray into the sink. A single shot of water hit the stainless steel with a ping. He reached over and turned the pressure to high.

A slight grin developed on Eli's face—a kid with a new toy.

"You're sick," Janice whispered.

Norman heard her. "Nurse, leave my surgeon alone. He's trying to concentrate."

Janice rolled her eyes and watched a stronger stream of water splatter the sink.

"There," Eli said, pleased with his calibration.

Janice placed a surgical mask over her mouth and was applying protective eyewear, like a hygienist about to clean teeth. She offered a mask and eyewear to Eli, but he waved her off. After ten years of general surgical practice, he'd had much worse splatter in his face.

Like a good patient, Norman bowed his head to present the operative site. The first shot was dead aim at the base of the largest cavity. The whole maggot colony blasted away and scattered across the floor.

Next, he aimed the applicator at a group of superficial maggots that seemed almost too easy. He smiled at Janice with complete satisfaction and thought he heard her gag.

What kind of doctor had he become? From a rising academic surgeon to a small time ER doc shooting maggots with a WaterPik.

One patient at a time, Eli told himself. Besides, what else did he have to do? No other patients had come to the ER. Hours remained in his shift.

After several more rounds, the maggot refuse began to pile up. Problem was, the maggots weren't actually dead. After being momentarily stunned, they'd begun to wiggle and crawl and look for a new home to eat. Janice called the night-shift housekeeping crew, a single-man unit consisting of Benjamin, the longest-standing employee from the time the hospital was built in the mid-seventies.

Eli heard Benjamin's mop bucket banging the wall as he approached. This was followed by the stomp of a boot. After a moment's silence, Eli heard, "Damnation to hell. How'd these maggots get in here?"

Benjamin knocked open the door with his foot and stood holding his mop like a shotgun. "After thirty-four years, thought I'd seen everything. Now we got maggots crawling under the door." He looked at Eli, bent over Tobogganhead's scalp like a neurosurgeon teasing brain. "What will these new doctors think up next?" He began stomping the crawlies again.

For the next fifteen minutes, Eli kept blasting away at the open pocks in Norman's scalp while Janice tried to stay out of the fray. He knew that removing the maggots was only a start. The whole top of his scalp was most likely a cancer, a neglected carcinoma turned happy maggot home. The lesion went all the way down to the skull and would need radical excision, skin grafting, maybe even plastic surgery to swing a flap from the shoulder for coverage.

Norman "Tobbaganhead" Felts would be in the hospital for days, possibly weeks. And it didn't take a social worker to figure out that he was a flight risk. Eli suspected that Norman would be hard to convince that the top of his head was eaten up with cancer. Once the "crawling" went away, so would Norman.

Between Eli's WaterPik blasts and Benjamin's stomps and mutters, the only other sounds came from outside the room—car tires squealing, followed by a series of escalating shouts.

"Which room is he in?" one of the nurses yelled from the hallway.

Eli knew this couldn't be good.

"Dr. Branch, we need you out here. Now!"

Janice opened the door. "We're almost finished." They all wanted to complete the maggot procedure, no matter what the emergency.

A nurse stood in the doorway, eyes wide. "They just dropped him off. Blood's everywhere. He may already be dead."

Eli listened as he finished the procedure on Norman's head. Calmly, he told Norman, "I have to see another patient now, but I want you to stay right here until I get back."

Norman had reached up with one hand and was barely touching the raw surface of his scalp.

"Okay, Norman?"

"Sure, doc. Whatever you say."

Eli ripped off his gloves and dashed into the hallway. The ward clerk and medical technician were standing outside the trauma resuscitation room, wringing their hands.

If the squealing car was connected to this new patient, and Eli was sure it was, the injury was most likely penetrating, a gunshot wound or stabbing.

And life-threatening.

He stepped into the trauma room and saw a young white male lying lifeless on the gurney. His left arm had fallen off the side and hung at a right angle to his body. The nurse had his right arm extended on an arm board attempting to start an IV.

"He's got a thready pulse, shallow respirations," she said, then blew out a pent-up breath. "I can't get this damn IV started, his vessels are clamped down."

Eli had faced this situation many times. As a chief surgical resident at Vanderbilt University Medical Center, he had directed trauma resuscitations on countless patients—car and motorcycle crashes, knifing victims, gunshots. But at Vanderbilt, he had the luxury of a Level One Trauma Center with specially trained nurses, a blood bank, and the ability to operate in the emergency room.

It was obvious to Eli why the young man's veins weren't cooperating. He had a bullet hole in the dead center of his chest. Strands of a long, gold chain necklace entered the wound. Rhythmically, the chain would catch taut, then release, as if keeping time with his heart.

What had been the boy's white tank top was now dark red. With each shallow breath, a frothy plume of blood blew out of the hole. Given the location of the entrance wound, the bullet had likely hit the heart.

If the boy was to survive, Eli immediately knew what had to happen.

CHAPTER THREE

The algorithm was as easy as a child's nursery rhyme.

A-B-C-D-E-F.

Control the <u>A</u>irway. <u>B</u>reathe for the patient. Re-expand the <u>C</u>irculation. Assess for neurological <u>D</u>isability. Finally, cut away all the clothes and <u>E</u>xpose any other injuries. If you didn't make it to one of these steps, then came <u>F</u>—Fatality.

Earlier that evening, when he arrived for his shift, Eli had passed through the small trauma room to assess the equipment—rudimentary at best. The ward clerk reminded him that they had not used the trauma room in over a year. That his zealous Boy Scout preparation was unnecessary. He could still hear her instruction.

Look, doc, traumas go to the medical center. Ambulances don't stop here. They ain't that crazy.

She had not considered what was all too real now. The drive-by delivery. A gang member shot. His buddies running from the police, scared shitless.

Eli's next actions took all of ninety seconds. He tilted the patient's head back, inserted a laryngeal blade over his tongue, and jammed a #8 endotracheal tube past the boy's vocal cords. He saw brief condensation of exhaled air on the Silastic tubing, hooked an ambu bag to the tube, and with his strong hand, pumped five quick breaths, each blowing a bloody spray from the hole in the boy's chest.

He gave the bag to a medical technician student, the name Brian stamped on his badge, to continue squeezing breaths into the patient's lungs. Janice, who'd gladly followed Eli from the maggot room, was struggling with the peripheral IV. So Eli doused Betadine on the boy's left shoulder, inserted a large bore needle beneath his collar bone, and pulled dark blood from the subclavian vein. He could do this procedure mostly with his right hand, using his injured left to balance the instruments. He threaded a wire, then passed a long central line catheter over it. Through the catheter, Janice infused a bag of Ringer's lactate, a balanced salt solution to treat his profound shock.

Eli checked the monitor for vital signs. The boy's heart was beating at twice normal speed, trying to compensate for a hypotensive pressure of fifty. His pupils reacted to light so at least his head wasn't dead—yet. Using a pair of trauma shears, Eli cut away the boy's shirt to reveal a single entrance wound.

"Help me roll him."

In tandem, Eli and Janice rolled the boy on his side so Eli could examine his back. Just as he expected. The bullet had exited through what was now a gaping wound, taking a piece of shoulder blade with it. As they rolled him back, Eli marveled that the boy was still alive.

"All right everyone." Eli nearly had to shout to get the emergency room team's attention. "If there's any chance he'll survive, we have to get this boy to the trauma center. Call an ambulance and get the on-call trauma surgeon on the line."

While the clerk scrambled to make the call, Brian, the med tech student, asked, "What's this?"

Eli shouted, "Don't!" when he saw a bloody gold medallion hanging from the chain necklace the young student pulled from the wound.

Too late. Blood gushed from the hole in the chest and the boy's blood pressure dropped to zero. The boy had survived this long because the chunk of gold nugget had plugged the hole in his heart. Now the dam was open. He would be dead long before the ambulance arrived.

"I'm sorry," Brian said, horrified. "I didn't know."

"Run in as much fluid as you can," Eli yelled to Janice. He stuffed a wad of gauze into the boy's chest wound. Although unlikely to help, any degree of tamponade would be a good thing.

When Eli pulled his hand back to start chest compressions, the soaked wad shot out of the hole like a Kleenex tossed into Old Faithful.

"I need a scalpel, rib spreaders, and four 0 pledgeted nylon on a cardiac needle."

By the look on Janice's face, Eli might have just asked for a million dollars, cash.

"We don't have all that here. What're you planning to do?"

"I'm opening his chest. That's his only chance."

While Eli delivered compressions, Janice returned with a scalpel, the disposable kind with a plastic handle, one that might have been sufficient to lance a boil.

At least it was sharp.

Janice pointed at him. "You can't open his chest with your injured hand."

Eli ignored her and nodded to the ward clerk. "Here, do compressions."

Wide-eyed, the clerk stared at the patient.

"Me?"

"Just press down like I'm doing."

They switched places and Eli took the scalpel. The best exposure to the heart would be a median sternotomy, through the breastbone, but he would need a pneumatic bone saw to cut through the sternum. He chose the left chest and incised the skin deeply, just below and lateral to the nipple, following the natural curve of the ribcage all the way back to the gurney. He plunged the knife deep along the top of the fifth rib. Once in the lung cavity, he was greeted with several liters of blood.

Now he needed that rib spreader. He tried to insert his hands between the ribs but they wouldn't fit. "Damn," he said, searching the room for a substitute instrument.

Benjamin had parked his cart just outside the door. He was watching the procedure.

"Bring me that two-by-four."

The custodian had rigged a short vertical plank on his cart with a sideways hook at the top to keep his mop from falling over. Startled, Benjamin stepped forward.

"Your cart, the two-by-four sticking up. Bring it to me."

Benjamin did as Eli said. He dislodged the plank and shuffled into the room with it.

Eli took the piece of wood and inserted it sideways between the ribs. Then, in one quick motion, he twisted it at a right angle and wedged the ribs apart. There was a pop and grind as ribs cracked and costochondral junctions tore.

Eli jammed his right hand through the gaping ribs, all the way to mid-forearm, and grasped the boy's heart.

With no blood in the muscular pump, the heart felt deflated like a balloon. He needed light to see into the boy's chest. An overhead procedure lamp hung from tracks on the ceiling, and he tried to knock the beam into place with his injured hand. But the light fixture was frozen. Without illumination, Eli had to find the problem by feel. His finger happened to slip inside a large hole in the pericardial sac. The bullet had entered the right ventricle and ripped a hole through the muscle. Eli plugged the hole with his finger. He felt the fine tremors of fibrillating cardiac muscle. The electrical impulse was intact but there was no blood in the heart to pump.

"I need two twenty French Foley catheters. And start charging the defibrillator."

Janice peeled plastic off the urinary catheter tubes and handed one to Eli. He inserted the tube through the hole in the boy's heart and inflated the balloon at the catheter's tip with fifteen cc's of water. Then, Eli pulled the tube and balloon back against the hole, effectively sealing it. With his fingers, he located the exit hole in the back of the heart and did an identical maneuver with the second catheter.

Eli knew this was a long shot. An incredible long shot. At the best of trauma centers, fully manned and stocked and waiting for a victim like this with penetrating cardiac trauma, the majority of patients would die anyway—despite the all-out effort.

And here I am, with a piece of nonsterile wood wedged in this guy's chest and a couple of bladder catheters in his heart.

He had no idea why the boy had been shot. It was easy to think the reason was crime related. A drug deal gone bad, a robbery attempt. But

Eli didn't care, at least not right now. He had to believe that each patient was an opportunity to make a difference. This was the boy's only chance. Eli was giving it to him.

"Charge to two hundred," Eli yelled.

Janice presented the defib paddles to him. "You're going to shock the heart directly?"

He knew, of course, that the paddles were made to be applied externally on the chest. Direct cardiac defibrillation was accomplished only with special intraoperative paddles used in cardiac surgery. Eli positioned the paddles for insertion through the rib opening. "Got a better idea?"

Janice shook her head. "I think all this is crazy if you ask me. The boy's dead."

"Everybody stand back," Eli ordered. The med tech student continued to squeeze the bag, so traumatized by the situation that he was on autopilot, like a robot.

"Drop the bag and get back, I said." This time he shouted his order.

He did exactly what Eli asked, then ran from the room.

Eli placed the paddles on opposite sides of the boy's heart. If there was some sporadic electrical impulse still present, maybe the shock would synchronize the currents and initiate contraction.

With the first shock, the heart flopped up, convulsed once, then nothing.

Janice charged to three hundred. Eli repeated the shock, with the same result.

"Turn it up all the way," Eli said. "This is his last chance. Eli repositioned the paddles, pressed hard, and delivered the final shock.

The boy's heart bucked, and then bucked again.

The cardiac monitor recorded this activity. Beep. Beep-beep.

No one moved. Everyone expected the heart to stop again. But it didn't. The bucking turned into regular, rhythmic contractions.

"Well I'll be damned." Janice wagged her head.

"Call the ambulance and get the trauma center on the line," Eli ordered. "For real this time."

•   •   •

During all this resuscitation, another observer went unnoticed. Once the center of attention, he was now all but forgotten. Norman "Tobog-ganhead" Felts stood just within the doorway of the trauma room. Rather than watch the emergency thoracotomy, he was eyeing the boy's cell phone the nurse had removed from a blood-soaked pocket and placed on a side table. It was one of those fancy phones that could do all kinds of things—play songs, take a picture, probably order groceries for you.

But he didn't care about the phone. It was the wad of cash rolled under the clip that Tobogganhead was interested in. He eased over to the corner, and with two pincer-like fingers to avoid the not-yet-dried blood on the casing, he picked up the phone. Then he slipped out of the ER, past the nurse's desk, and out into the sultry night.

CHAPTER FOUR

At the same time that Eli Branch was inserting tubes in the boy's heart, a black sedan traveled south on Interstate 240 toward the community hospital in Whitehaven where Branch was on call. The driver had a tiny speaker clipped over his left ear, and his passenger dialed through frequencies of a police radio scanner. Both occupants were in their early fifties, wore dark suits, and had a recent shine on their black shoes. They were fit, kept in shape as part of their job, but in the sitting position, guts bulged over their belts a little more than they wanted. They did more traveling now, more talking about the days when they saw real action.

During the drive, they listened to various calls on the scanner: a warehouse fire in Southaven, a domestic dispute at the Majestic Gardens apartment complex. Nothing out of the ordinary, nothing too exciting.

They listened more out of habit—or maybe boredom. They didn't care for music. Talk radio was fairly dead that time of night unless you wanted to hear that the garbage strike was a racial issue with mounting implications for Memphis politics.

The suits were from Washington, D.C., and neither could care less about political tensions in the Mid-South. The healthcare scene was foremost on their minds. Or at least one recent episode of care that had ended in the death of a patient during robotic surgery.

Static on the scanner crackled, then a clear voice came through.

"He's got a blood pressure right now but I doubt it'll last. He's been down a long time."

"What are you doing to keep him alive? Over."

"I've got two Foley balloons inside his heart."

After a brief silence. "Excuse me? You've got what?"

"Just have cardiac surgery ready to go. This guy needs to go straight to the OR if we can get him there alive."

"Will do, Dr. Branch. Good luck."

The driver of the black sedan peeled off his ear piece. "Did she say Branch?"

"That's what I heard."

He checked his sideview mirror as though he might change lanes, or direction. "You think it's our Branch?"

"Balloons in a patient's heart? Has to be." The passenger shook his head. "Branch could pull off something like that."

"Yeah, like the fire he started in the OR a couple of months ago. Used the flames as a weapon to take down his adversary and then extinguished it like a grease fire in the kitchen."

The men had hoped to connect with Eli during middle-of-the-night dead time at the small ER. "Now, we'll have to intercept him at the medical center," the driver said as he pulled into the right lane. He took the nearest exit and started to double back toward downtown.

"What're they talking about, balloons in the heart?"

"Hell if I know. But that's why we need him on this investigation. He can pull off that kind of shit."

"Trouble seems to follow that guy, you think?"

The driver gained speed on a straight stretch of highway that ended with the first glimpse of lights from downtown Memphis. "Yeah, but he has no idea the trouble we're bringing."

Outside the trauma rooms of Mid-South Medical Center, chief surgical resident Susan Morris disconnected from the ambulance call and punched in the pager number of the on-call cardiac surgeon. She turned to her third-year trauma resident, who was eating donut holes like popcorn.

"Remember Dr. Branch?"

Donut Hole looked up from his bag of breakfast left over from the day before.

"The guy who got stabbed in the neck? Had his arm slit open in a fight with that biotech company?"

He said this while spewing plumes of powdered sugar with each hard consonant. "He was all over the news. Who doesn't remember him?"

"You won't believe what he's bringing in," said Dr. Morris.

"Oh shit, what?"

"He's doing an ER shift somewhere in the boondocks. Gets a drop-off GSW to the chest. Cracks him open. Sticks two Foley catheters in the heart."

"No way the guy's alive," he said, popping his last donut hole.

"Branch shocked his heart with external defibrillator pads."

"Damn, I didn't know that was possible."

"It's not supposed to be. But he says the guy has a pulse."

"How far out?"

"Whitehaven, below the 240 loop. Ten minutes."

Donut Hole stood, brushed the white dusting off his green scrubs. "I'm calling the interns and medical students. They've got to see this."

The black sedan caught up to the ambulance on Interstate 240. The agents had learned from the police scanner of the ambulance's route and followed it to the medical center. Knowing it would be a while before they could approach Dr. Branch, they parked, leaned against the sedan, and watched the ambulance back into the trauma bay. When the ambulance doors swung open and the stretcher rolled out, Eli Branch was sitting on top of it, straddling the patient, his arms and scrubs covered in blood. A rush of people pushed the stretcher and it disappeared inside Gates Memorial. The feds waited.

CHAPTER FIVE

"His pressure's starting to drop," Eli said as the back doors of the ambulance opened.

When he looked up, he saw a mass of medical personnel standing in the receiving area of Gates Memorial's Emergency Department, as though awaiting his arrival. He was glad to see the familiar face of Susan Morris among them.

"Hope you got an OR ready." Eli held up both catheters, the patient's lifelines. "I'm not sure how much longer this will hold him."

"Go straight up," Dr. Morris said. They pushed the stretcher inside the emergency room and Morris pointed to an open elevator at the far end of the room.

Eli noticed camera phones pointed his way. A young woman with a more professional appearing camera was clicking off flash shots.

As Eli rode past on the stretcher, a surgical resident sporting a thin mustache of powdered sugar explained to a group of interns and medical students how Dr. Branch had devised a way to keep the patient alive—despite a lethal cardiac injury. One of the female medical students grimaced at the blood that covered Branch's arms and legs and had sprayed about his face. "If the patient has hepatitis or AIDS," she said, "that doctor's hosed."

Like spectators at the eighteenth hole, the crowd closed in around the elevator as the cardiac surgery team maneuvered the stretcher with Eli still straddling the patient. The emergency department became quiet as the doors closed and the elevator ascended to the third floor operating rooms.

Ten minutes later, the cardiac surgeons took over the care of Eli's patient. After washing the dried blood off his arms and face at the scrub sink, Dr. Eli Branch entered the surgeons' lounge. He felt strange doing so, having been terminated from the medical center only two months earlier. Except for a resident lying face down on the couch, the lounge was empty. He relived the brief time as a new faculty member when he was greeted here by his fellow surgical colleagues as they congregated in the lounge between surgical cases.

Without rising from his stupor, the sleeping resident flopped sideways on the couch. Eli remembered how exhausted he'd felt during surgical residency at the end of a thirty-six-hour shift. In many ways, it was a good feeling—to be physically depleted after successfully accomplishing the task. Problem was, as a resident, the task came every third night. You were either pre-call, post-call, or on-call all the time. At times, after a particularly grueling shift, he had made it as far as his apartment and lain down for the night on the floor just inside his door. Once, he fell asleep in his car in the hospital garage, his forehead against the steering wheel for several hours until a security guard knocked on the window.

The adrenaline rush that comes with trying to save a life had now subsided, and Eli felt the familiar drag of exhaustion. He saw the piles of fresh scrubs in the linen rack. That's all he wanted, a nonbloodied pair. He planned to change from his scrubs and leave quietly down the back stairwell. He had done all he could do for the injured boy. The cardiac surgery team would take care of him, Eli told himself. But before he could grab a pair of scrubs, two men, dressed most inappropriately for the surgical suite in dark suits, entered the room and stood between him and the clean surgical attire. And they weren't moving.

"Dr. Branch, we need a moment with you."

The words brought Eli an instance of déjà vu. Maybe it was the time of night or the wake of a trauma resuscitation thrill ride. But when the man removed a leather wallet from inside his coat pocket and flipped it open to show Federal Bureau of Investigation, Eli's déjà vu turned to stark reality.

These were the same men who'd helped close the corporate biotechnology scandal, a weeklong nightmare that cost Eli his job, the use of his left hand, and possibly his surgical career.

"It's good to see you again, doctor. Looks like you're up to your elbows again."

At this comment, the larger of the two men snorted.

Eli failed to see the humor. "I thought we were done. The biotech investigation is over."

"Nothing is ever completely over, Dr. Branch. We informed you last time that we would call on your services again." The man looked at Eli's blood-covered scrubs. "This time, you practically came to us," he said. "Go change clothes, we'll buy you a cup of coffee."

What Eli wanted was a bed in a dark room of his apartment with the air conditioner on full blast. Not a cup of coffee. After his job demotion and the dramatic cut in his salary, he no longer lived in plush Harbor Town. His new apartment was a little farther south and not in the best part of town, but it would do for now. At least he still lived by the Mississippi River. He longed now for a view of the water from his tiny balcony. He would fry a couple of eggs, maybe a half pound of bacon, and then hit the sack.

Instead, he had two suits wanting to talk "investigation." All of this because he'd exposed one of the most pervasive biotech corruptions in medical history, which also took down several academic accomplices— one of whom happened to be his former boss and chairman of the Department of Surgery. Now, the feds wanted him on the inside, their inside, where it was crowded and wrapped in red tape.

The agents had indeed told him they would call again. Eli wasn't sure whether he believed them or chose to deny the possibility of further involvement. Since he'd last seen them, he had planned to make enough income to pay his rent, catch up on the monthly nursing home payments for his brother, Henry, and complete rehabilitation of his hand so he could hopefully operate again.

On good days, he believed he could regain full function and return to the OR. Maybe go into private practice, or even sneak back into academia. On bad days, which seemed to be ever more frequent, he thought his hand and his surgical career were shot forever. So much for his dream of becoming the star academic surgeon. Now, he was worried more about supporting his mentally challenged brother. What would happen if his sporadic emergency room shifts were not enough to pay Henry's nursing home rent and Henry was forced to leave the institution? He shuddered to think of the consequences.

Eli changed scrubs in the dressing room and returned to the lounge. The sleeping surgical resident was gone. The two feds sat on the couch. One wore a moustache that curled over his top lip and needed a trim. He strategically placed a cup of coffee into Eli's right hand—old black coffee from a carafe in the lounge. But at least it was hot.

"What do you know about robotic surgery?"

Eli took some of the coffee. More of a drink than a sip. "You came here in the middle of the night to ask me about robotic surgery?"

"Is it safe?" Moustache asked. "Should it be done?"

Eli knew this was leading somewhere. These weren't the type of guys to be curious for no reason. *Something must have happened*, Eli thought. *I haven't seen the news or read the paper. I just don't know about it yet.*

"Is the robot better than an actual human?" Moustache's partner asked.

Based on this question, Eli knew that the concept of robotic surgery was lost on them. At least he could clarify. "Robotic surgery is being used increasingly," he said. "It is very safe and effective and, in fact, easier on the patient."

Eli immediately felt as though he was defending the new, cutting-edge technique, although he'd never been involved in a robotic procedure himself. He decided to get more specific.

"Especially for prostate surgery. Are you having problems with yours?" Eli smiled, took another gulp.

They ignored his question.

"What about for . . . ." The agent stopped and checked his notes. "Hysterectomy?"

Eli thought a moment. He knew the uterus could be safely removed with that approach. "Sure."

"What's the advantage? Or is this just another marketing tool?"

"Think of robotic surgery," Eli said, "as very advanced laparoscopy. You know, small incisions, a camera inside the abdomen. The instruments are controlled through a computerized robotic system that allows for greatly enhanced precision. Manipulation of the tissue is state-of-the-art—and the surgeon doesn't even have to get his hands wet, if you know what I mean."

They didn't know what he meant. Hadn't a clue. That's why they'd come to Dr. Branch.

The large man leaned forward. "Enough of the introductory questions." He planted both elbows on his knees, fingers locked. "Yesterday, here in Memphis, one of these robotic uteroectomies was done. The uterus came out but the patient didn't. She died on the table."

"I'm sorry to hear that."

"Yeah, so was her family, I'm sure. She was only fifty-three. Had a husband, kids."

Eli put his cup down. "You came all the way from D.C. to tell me surgery can be dangerous?"

They chose to follow that line. "So you think this type of surgery is dangerous?"

Eli became defensive of his own profession, even though lately he felt like an outsider, skirting the fringes of medicine.

"All operations have risks, whether assisted by a robot or not. A death happens so rarely now that people forget about the possible complications. And when they do occur, no one seems to understand."

"What if I told you two deaths have occured? Same hospital, same operation, same surgeon?"

Eli wanted to steer the discussion elsewhere. These questions made him think about his own fallibility as a surgeon, a theme that increasingly haunted his thoughts.

Instead, he asked, "Same robot?"

They hesitated, which for them was tantamount to laughter.

Moustache said, "Funny you should ask that. We've already talked to the surgeon. Lady doctor, real nice."

The big man cleared his throat. "Yeah, very nice."

"Anyway, she says it wasn't her fault. Blames the death on the robot."

"The robot?" Eli asked.

"Says the machine started moving, doing things, beyond her control."

The big man winked at Eli. "Killer robot."

Eli did not respond. The "robotic" portion of the operation is always under the surgeon's control. To blame it on the instrument was most unusual. A shot at an easy way out of a career-threatening situation.

"Any comments about that?"

"I don't have enough details to comment," Eli said.

The two men made eye contact with each other and nodded simultaneously. "There's another little detail we haven't told you yet."

Eli waited as Moustache checked his notes.

"The name Liza French mean anything to you?"

Eli clenched his jaw.

"*Doctor* Liza French," the agent added, as though the prefix was needed to jog Eli's memory.

Eli knew she had recently taken a position at Gates Memorial. He had kept up with advances in her robotic surgery research, but had not seen her again in nearly ten years since they were interns together. He had tried not to think of her.

"You think there's some connection between us?"

"If you say so, doc. All we know is she personally asked us to notify you."

"Why me?"

"You know why."

Eli didn't want to hear this again. How just weeks ago he'd exposed the corrupt company, Regency Biotech International, while running from an ill-conceived police search that pinned him as the main murder suspect. What they didn't know was that he needed to take care of his institutionalized brother, work on rehabilitating his hand, and land a steady job as a surgeon in this town.

"Frankly, doc, you don't have much of a job anymore."

Maybe they did know.

"You can't operate—"

"Hey," Eli said, raising his left hand, a fresh scar down the length of his forearm. He pointed in the direction of the operating room where he had delivered the injured boy, "Did you see?"

"Okay, let's put it this way. You can't operate on people who actually consent to your operating on them." He cleared his throat. "You're work-ing shift-to-shift in an ER out in the, how you say it? Boondocks?"

Eli thought about the previous night's call. Waterpiking maggots seemed preferable to getting involved in this mess. Especially since his previous foray into the dark side of medicine had gotten him shot at, sliced open, and stabbed.

"We'll put you on a steady income, with benefits. And health insur-ance." Moustache gestured to Eli's hand. "Which it looks like you could use about now."

That got Eli's attention. He had been paying for his rehab out-of-pocket. But he remained silent, wondering what else they had to offer.

"We're being gentle here. We have ways of requiring you to assist us if you prefer we open that can of worms." The big man sneered, proud of using such a clever expression.

"All you've told me is there have been two deaths during surgery by the same surgeon. What am I supposed to do with that?"

"You seem to be able to figure out these tricky little situations." They got up to leave. "We'll be in touch."

CHAPTER SIX

Police detective Nate "The Lip" Lipsky got the call soon after he sat down for his first cup of coffee. He liked to sit at his desk a few minutes each morning and think about the previous day and the day ahead. A Memphis homicide investigator, he enjoyed this brief time of humaneness before his day became veritably inhumane. He needed his coffee this morning, craved it.

He chewed the first few sips, an act intended to activate his taste buds and scrape off the caffeine receptors. He'd come home late the night before after investigating a potential homicide that turned out to be a heat-related death behind a Dumpster on Poplar Avenue. He drank four beers, watched a *Taxi* rerun and an old episode of *Kojak*, and fell asleep in his recliner. Woke at two thirty and couldn't go back to sleep until thirty minutes before his alarm clock screeched, at which time, of course, he was sleeping like a baby.

His desk phone rang and he grabbed it, not wanting to suffer another shrill ring.

"It's too damn early."

"Good morning to you, Nate."

The only person who ever called him by his first name was Phil Doster, the officer who delivered assignments like a warm batch of glazed doughnuts. Lipsky didn't much like the name Phil or the fact that Doster's voice had never lowered, like he'd skipped puberty altogether.

"Got a homicide for you down on Second."

"You'll have to sell it better than that, Phil. Homicide these days means heat-fried brains."

"Workers found the body strung up in an old cotton warehouse."

Lipsky took a gulp of brew; the luxury of sipping was gone. "I could've tolerated your whiny ass much better if you'd called after this cup of coffee."

Like a schoolgirl, Phil said, "I'm sorry, Nate."

"Strung up?"

"Yeah, that's what they said."

"Who's they?"

"Couple of patrol officers. They're on the scene now."

Downtown Memphis was coming alive with steady but not yet congested traffic. Lipsky drove past the Front Street Deli. A couple at retirement age emerged with tall cups of coffee-to-go. The woman wore a camera around her neck. Tourists headed to Graceland, or Sun Studio, or maybe to catch the Peabody ducks, unaware that a few blocks away, a body was "strung up."

For a homicide detective in Memphis, there was always business somewhere, and lately business was booming. A bump in violent crime during the hottest part of the summer was to be expected, whether in Memphis or Boston or Wichita. But this heat wave had been extreme. Temps over 100 degrees for days in a row. And not that dry heat like out West. Yesterday hit a dripping 104.

Violence wasn't occurring in only the bad parts of town, either. A housewife in Central Gardens stabbed her neighbor with an ice pick because she wouldn't let her borrow a couple of eggs. Ice pick injuries were way up, a sign of the times. Homemakers were filling Tupperware bowls with water and freezing them for extra ice. Then they'd find some rusty old ice pick in the back of the drawer to bust up the bowl-sized blocks. Ice picks lying around are a dangerous thing, Lipsky thought. They're sharp and thin, and a mild-mannered housewife can drive one six inches to the hub.

All heat-related deaths had to be evaluated for potential homicide, a tricky endeavor since heatstroke left no external marks. Most likely, the guy found under the bridge or the old woman alone in her house was a heat death—but maybe they were popped on the head or poisoned or stabbed with an ice pick, leaving a wound no larger than a pimple.

Lipsky had driven this route so many times he no longer noticed the old warehouses that used to be the centerpiece of the world's cotton market. He passed an historic warehouse with the painted letters "F. G. Barton" fading into aged brick. As a child he'd watched barges float mountains of white bales down the river toward New Orleans and the Gulf. So much had changed since then. Cotton was traded electronically now, phantom bales floating the Internet, with the old warehouses a decaying reminder of the city's past.

Halfway down Cotton Row, two squad cars, each with strobing blue lights, were parked on the sidewalk in front of a slender brick building with a rusted-out garage door. Lipsky pulled to the curb and stepped from the car. As if from nowhere, a disheveled man in a tattered goose down vest and no shirt was all but in his face.

"There's deadness in there, I'm telling you. Deadness."

The man's breath reeked of decay.

"Get back," Lipsky ordered. "Unless you want me to lock you away."

The man took a step back, and Lipsky saw that he wore army fatigue pants and running shoes likely plundered from the garbage.

"I saw it. In the eyes."

The man stretched his arms to both sides and gazed trance-like toward the sky, as if he was a street preacher delivering an end-of-the-world message.

"The world is on fire."

Then he looked directly at Lipsky and started walking backward.

"It's here. The burn is finally come."

CHAPTER SEVEN

Lipsky felt his heart rate slow as the man walked away. He'd experienced abrupt street confrontations many times before and was surprised that this time he'd let his safety zone be breached. One of the police officers approached him.

"Sorry about that, detective. That old geezer's been hanging around trying to get a look."

Lipsky recognized the officer. "Didn't bother me, Riley. What you got?"

A large, metal door that opened from the bottom made up the front wall of the warehouse. They entered through a single door off to the side. Lipsky adjusted his eyes to the only light streaming in from two corner windows placed high on opposite walls. Floating dust reflected the two columns of light that converged mid-room on their subject, a suspended body, arms out to the side, head tilted back at an unnatural angle.

Officer Riley flipped on his flashlight and ran it across a large metal beam. From it, a turnbuckle held heavy chains and two taut leather straps that formed an inverted V and looped under the victim's arms. The body was suspended by an old cotton scale. An orange lever had come to rest at 175 pounds.

"Now that we know what he weighs," Lipsky said, "what else can you tell me?"

"No forced entry," Riley said. "No sign of a struggle."

"How long he's been here?"

"Couple of workers came in an hour ago. Said they hadn't been inside the warehouse in months but came in this morning to retrieve some stored equipment."

"What did they know?"

"Not a lot. Saw the body. Called nine-one-one from a cell phone."

"Got numbers for them in case we need to talk?"

"Of course. Both the cell and the company they work for."

The second officer, quiet until now, whispered to his partner, "And the fresh blood?"

Lipsky knew the guy was a rookie. After twenty-two years on the force, he could spot them day one.

"Speak up," Lipsky told him. "No secrets here."

"We don't know what to make of it," Riley said. He shined the flashlight on the floor beneath the corpse's hanging feet.

"Tell you what," Lipsky said, "I can't see shit in here." He turned around. "Does that big door open?"

After Riley released a metal latch along the floor, he and the new recruit strained to lift the rusty door and get it started rolling up and back into its frame. It made a terrible racket, screeching and bucking as though it hadn't been opened in decades.

For moral support, Lipsky pushed up with one hand. As the door gained momentum, its weight carried it the last few feet. Light flooded the room. The opening faced west toward the Mississippi, and traffic on Second Avenue seemed only a few feet away. The body hung in full view from the street.

"We thought about opening it but didn't want a bunch of rubbernecking."

Lipsky turned toward the body. "They'll get over it."

What had first appeared as an indistinct figure suspended in midair was now visible as a young male, mid-twenties, wearing a stylish short-sleeved shirt. A gold chain hugged the man's neck. By the way his head flopped back, his neck appeared broken. His right tennis shoe and sock were missing, the pants leg of his blue jeans ripped up to the knee.

"This is what we wanted you to see," the officer said and pointed with his flashlight to the victim's foot. Blood had dried between the toes and pooled on the concrete below. A footstool sat beside the blood. Lipsky imagined the killer using it to position the body, then cover his tracks. On top of the stool, as if on display, was a piece of bone. Lipsky squatted like a baseball catcher and studied it. The bone was oddly shaped, like a little boat, but cut in half, exposing the spongy marrow inside.

Lipsky turned his head toward the officers. "What the hell?"

"That's what we thought," the rookie said.

Lipsky studied the foot a little closer. A clean, horizontal slash had been made in the skin, leaving a small cavity inside the tissue where the bone had been extracted. Next to the bone lay a square piece of paper. Without picking it up, Lipsky could see that the paper was coarse, thicker than typing paper. Sketched on it was a small oval object cut into two pieces. A quick glance at the piece of bone revealed an exact likeness. Even Lipsky could tell that the rendering was of artistic quality.

Lipsky stood up. His back popped, his hamstring started to cramp, and he felt light-headed. Sleeping in a recliner after a few beers was not as kind to him as it used to be. He closed his eyes to find balance.

"You okay?" Riley asked.

Lipsky opened his eyes. "Damn heat's getting to me."

"Weather Channel says it's the worst heat wave to hit the Mid-South since they been keeping records," the rookie said.

Lipsky felt a twinge of nausea. "Thanks for telling me."

A car horn blew on Riverside Drive. Lipsky looked up to see cars at a standstill in both directions as drivers gawked at the body. On the river just beyond the traffic, two guys on the deck of a tugboat passed binoculars back and forth.

The rookie stepped into the street to start traffic flowing again. His complex arrangement of hand signals looked as if he was guiding aircraft into a hangar.

Riley peered at the bone. "What do you think?"

Lipsky shook his head. "Someone went to a lot of trouble to string this poor bastard up like that."

"And the foot?"

"Hell, if I know. A bone cut out and put on display for us? Even took the time to draw the damn thing."

"Like the perp's trying to tell us something."

Lipsky turned toward the street. Despite the rookie's efforts, the traffic was barely moving. A collection of boats had now gathered along the waterfront.

Lipsky circled behind the victim and noticed a lump in the man's back pocket. Riley handed him a pair of gloves. Lipsky manipulated the wallet out of the pocket and opened it. The gloves were too big for his stubby fingers and the extra folds of latex made it difficult to remove the driver's license. He read the victim's name. The date of birth indicated that he would have turned thirty in three months. His address was only three streets over from Lipsky's home in Midtown.

There were two credit cards, an old Blockbuster card, and a photograph of an attractive young couple lying in a pile of leaves. Lipsky slid the photo back in its slot and removed a business card.

BOARD OF CERTIFIED REGISTERED NURSE ANESTHETISTS (CRNA)

He flashed the card toward Riley. "This guy's a nurse anesthesia whatchamacallit. Probably works at the medical center." Lipsky studied the body again. "He's the one asleep now."

"We need to cover the entrance," Riley said. "The forensic investigation will take a while. By then, we'll have a mob out front."

With Riley's help, Lipsky pulled on the metal door from the outside. It slid down easily this time and banged into the concrete. Behind them, someone said, "The city's dying." The street person had returned, arms spread wide, and way too close.

Lipsky stepped back as both officers closed in on the man.

"We're all going to burn," the man said. "Then the rains will come and wash it all away."

CHAPTER EIGHT

Victorian Village is a small group of unoccupied museum-like mansions from the 1800s nestled between the rough side of Jefferson Street and the bad side of Washington Avenue. Interrupted wrought iron fences separate this shaded, otherworldly place from the aimless foot traffic milling about its borders at all hours. Complete with pre-Civil War accessories such as stables and slave quarters, most of the mansions have been turned into museums offering guided tours and gift shops. Gardens with picturesque fountains are popular locations for summer weddings. One of the houses supported a tower on the roof so that its original owner, a merchant, could watch his supply boats drifting in from the Mississippi River.

Although Eli had never entered the village grounds, he was familiar with the location of the Victorian-era mansions. For three years while attending the University of the Mid-South Medical School, he lived one street over in a medical fraternity house on Jefferson. The morning sun had begun to bake the pavement as Eli parked his car along the curb on Adams.

Eli admired the three-story Victorian mansion belonging to Dr. Liza French, the only privately owned mansion in Victorian Village in which the owner took residence. The house was unique within the village, its exterior resembling Italian Villa architecture with arched windows and a stone block stucco façade.

At five minutes past eight on a Tuesday morning, Eli assumed she would be home. The federal agents had assured him that Dr. French's medical office was closed and her hospital privileges suspended until further notice. He delivered three loud raps on a lion's head door knocker and waited.

A few seconds later, he saw the curtain of a floor-to-ceiling window part briefly and then close. A young woman opened the door. She wore a button-down white shirt and black leather skirt well above her knees, which showed off her striped see-through hose. She was barefoot. Her skin was an exotic deep caramel brown, a mixture of black, Creole, and—based on the way she snarled at him—witch.

"Did you knock on this door?"

Eli looked at her as though the answer was obvious.

"I know who you looking for, my dear." She stepped out from the threshold, cupped her wrist around Eli's arm and turned him back toward the street. "But it's much too early. Go home, or wherever it is you go, and come back later. Much later."

Out of courtesy or politeness or the firm cadence of her leather-skirted hip bumping against his, Eli let her escort him until they were halfway to his car. Then he stopped her.

"This is very important."

She smiled, bumped his leg with her knee. "It's always important," she said, as though an unexpected visit to this address was not the least bit unusual. "Believe me, I know."

She tugged his arm again toward his car. Eli heard a knock against one of the windows, and he turned to see Liza French standing behind upstairs glass. Dressed in workout clothes, she drank from bottled water, acknowledged Eli, and closed the drapes.

"Well now," the young woman said, as though impressed, "looks like the doctor wants to start early this morning."

CHAPTER NINE

The exotic young woman led him into a receiving room. Eli assumed the proper term was parlor, although his knowledge of Victorian style was scant, at best. Ornamental lamps sat on tiered tables, and the walls were stenciled by hand. The room looked as if it belonged to an old woman who hadn't touched anything in years.

"Would you like to sit on that fancy couch?"

"Sure," Eli said. He approached what she called a couch but what resembled two chairs turned opposite each other and glued side by side. He sat on one side, she on the other, so close that Eli heard leather peel from her hip.

The cushions were too firm and the curved wooden arm rest was hard as bone. Eli was more accustomed to U-shaped sectionals that accommodated a crowd on game days or could sleep four comfortably.

"You look older than most of the medical students."

She spoke a mixture of broken English and street slang. Eli guessed her speech was put on for effect. To his surprise, her dialect was working. Sexy as hell.

She tilted her head. "How come's that?"

"I finished medical school ten years ago."

"What is it you do then?"

Eli looked at the curved staircase, and wished Liza would descend. "I'm a surgeon."

Eli felt her hip quiver.

She put her hand on his knee. "Dr. French is moving up a notch."

Eli found it difficult to follow her conversation. She was obviously referring to a part of Liza's life of which he was unaware.

"Why did you think I was a medical student?"

"Oh, don't you know, she's very fond of them."

"Okay, Layla," a voice came from the staircase, "that's enough."

Layla quickly scooted away from Eli as Liza French descended the stairs in short bouncy jogs. She wore a tight, peach-colored top that stretched and clung to her upper body, the sleeves reaching to mid-forearm, her midriff exposed, tanned and toned. A similar fabric, but in black, sculpted her butt to mid-thigh.

"Could you get us some tea, please?"

Layla stood, said "Certainly," and stuck her tongue out as she left the room.

Liza stopped at the bottom of the stairs. She put both hands behind her and arched her back as though stretching for a morning run.

"They found you rather quickly."

"Hello to you too, Liza."

She smiled and released a breath. "Forgive me. I seem to have lost my manners over the last day or so."

"Manners?" Eli said, "We both know you never had any."

She ran her fingers along the banister. "How long has it been, Eli? Ten years?"

He wondered if those few minutes in the hospital linen closet, early one morning after a long, treacherous night on call, invaded her thoughts as often as they did his.

"Ten years? Something like that."

Her hair was casually arranged in short spiky curls. Eli remembered her as a redhead. Now she had silver highlights. The touch of gray gave her a mature, sophisticated look. Then he realized his eyes were loosely wandering down her workout clothes. Her top had Body Glove written across her chest. It certainly fit her like one.

Liza followed Eli's lead and glanced down at her clothes. "I'm going out for a quick run. It's the only way I can forget what's happened."

Eli held open his hands. "And here I come to remind you."

She hesitated as though reluctant to get him involved. "I want to talk to you, Eli."

"I seem to have acquired a habit of getting in the middle of things."

Liza smiled. Layla reappeared in the doorway carrying a fragile tray and tea cups.

"Tea?" Eli asked.

Liza directed his attention to the Victorian-laden antiquities around them. "Well, yeah."

"I'll take coffee, myself. If you have it."

"Only tea in this house, doctor." Layla placed the set on a low table. Little white frosted cookies surrounded two delicate china cups. Liza sat on a fancy footstool across from him.

Relieved that she didn't sit next to him in the awkward side-by-side chair, Eli was ready to discuss the robotic operation gone bad. Instead, he picked up his dainty cup as if making a toast. "When in Rome." He took a sip. It tasted like triple strength Lipton's. He dumped in a teaspoon of sugar, gestured to the room's interior design, and said, "What's all this?"

"You don't like my décor?" Liza asked.

"Not exactly my taste. But then again, I don't have any."

"The Victorian era is my passion. Always has been, since I was a girl."

Eli said nothing.

"You must have a passion, Eli. What is it? Golf, sports cars, women?" She didn't wait for him to answer.

"When the robotic program took off, I put everything I had into this old mansion. Two years it took to restore it."

"What happened, Liza?"

She placed her delicate cup back on its saucer and stared at it. "Everything was going beautifully. The robotic surgery program was back on track, patients were doing very well. They were all so happy with the outcome, Eli."

She obviously wanted to flaunt her success first.

"The incisions are so small. Patients have very little pain. I have patients booked out three months."

Her face lit up like a child's on Christmas morning.

"Did you know my program has more referrals than any in the Southeast? Second only to the program in Boston?"

"What went wrong?" Eli asked, trying to get her to focus.

"It's the damn machine, Eli. Has to be."

Her hand jerked, rattled the saucer, and tea spilled on the table.

"The operation was going so smoothly, just like all the others. We were ready to close. Then something went terribly wrong. It's like I had no control of the robot. No matter what I did, the trocars continued to move until they were ripping and tearing the tissue."

Liza made jabbing motions with fingers to emulate the doomed operation. Her face was red and tears pooled in the corners of her eyes.

"One of the instruments hit the aorta and blood was everywhere."

Liza was calm again.

She looked at Eli and said, "It wasn't me. You have to believe that."

CHAPTER TEN

Eli took a sip from the china cup. Even though he was not a tea drinker, it seemed as though Layla had added too much cream. He wondered what else she might have put into it.

"We haven't spoken in ten years, Liza. Why do you want me involved in this mess?"

"You make it sound so sinister, Eli. I know you've investigated problems like this before. I've seen you on the news."

"I was just in the wrong place at the right time. I have no investigative training. You need to hire a professional, starting with an attorney."

Liza closed her beautiful green eyes, then opened them only halfway, making them lazy, seductive, impossible to look at without feeling the sting. Eli had suffered this look before, and he did not want to see it now. Though some called it bedroom eyes, he knew Liza French never confined herself to one room.

"I'm in trouble, Eli. My privileges are suspended. They're threatening to permanently close my robotic program."

Her green eyes were now on fire.

"I need your help."

As hard as it was for Eli to admit, he and Liza had a lot in common. He had lost his hospital privileges, his whole research program. He watched Liza pick up her cup and stir in another lump of sugar. *At least you have use of both hands.*

"It's not like I'm a stranger, Eli. I thought you might remember. You know."

He didn't want to go there, not now.

"How exactly do you think I could help?"

She leaned closer to him, and in a half whisper said, "Convince them it wasn't my fault. It was device failure. Show them that the robotic instrument is responsible for this death. If you can prove that, then the blame will be off me and I can continue my work." Liza stood and caressed the rim of a lamp shade. "I may have to move. Completely start over, I don't know. But at least I'll have a chance."

Her gaze returned to him and Eli considered his options. Federal agents had approached him because of his experience with corruption in the biotech industry. Now a former colleague, acquaintance, whatever the hell she was, was asking him to clear her name.

Both of us want the same thing for ourselves.

And there was the promise of steady pay for this job. No more all-night ER shifts, which he had no interest in ever doing again.

Liza stood and handed him a business card. Renaissance Robotics was written in bold letters, with New York, New York printed under it. Below this was a local address for the company in Memphis. And in much smaller letters, in parentheses, a division of Regency Biotech International.

Liza pulled her foot behind her and toward her head in a ballerina sort of stretch now. She released her foot, turned sideways and leaned forward to touch her toes. She looked up, caught him staring, and said, "The company has a branch office here, you won't have to go very far."

Regency Biotech International. The parent company of Renaissance Robotics. Eli knew RBI well. After the biotech investigation that cost him his academic career, RBI was forced to close all its divisions. Except its robotics department. The one remaining focus of the company was Renaissance Robotics.

The visit by the federal agents made more sense to him now. Their investigation of RBI continued. Same song. Different verse.

"I can't just walk up and say, 'Hey, I'm here to find out why your robots have become so unruly.'"

Liza approached him, lightly traced the V-neck of his scrubs with her fingertip. "The Eli I used to know was pretty crafty. You'll think of something."

Then she turned away, held tight in black spandex.

"I might think of doing nothing at all." It sounded like an empty threat.

Liza stopped but did not turn around. "On the second Monday of each month, the Madison Hotel hosts a medical conference. Renaissance Robotics has taken this opportunity to hold workshops on robotic surgery there. It draws surgeons from across the Southeast and the nation."

Eli wondered where she was going with this. He waited for more information. Then he realized that tomorrow was the second Monday.

She turned where he could see her face, and other parts, in profile. "Maybe the workshop still has an opening."

CHAPTER ELEVEN

The Madison Hotel is a small, five-star luxury hotel on Madison Avenue in downtown Memphis. A former bank building, the sixteen-story structure built in 1905 was renovated nearly one hundred years later with European flair.

The bellman greeted Eli and held the door. The ornate lobby displayed a colorful décor with plush seating. Discreetly placed in the corner of the lobby, a marquee announced the meeting.

Renaissance Robotics presents:
A Workshop in Robotic Surgery
Continental Ballroom—Third Floor

Eli took the stairs. He purposely arrived late so that he could sneak in the back just as the conference started, hoping to get a last-minute registration. He figured the attire would be business casual, so he had thrown a tweed jacket over a white button-down shirt and slipped on a pair of loafers. Stylish but comfortable. In the reception area, he approached the registration desk attended by two young women, both in their mid- to late-twenties, tanned, all smiles, with perfect makeup and grey business suit skirts well above their knees. Handpicked by the company, Eli thought. They would know nothing about robotic surgery, nothing about biomedical device production, but would attract attention from anyone who walked by. Eli hoped to use this to his advantage.

"Good morning," they called in a near-synchronized greeting.

He stopped in front of the desk. One of the young women held a clipboard with names of the registrants while the other arranged preprinted name badges in plastic clip-on holders. A table piled high with pastries, fruit, and coffee sat to the left of the registration desk. On the opposite side, Renaissance Robotics displayed its brochures. Behind the smiling young women, through the closed conference room doors, Eli heard the crescendo of a musical passage as though a movie was starting.

They addressed him, in tandem. "Welcome, doctor. Your name please, doctor." You could tell they liked to say "doctor."

Without hesitation, Eli said, "Hunter. John Hunter."

He had never used an alias before. Never had the need for one. But his name had been all over the papers a few weeks before and the biotech company would not want him as a workshop participant, he felt sure. He wanted to remain anonymous as long possible. The fake name rolled out so effortlessly, even he was surprised by it. Then he realized that the name he had chosen was anything but anonymous. John Hunter was the influential surgeon in the mid-1800s who brought science into the surgical discipline.

Well, at least the name would be anonymous to them. He let the clipboard woman search her list of registered names. A little anxious, she crossed and recrossed her skirt-bound legs.

"Is there a problem?"

"Well," she said and glanced at her partner. Eli knew that most if not all of the workshop participants would have traveled from out of town and therefore were preregistered.

"We can't find your name and we don't have your registration fee of four hundred fifty dollars."

"Yeah," the other one said, "four hundred fifty."

"My assistant mailed in the registration and the fee several weeks ago."

The girls scrambled to the list again, flipping pages, searching their desk for lost paperwork.

"I'm sure you'll find it." Eli was already moving toward the conference hall.

"But you need a name tag, sir."

Eli winced at the "sir" and grabbed a name tag. "I'll fill it out," he said, holding it above his head as he disappeared into the meeting room.

Except for the PowerPoint presentation on a large central screen, the room was dark. Eli let his eyes adjust and took an open seat in the back row between two attendees riveted on the screen who did not acknowledge his presence. Seven rows of linen-covered tables filled each side of the room. Most of the seats were occupied. He guessed the room held between fifty and seventy-five people.

In the center of the room, the tables were pushed to the side, making room for a plastic drape suspended from poles, a rectangular indoor tent. It appeared to hide a large object beneath. Behind the lit podium, a man in a business suit and slicked-back gray hair advanced the next slide.

"I'm Michael Bass, CEO of Renaissance Robotics. You've been watching a brief presentation about our company. Now, I am pleased to tell of our contribution to the history of robotic surgery." The next slide was bulleted for emphasis.

- **The first in the Southeast to bring robotic technology into the operating room.**
- **A leader in robotic hysterectomy.**

Bass flipped through slides on the history of robotics. A bit on the theory behind robotic technology, aspects of robotics that made robotic surgery such a powerful innovation with its three-dimensional precision movements. Bass even made reference to a potential use of the technology in the military: robotic devices to disarm bombs, unmanned vehicles to rescue soldiers wounded in combat.

Eli noticed a conspicuous absence of any reference to RBI, the parent company of Renaissance Robotics. An intentional disguising, he suspected, due to RBI's recent negative publicity and its desire to establish Renaissance Robotics as a separate entity. Of course, there was no mention of the recent operative death, or the death six months ago, both during robotic hysterectomy, the pioneering procedure of the company. Eli wondered if any of the attendees knew about the failures yet.

A few minutes later the presentation ended and the lights came on. Full light revealed the space to be a ballroom, chairs of blue linen with gold accents and long draperies framing floor-to-ceiling windows. Bass moved down the stairs from the podium carrying a handheld microphone. The attendees sipped coffee and watched him stop next to the tent-covered structure.

"Now let's get to what you're all here for," he said. "Nathan, please unveil our instrument."

His assistant untied a single rope and the plastic covering dropped gently to the floor.

"This, ladies and gentlemen, is the new Veritas surgical robot complete with the very latest in robotic engineering."

The entire module was set up to simulate a real operating room. A mannequin lay supine on an operating table, four stainless steel trocars piercing its abdomen. Two large plasma video screens were positioned on each side of the table to receive transmission from the intraabdominal camera. The screens revealed the stationary trocars inside the abdominal cavity, beset with anatomically accurate organs—liver, gallbladder, and uterus. Fifteen feet from the mannequin sat the robotic console, resembling a space-age flight simulator, with screen, hand controls, and custom-fitting seat inside the cockpit.

"We have simulated an actual OR environment with cameras inside the dummy's abdomen. The robotic movements will be projected on high-definition screens."

Bass pointed these out for the audience.

"Many of you have seen the previous model of Veritas, and some of you may be utilizing it already in your own practices for robotic surgery. A show of hands for those of you who have used the Veritas."

Out of the entire room, three hands went up, then a reluctant fourth. *So most had come just to see what robotic surgery was all about. But they, unlike me,* Eli thought, *were here to see the advantages it could offer for their surgical practices, not to investigate what could go wrong.*

"I'll start with the basics," Bass said as his assistant exchanged his handheld microphone with a headset unit, allowing the company's CEO to more freely demonstrate the technology.

He then explained the efficiency of the self-contained robotic console and how it could translate coarse, unrefined, two-dimensional human movements into a fine, three-dimensional, symphonic choreography. Eli thought that the dance reference was a bit exaggerated.

In his seat, Eli sketched the arrangement on a pad of paper the hotel provided for each attendee. He drew the robotic console, and several feet away from it, the patient. He filled in the position of the scrub nurse next to the patient, and a medical student and a surgical resident hugging the table as in a traditional operation. Away from the table, he filled in the space for a circulating nurse. He counted six surgical personnel in the "operating room." Then he sketched in the seventh person, the surgeon, sitting at the robotic console. He imagined Liza French there, her back arched, intensely watching the movements on the screen.

Eli wondered how it had all gone down the day her patient died. Who first noticed a problem? Was there any warning at all? Maybe it was a deceptively quiet and calm operation, suddenly giving way to chaos.

"I don't know about you, but I think this robot surgery is a bunch of crap."

Startled, Eli looked up at the man beside him.

"I like to feel the tissue in my hands, know what I'm saying?" The man was squeezing his hands, open and closed, as if testing farm produce. Eli wondered what training program had allowed him to slip through and become a surgeon. As the man continued to rant about the ills of robotic surgery, Eli noticed that the workshop participants had moved out of their seats and were gathering around the robotic simulator. The CEO, Bass, had called everyone up for a "live" demonstration. Eli stood and took the long way around the conference tables, hoping to lose his chatty neighbor. The man tracked him anyway.

What followed next was a robotic dog and pony show. The assistant sat inside the console and maneuvered the hand controls. Tiny movements of his fingertips were translated to the intraabdominal trocars and materialized on the high-definition screens. Bass narrated the show while specifying the details with a laser pointer.

"Nathan is demonstrating the three hundred sixty-degree range of motion that's so easily attainable with the robotic controls. Those of you close to the console step up and observe the minute hand movements that translate into such fluid motion."

Eli stepped forward and watched the assistant, introduced as Nathan, work the controls. The young man watched a screen inside the console that showed a picture identical to that displayed on the audience's freestanding screens.

"How many of you perform cholecystectomy in your surgical practice?"

Not surprisingly, nearly every hand went up. Removal of the gallbladder was one of the most commonly performed operations.

"Wait until you see the ease of robotic cholecystectomy. You'll never want to go back."

Eli watched the president of Renaissance Robotics. He definitely knew his stuff—the technology, the instruments. But he was a little too smooth—a bit too much the used car salesman.

"With the robotic system, you can lock a trocar in place for retraction of the gallbladder fundus; another lock on the infundibulum, and you start the dissection. Without an assistant, if you like."

Nathan demonstrated these moves, then switched to another hand control. But as he did this, one of the trocars dislodged and ripped the gallbladder off the surface of the liver. Several of the attendees around Eli gawked at each other in surprise. Throats were cleared. If this had been a real patient, the bile duct would have been injured and the liver would be bleeding like hell.

For a moment, even the president of Renaissance Robotics was without words.

Eli's newfound buddy leaned closer to him, so close he could feel the guy's breath on his ear.

"Told you this robot surgery is a crock of shit."

The assistant, carried on as though nothing had happened. Because the cholecystectomy had been completed, albeit violently, they moved on to the next demonstration.

"Now let's switch gears and show you how easy it is to remove the spleen."

A few attendees snickered. Eli heard one say, "Yeah, right."

The splenectomy did in fact go very smoothly, and Eli was impressed with the advantage afforded by the robotic technology over traditional methods.

At the end of the demonstration, the attendees broke for lunch and filed out of the conference room. The company had reserved a large room at the Rendezvous Restaurant a few blocks away. Eli knew that many in the group would taste real Memphis barbecue and dry-rubbed ribs for the first time. He envied them, but he stayed behind to ask the company's CEO a few questions. But when Eli located him, Bass was walking out at the head of the group, the two young women from the registration desk at his side. Soon, Eli was alone in the room except for Nathan, who was wrapping an extension cord into a tight coil.

Eli approached him. "I enjoyed the demonstration."

"Yeah?" he said and continued to loop the cord over his hand and around his elbow. "Glad you liked it."

Eli noticed a tattoo of three slender animals, like rodents, on his bulging bicep. Nathan looked more like a roadie than employee of a biotech firm.

"I can certainly see the advantage of the robotic technology," Eli said, trying to warm up to him.

Nathan said nothing.

"I was wondering, is there ever a disconnect between the surgeon's movements and what the robot delivers?"

Nathan moved to one of the digital screens and began lowering it on its tripod base.

Eli tried again. "It seems that one misplaced trocar or one errant move could—"

The assistant turned to Eli and said calmly, "I just load the truck, okay. You'll need to ask my boss questions like that."

CHAPTER TWELVE

Liza stopped in the doorway of the executive conference room on the fifth floor of Gates Memorial Hospital. Three men sat watching her from the far side of a heavy oak conference table. Two of the men wore dark suits. She knew one of them. Robert Largo, chief of staff at the hospital. He addressed her first.

"Have a seat, Dr. French."

The third man wore a light tweed jacket over a button-down shirt. No tie. Liza recognized his signature look from the newspaper. Gordon Daffner, president of the University of the Mid-South.

Dr. Largo had called Liza to tell her of the meeting. They expected a swift lawsuit from the deceased patient's family and wanted to waste no time in getting the facts down. The chief of staff motioned to a chair opposite the three of them.

Liza had been in this conference room before to present her Program of Robotic Surgery to the board of trustees. She remembered being comforted by the rows of books in dark-paneled cases along the wall. This time as she took her seat she felt no comfort at all.

Largo began with brief introductions. "Dr. French, you know our president, Dr. Daffner."

Daffner rose, extended a hand across the table. "Doctor."

Liza started to say "president," then, "Dr. Daffner." In an awkward moment, she said nothing.

Largo cleared his throat. "This is attorney Mitchell Downing, head of legal affairs for the hospital."

Downing didn't get up. He nodded, then opened a legal pad as a signal he was ready to start transcribing.

Largo began the meeting. "The events of the past twenty-four hours have been most unfortunate, as you know. Not only did we suffer an intraoperative death, but—"

At this he stopped, as though he didn't yet accept what had happened.

President Daffner put his fingers to his lips in the shape of a triangle. The lawyer, pen poised to paper, stared at Liza, eagerly awaiting her reaction.

Largo continued. "The complication, at least the initial chaos, was broadcast on the Internet."

The chief of staff shook his head in obvious regret of the decision to contract with SurgCast. "We are receiving numerous calls from patients."

"Calls?" Liza asked.

"Yes, calls, Dr. French. Patients are canceling their appointments and their operations. And it goes beyond just the OB/GYN department."

Downing removed a newspaper from his briefcase, slid it across the table. It came to a stop in front of Liza. On the front page, in bold letters:

Second Operating Room Death at Gates Memorial Hospital

The subheading was even more damning:

Botched Procedure Broadcast Live on the Internet

Liza blew out a pent-up breath.

She knew this would be the end of her robotic surgery program. She couldn't yet fathom what this meant for her career, much less the reputation of the hospital.

Largo reached across the table for the paper. He handed it back to Downing and said, "We want to hear from you what happened in the operating room."

They waited for her answer.

It was hard for her to even think about the operation without seeing flashback images of uncontrolled hemorrhage, the ensuing chaos, her looking at the clock to pronounce the time of death. She knew these men represented the interests of the hospital and the university, but Liza did not feel as though she was among allies.

"The case was proceeding very well," she began. "A routine hysterectomy, really."

Downing cleared his throat, the first of many interruptions. "How many of these," he stopped and made double quotations with claw-like fingers, cases have you performed, Dr. French?"

She knew where he was going with this. He obviously wanted to invoke the incident from six months ago.

"Mr. Downing, I have completed over two hundred hysterectomies, if you must know."

French and Downing locked in a stare down.

"And how many with the robot?"

After a brief hesitation, "Twenty."

A grin appeared on the attorney's face as though entertained by his next question.

"Does that number include only the patients that lived?"

Largo put both hands firmly on the table. "That's enough. We're all aware of the death that occurred a few months ago. Fortunately, we moved past that without a scratch. Let's focus on this case, shall we?" He glanced at Downing. Then he said, "Please, Dr. French, continue."

"I had removed the uterus and was about to start closing. My assistants began removing the instruments from the patient's abdomen."

Liza stopped.

They waited.

"All of a sudden, there was blood everywhere."

"Blood, everywhere?" Downing repeated. "Can you be a bit more specific, Dr. French?"

"We had not yet removed the camera from the patient's abdomen. I saw a flash of blood. Then, the entire screen was red."

"Where were you at that moment?"

"I was in the OR, of course."

"What I meant was," Downing clarified, "where in the operating room?"

"I was at the robotic console, monitoring the procedure. What are you getting at?"

"Is monitoring the same thing as supervising?"

Irritated with his questions," Liza asked, "What?"

"Were you in control of the operation, Dr. French?"

"Yes, I was."

Downing hesitated a moment. "What else was going on in the room?"

"The nurses had begun to count the instruments, usual proceedings for the close of an operation."

Until now, the president of the University of the Mid-South had not spoken a word. "Were personnel from SurgCast still present?"

Liza immediately knew the focus of his concern. A hospital-related death was one thing. A worldwide Internet preview of the death, boasting the university's seal, was leagues above the concern of one individual or one family.

"Yes, sir," Liza answered, "they were filming the procedure."

President Daffner closed his eyes, pressed his fingers together so tightly beneath his chin that the skin turned white.

Downing struck again. "Why did you not supervise removing the trocars?"

"That is a routine part of the procedure. I allow the surgical resident to remove the instruments."

"Doesn't sound routine to me, Dr. French. Isn't this when the patient died?"

Liza had already answered this question before. Or thought she had.

"Describe to us how this could happen, please."

"I don't really know."

"You don't know? You're the attending surgeon. Your patient dies on the table, and you don't know what happened?"

Liza was hesitant to speculate. After the death, she had drilled Thomas Greenway, her chief resident, with these same questions. Cate, the medical student, was still too traumatized to give any detail.

"The autopsy should define the injury," Liza added.

Largo leaned forward. "Humor us, Liza. What do you *think* happened?"

"One of the trocars must have injured an artery. It hardly seems possible because the trocars were being withdrawn, not plunged deeper into the abdomen."

"What were you doing at the exact time the instruments were removed?" Largo asked.

Since Downing had already posed that same question, he gave Largo a what-the-hell kind of look.

But Liza gave a very different answer to Largo.

"I was answering an e-mail question from a prospective patient."

Largo leaned forward, looked as though he might throw up. "An e-mail?"

"Yes." By the looks on their faces, the men did not know that e-mailed questions were allowed during operations webcast by SurgCast. "We had time for one more question. I was answering it when the problem occurred."

Downing dropped his pen on the legal pad. "We might as well write the check. Pay them whatever they ask for."

They wanted him to explain.

He did.

"We can't defend this. Our surgeon is playing talk-show host while a trainee finishes the operation? And I mean finishes it."

He glanced at Largo, then the president. "Hope you have millions in malpractice reserve. That's what it's going to take."

Liza wasn't ready to concede. "I believe the surgical instrument contributed to the death."

"Excuse me?"

"This had to be a malfunction of the robotic equipment."

"Dr. French, I reviewed your statements after the first death, six months ago," Downing said. "You claimed device failure in that case as well."

"That's right and—"

Downing cut her off. "I have researched the company's records. They have had no other such claims. Their quality control is excellent. Spotless, actually."

This squeaky-clean talk made Liza nauseous. "I'd like to switch to different equipment for future robotic operations."

"Future operations? You don't get it, do you, Dr. French?"

Liza sensed they weren't telling her something. Something big. She had expected her robotic program to be in jeopardy. And suggesting an alternative plan was her only hope for saving it.

Largo delivered the news. "We're forced to withdraw support from your program, Liza. There's no way to continue the program given the negative press. Besides, we have larger issues to face."

Largo hesitated briefly, but just long enough for Downing to take over.

"We received a call yesterday. Criminal charges have been pressed against you and the hospital." Downing allowed a slight grin to cross his face. "Your little incident has attracted the attention of the FBI."

CHAPTER THIRTEEN

Fourth-year medical student Cate Canavan unlocked the deadbolt and entered the Poplar Avenue Free Clinic. Behind her, a line of patients ten deep waited to enter the same concrete structure that, for years, had supplied the same clientele with discount beer and tobacco. Some of those now gathered had slept there through the night, at the edge of the parking lot, asphalt still baking from the previous scorcher.

She saw a couple of familiar faces. Foster, the kind man who came to the clinic more out of habit than medical necessity. He'd never embraced the reality that the beer and tobacco store was no more. Beside Foster stood The Meatman, four of his left fingers chopped off at a slant from an improperly wielded meat cleaver. Most people called him Meat. Cate thought The Meatman sounded more proper.

It was twenty minutes after six o'clock in the morning. The clinic usually opened at eight. By then, the temperature would be soaring to near ninety degrees, and Cate's homeless patients were already hurting. She turned to face the line and saw others crossing the four-lane avenue toward the clinic. Cate watched Mary Macklin pushing her shopping cart across the pavement, mumbling to herself as usual. In her path stood Joey the Flicker, named for the cigarette lighter in his left hand that he nervously flick, flick, flicked. The tip of his left thumb was a seared leather rind. Mary banged the cart into his leg and Joey stepped aside.

To no one in particular, Cate called out, "Just give me a few minutes." Then she closed the door behind her. She felt the immediate rush of cool air. Even though the city had mandated that lights and air conditioners be turned off in unused buildings, she was glad she had left one of the window units on overnight. She knew the clinic would soon be full of bodies trying to escape the heat. She turned the unit on high.

A young man, mid-thirties, his hair long and dirty, stood at the window with vacant eyes fixated on her. She gave him an unconvincing smile and turned away.

Since the clinic had opened six months before, this morning marked the first time Cate was there alone. The free clinic was a project she and a handful of students had imagined their first year of medical school. It was their way of righting the injustices of health-care disparity among the uninsured poor. Now, three years later, after raising money to buy the building, gaining the support of a few medical school faculty members, and fighting a court-ordered injunction citing the building code, the Poplar Avenue Free Clinic opened. Finally, it was gaining a reputation as a compassionate emergency room alternative for care of the city's most indigent.

Through those three years, however, only a handful of other medical students had stayed the fight. Faculty attendance and supervision at the clinic were scarce and infrequent. Most of the burden fell to the few dedicated students and Cate took on more than her share. While her classmates were kicking ass on specialty rotations so they could get the best residency spots, Cate signed on for two months of indigent clinic rotation, time she feared would be highly suspect as "unfocused" to most top-notch residency review committees.

She peered through the dirt-speckled window. As a female, she felt frightened being alone while a mostly male group waited outside. But she knew that these were the people most in need of care and that she was the only one to provide it. She felt strangely comforted by the sight of Mary pushing her cart past the line, mumbling the select words that comprised her favored vocabulary.

Mary Macklin had become an unsolicited assistant in the clinic early on after proclaiming that she had been a "full-blown" nurse in a previous life. Every day, she pushed herself past those waiting, as if she had risen above them, even though she was just as needy as they, if not more so.

The clinic space occupied one large square room that led into a small break room, added on during the renovation, its pantry serving as a medical supply closet. Curtains hanging from the ceiling on sliding metal tracks provided the only privacy for a patient during an exam. A metal desk at the entrance marked the reception "triage." Since the heat wave began, all who came—after receiving a number specifying the order in which they would be seen—got to wait in the luxury of air-conditioning.

So far, the Poplar Avenue Free Clinic had been lucky and missed the rolling blackouts initiated across the city. Although the clinic lacked sophisticated equipment, surplus and slightly-out-of-date medical supplies had been donated from hospitals throughout Memphis. This outward act of benevolence definitely furthered the best interest of these hospitals if it succeeded in keeping just one more uninsured patient from adding to their already crowded emergency rooms. Cate's clinic had IV fluids, antibiotics, and samples of antihypertensive medicines from generous pharmaceutical companies. Even the fire department had pitched in, donating an early model defibrillator. Cate thanked God she had not had to use it—yet.

There were even a few pills of Viagra to hand out. Cate had sequestered this box in the back cabinet, consciously choosing not to take on erectile dysfunction as the clinic's main medical mission. She shuddered to think of the consequences of resurrected sexual function in this group.

Cate entered the break room to assess the dwindling supply of bottled water. She turned on the light and immediately noticed that a wicker basket had been placed on the table. A large plastic daisy projected over the handle with "Congratulations" stamped in the fluorescent yellow circle.

Cate smiled at the basket's wrapped goodies—two bags of Doritos, a Pay Day candy bar, a Butterfinger, and a giant frosted oatmeal cookie wrapped in cellophane. All the things *you* like to eat, she whispered, and laughed at her brother's choice of health food. She had given her brother a key when he volunteered to do minor carpentry inside the clinic, which he completed late one night after work. Cate knew the basket was his way of acknowledging the stress she was under lately. He didn't quite understand that she had been granted only an interview for a potential residency position in OB/GYN, not the position itself, even though the interview was for one of the premier programs in the country. She assumed he had dropped the basket off before dawn, coming through the back entrance so he could avoid "those people," as he called them. At least her brother was around and still cared. They had each other, the only family left.

Cate found a granola bar hidden at the bottom of the basket and she ate it quickly. She would hand out the rest of the food to the patients.

Her peaceful one-minute breakfast was interrupted by the cymbal-like crash of a grocery cart knocking against the front door. "Get your nasty ass hands away from me." Then, Cate heard an abrupt shift to the singsong voice of an angel, "Dr. Canavan, I'm here, open up."

Cate rushed from the break room to open the door. *Mary's off her meds again,* she thought. *This is going to be a wild day.*

As Mary banged her way into the clinic, she delivered her final greeting to those waiting, something about the ills of what she called Afro-Americana rap music.

Her faded orange sundress stopped above her knees, revealing a fetching pair of brown lace-up boots. Cate noticed her legs had not been shaved in months.

"They out there drinking that Colt 45 malt liquor is what they doing. Colt 45 malt liquor."

"It's okay, Mary. Let them be for a minute." Cate noticed that her cart was full. "What have you got there?"

"Umbrellas. Bunches of them."

"I see that."

Umbrellas of all sizes and colors filled the grocery cart. All were used and had bare metal spokes sticking out. Mary removed one, opened it, and twirled it over her head like Mary Poppins.

"Where did you get all these?"

Mary smiled and curtsied. "From the garbage. There's lots of garbage out now, you know?"

Cate nodded. "Yes, I know."

"Figured we could sell them to folks, keep the sun off their backs."

Cate tried not to laugh. "We won't sell the umbrellas, but I bet the patients will be most appreciative." She pointed at Mary's cart. "Pull it over here and we'll get started."

When Cate turned back, Mary was using the umbrella like a cane to prop herself up. She looked very serious and asked, "You see that prego out there?"

"Excuse me?"

Mary dropped the umbrella and held both hands way out in front of her belly. "Big old fat prego. Probably been drinking Colt 45 malt liquor."

Through the front window, Cate saw Mary's "prego." Halfway down the line, a teenage girl stood with both hands on her distended abdomen. She was much too thin to be carrying a child. A sleeveless cotton blouse stretched over her gravid abdomen. She wore no bra. Definitely not maternity clothes, Cate thought. *Probably no prenatal care either.*

One of the male patients circled the teen, gawking.

"Those whore daddies out there did it to her, Dr. C. Guarantee."

Cate tried to ignore Mary. "The pregnant girl needs to be the first patient in," Cate said. "I'll finish setting up, but I need you to go out and get her."

The cart-pushing, blaspheming clinic nurse continued to stare out the window.

"Mary," Cate said, loud enough to get her attention, "I need you to do that for me."

Mary started for the door, pushing her cart in front of her.

Cate grabbed the cart's handle. "I'll keep it here."

Reluctantly, Mary released the cart and walked outside.

Relieved that there would be a few moments before the patient came inside, Cate needed time to think. A pregnant *teenager* no less. From the looks of her, she was well into her third trimester, possibly term. And likely suffering from dehydration, or worse, heatstroke. Even though Cate was just months away from starting her OB residency, this was a far cry from the controlled environment of the prenatal clinic or the delivery room.

I'll need to start an IV and give her fluids, Cate thought. *Hopefully she's not having contractions. Or in active labor.*

Her mental planning did not last long before she heard shouts from outside.

"Let go of her, you pimp whore dog."

Cate ran to the front window. Mary had carried one of the umbrellas with her and was swinging at two men, who now cowered away from her.

"Can't you see she's impregnated with child?"

Cate knew she had to defuse the situation quickly. She had seen Mary on the wrong end of a fistfight before and it wasn't pretty. She opened the clinic door. "We're ready for the first appointment," she said. She pointed to the young girl. "You're right on time, sweetheart. Please come in."

Mary gave her a gentle slap on the bottom and the girl approached the clinic door.

"Hey, why does she get to go in first?"

"Yeah. My appointment was sooner than hers."

Cate held up both hands in surrender. "Everyone will have a turn, I promise."

There was some mumbling and cursing, but all returned to their places in line. Cate was young and only a student, but in this clinic she assumed an authoritative position and the patients responded. She knew they thought of her as their doctor.

Inside, Mary tried to lead the patient to a stretcher, but the girl collapsed in a chair by the door instead. Cate knelt beside her and pinched the girl's wrist to feel her pulse. She looked even younger close up. Sixteen. Maybe. Her pulse was rapid, her breathing shallow, eyes wild with fear.

"What's happening to me?"

Cate placed her hand on the girl's knee. Her skin was warm and dry. "You're dehydrated. I need to start an IV." As she said this, Cate glanced at the girl's arms. Needle tracks pocked the inside bend on both sides.

Mary noticed them too. "Colt 45 malt liquor and then some."

"My name is Cate. What's yours?"

"You're not going to turn me in, are you?"

"No," Cate said and then waited for her to answer.

"My name's Deanna."

"I won't turn you in, but you have to help us, Deanna. When's the last time you shot up."

She looked down at her right arm where a fresh track lay red and infected. "I don't know."

"Deanna, it's important. This could hurt your baby."

The girl pushed Cate's hand off her knee and stiffened up. "Baby? What baby?"

Cate took Deanna's hand and placed it on the most protuberant part of her abdomen. "Your baby."

The girl stood up abruptly, knocking Cate back. "Y'all go to hell, I ain't got no baby."

Mary stepped forward, but Cate stopped her before she opened her mouth.

From the sudden movement, Deanna was now light-headed and looked as if she might faint. She swayed back and forth like a tree in the wind.

"Sit your ass down," Mary said. She helped the girl by pushing on her shoulders. "That Colt 45 malt liquor done turned your baby into a snappin' turtle."

Deanna heard none of this. Her eyes had rolled back, fluttering.

"Mary, run to the break room and get me a cold washrag."

Mary shook her head and mumbled. "Turtle won't let go till lightning strikes." She made a song of it. "Turtle won't let—"

"Mary, *please!*"

Mary waddled toward the break room and Cate grabbed an eighteen-gauge needle and a bag of saline. Not only was Deanna's life in danger, but so was her baby's. Dehydration would induce premature contractions and ultimately labor. The last thing Cate needed was a premature drug baby showing its head at the free clinic.

With a closer look at Deanna's abdomen, Cate estimated seven months. Eight at the most. The baby could possibly survive, even now, with the help of a neonatal ICU, and if it were not too deformed from all the drugs.

Cate wrapped a tourniquet around Deanna's arm and swabbed it with an alcohol wipe. The needle tracks were a daunting sign. Her veins had likely been all used up. She slapped the back of Deanna's hand and a tiny but distended vein appeared. It was much too small for an eighteen-gauge needle so she chose a smaller twenty-two-gauge instead. All she needed was a bag of fluid hanging to keep her conscious on the way to the hospital.

Mary returned with a heavily soaked towel and slung it around Deanna's head like a turban.

Cate got a flash of blood on the first pass and threaded the IV. She connected the bag and watched the fluid flow in. Deanna's pulse was still rapid and weak. The way the girl sat, both legs flung apart, allowed Cate a quick and easy exam of her perineum. She raised the tattered hem of Deanna's dress just enough to see thin bloody fluid smeared between her legs. From outside the clinic, Cate heard whooping and hollering and someone clapped behind her. Three male patients stood at the window, watching.

Mary went on the attack. "Get y'alls nasty asses away from there."

Cate grabbed the basket her brother had left, went outside, and distributed the remaining food. While the patients were distracted by the snacks, Cate flipped open her cell phone and dialed the emergency room at Gates Memorial.

The ER clerk answered her call, a cacophony of beeps and chatter in the background.

"This is Cate Canavan. I need to transfer in a patient. She's a—"

"Hold, please."

Waiting for the chief resident on call to come to the phone, Cate reentered the clinic. Mary was holding the big frosted cookie to Deanna's lips, trying to get the unconscious girl to eat.

"Gates ER. Dr. Morris speaking."

"Hi, I'm a fourth-year student working at the free clinic."

The resident groaned. "This can't be good."

"Young girl, pregnant. Needle tracks all over. No prenatal care. She's really dehydrated. And blood-per-vagina."

Cate heard an audible sigh on the other end of the phone. "What a night. First, we had an open cardiac massage roll through the door, the doctor straddling the boy's chest with balloons in his heart. Now, you call, with only thirty minutes left on my shift."

"She's really sick, near unresponsive."

"How you getting her here?"

"She needs an ambulance. Can you send one?"

"I'll call one, but the paramedics had a busy night. They're back out on other calls. Might be a while."

Cate looked at Deanna. Her condition had worsened, each breath rapid and shallow. Even her black skin looked pale. If she had the baby here, it would likely not survive and the mother's life would be in jeopardy as well.

The chief resident added, "And someone will have to cover the cost, you know."

That did it.

"Forget the ambulance. I'll get her there myself."

"We'll be ready for her, but I need the name of a transferring physician. Preferably an OB/GYN."

Cate knew this problem would eventually surface. The clinic had attending physician backup only half the time. The only name she could think of was Liza French. Dr. French had allowed Cate to list her in the clinic's brochure although the gynecologist had never set foot in the clinic.

"Dr. French is the admitting physician."

Cate hoped the ER shift had not yet been informed of the operative death. She wanted to forget the dreadful operation and was glad to be distracted by this sick patient.

A few moments hesitation. "We were told Dr. French's privileges have been suspended."

"Only her operative privileges," Cate lied. "She can still admit to the hospital."

"Whatever, just get the girl here."

Mary helped Cate move the girl into the clinic's only wheelchair. They rolled her to Cate's car, a '99 Ford Explorer that her mother had bought her in college. They laid Deanna in the backseat and Mary jumped in beside her. Reluctantly, Cate allowed Mary to ride along. The trip to the hospital would take less than ten minutes. It would take longer than that to get Mary out of the vehicle.

Before speeding off toward Gates Memorial, Cate noticed that more patients had gathered outside the clinic. One of her classmates would arrive at eight o'clock, in less than an hour. Cate called out to the patients, promising them she would return.

CHAPTER FOURTEEN

Gates Memorial Hospital is a 554-bed, level one trauma center located in the heart of downtown Memphis. Gates provides tertiary care to a largely indigent population and brings the most complex procedures and operations to the city's most ill. Memphis's Knife and Gun Club contributes a steady annual supply of penetrating trauma cases to the hospital. These patients train residents and medical students across multiple disciplines of surgery and medicine at the University of the Mid-South Medical Center each year.

Although Gates Memorial is recognized for its trauma and critical care, the hospital boasts the most active OB department in the region, with over a thousand live births annually. Based on this volume, the medical school made financial commitments to support select innovative programs, the most noteworthy being Liza French's Program of Robotic Surgery.

Another program selected by the board of trustees was a research initiative called the Program of Molecular Oncology. The first recruit to this multimillion-dollar program had been Dr. Eli Branch, a young surgeon who'd just finished a near decade of surgical training and cancer research at Vanderbilt University.

That was six months ago.

Since then, Dr. Branch had become entangled with a corrupt biotech company, discovered that his own father had been involved in the illicit transactions, lost his research program after his lab assistant was murdered, and—most horrifying to a surgeon—had his left hand maimed in a knife fight.

Through all this, his life was endangered, yet he was heralded a hero by those in the medical center because he had exposed the biotech company. The national media caught the story and suddenly Eli Branch became prime time.

Everyone has fifteen minutes of fame, they say.

Then it's gone.

Way gone.

The media's exposure of the biotech company and its ties to Gates Memorial was a little too much for the hospital's administration. The discovery that his late father was coconspirator in the illegal operation had tarnished the once prominent name of Branch in the medical center. The day after the news broke, Eli had his Gates Memorial Hospital privileges revoked.

This was the reason for the casual, just-a-visitor attire that Eli wore to "visit" the patient he'd brought to Gates Memorial just thirty-six hours earlier—his hand around the boy's heart. Yet he knew hospital security would likely keep him from entering the hospital. Eli assumed that a memo, probably with the same photo used by the medical center newsletter that announced his recruitment, had been circulated to security and those with a need to know.

Eli opened the door of the North Research Building. He knew the custom was for the first person in the morning to leave it unlocked for the next. At Gates, as at most medical center complexes, all buildings were connected internally by bridges, hallways, and tunnels. An intruder had to know only which doors were left unlocked and unattended. Eli was willing to take the risk. A code of strict patient continuity and follow-up had been instilled in him since his early days as a medical student. He planned to find his patient, the young boy, and make his rounds, hospital privileges or not.

In the main corridor of the research building, he passed the door to the laboratory that he'd occupied for all of two weeks before his dismissal from the medical center. The door was locked. He peered through the small square window to see long, empty Formica-topped lab benches.

The research building connected to the hospital by a series of underground hallways used primarily by housekeeping and power plant operators. He entered a passage used to transport the hospital's newly dead toward the morgue—a separate building altogether, lest the dead and the living cross paths.

A few turns later, the bare concrete floor changed to carpet and Eli reached the radiology department, a signal he was in the main hospital. Three short flights up and he would be in the surgical ICU. He opened the door to the stairwell.

"May I help you, sir?"

A security guard stood behind him. The timing was bad, but to Eli's advantage the guard was young. Eli was betting on less than six months on the job.

"Yes. Can you tell me how to get to the intensive care unit? My brother's there," Eli lied. "His nurse just called me for visiting hours."

Confused, the guard checked his watch.

"He's on life support," Eli continued. "They said I could spend some time with him.

"Up the stairs to the third floor, take a left."

Inside the ICU, Eli located the boy's assigned name on the whiteboard. He remembered the randomly selected name as the nurse called it out on the way to the OR the previous night.

Stat Virgo.

Room six.

The staff chose astrological signs for their currently unidentified patients. Next would be automobile types (Stat Taurus) followed by colors (Stat Mauve) and then it would cycle back again to the cosmos.

Eli went straight to room six. If he walked through the ICU corridor with purpose, like he was supposed to be there, he knew the staff would be too busy to stop him. At least it had worked when he'd entered the emergency room thirty-six hours earlier. But at that time he rode in on a gurney, administering open cardiac massage to the patient he straddled. Hard to detain someone in that position.

Stat Virgo was indeed hooked to life support, tubes in every orifice and out both sides of his chest. All a good sign. Meant that the boy had survived the night. Eli reached under the sheets and found the boy's wrist. A radial artery catheter was secured to his skin. Eli gently squeezed his patient's hand.

"Good morning."

A doctor Eli didn't recognize stood behind him flipping through the patient's chart. "Cardiovascular Surgery" embroidered his long white coat in red letters. He put the chart down, approached the patient's bed opposite Eli, did a double-take.

"You're Branch, aren't you?"

Eli extended his hand.

The cardiac surgeon shook it, pointed to the patient, and said, "Don't know how the hell you did it, but you saved this boy's life."

"Lucky," Eli said. "But I'm glad he made it."

"He made it all right. That contraption you rigged, pretty clever. I've read about using a catheter balloon to plug a cardiac injury, but I've never seen it."

"It was long shot," Eli conceded.

In silence they stared at the boy, who was in a drug-induced coma, his chest rising rhythmically with each breath.

"One of my fellows plans to write this case up for the next big trauma meeting," the cardiac surgeon said. "We want you to be one of the authors."

Flattered, Eli was pulled back to the lure of academic surgery for a moment. Trips to research meetings, journal publications—all in the name of publicity for the surgery department and the hospital. But publicity was exactly the problem.

"Thanks," Eli said, "but don't bother. I no longer have an academic affiliation. Hell, I'm not even supposed to be in the hospital."

The patient's nurse entered the intensive care room. She nodded to the cardiac surgeon, glanced at Eli, and hung another bottle of IV fluid.

The surgeon asked, "Did our patient have any fever overnight?"

Eli took advantage of the distraction. He had accomplished what he came for. At a time of multiple, often disjointed specialties caring for the same patient, but with little primary care, it seemed natural, a necessity really, for at least one of these doctors to actually lay hands on the patient.

As Eli stepped from the room, the cardiac surgeon nodded to him. He planned to leave the hospital through the emergency room. Enough chaos there that no one would impede his exit. The emergency room staff secretly hoped everyone would leave. It was those trying to get in that attracted attention.

Entering the ER, Eli saw that current attention was directed to a young, pregnant girl being wheeled in on a stretcher. She appeared to be in active labor. Beside the girl, a young woman escorted the gurney. Eli recognized her as the medical student lauded in the newspapers for starting a free medical clinic. Located in Midtown, as Eli remembered. Primarily for the indigent.

A male OB resident intercepted them and took hold of the gurney. "We're taking her straight to Labor and Delivery," the resident announced.

The medical student kept a firm grip on the gurney.

The resident stopped pushing the stretcher. "We've got her, Cate. Thanks."

Cate let go and watched the gurney disappear into the elevator.

Eli knew exactly how she felt, having watched his own patient disappear into that elevator the day before.

Cate stood near the exit. Eli passed her. Then he stopped.

"Is the girl from your clinic?"

Cate stared at the elevator doors. She breathed fast as though just finishing a sprint. "I'm sorry. What?"

Eli introduced himself. "I read about your clinic in the paper. Are you doing high risk OB there, too?"

She smiled. "I'm Cate Canavan. And no, teen deliveries are a little much for us."

Eli turned to leave.

Cate stopped him.

"Dr. Branch, we really need a surgeon to be involved with the clinic—if you have any time."

Eli thought about it. The free clinic couldn't be any worse than working the ER. He turned, winked at Cate, and said, "Maybe I'll stop by."

CHAPTER FIFTEEN

The old wrestling arena was empty. Rows of folding chairs encircled the ring, which was elevated four feet off the concrete floor. A single bare bulb illuminated the mat, casting shadows off the ropes to the ghost audience.

The sight of the ring flooded Lipsky with the glory days of professional wrestling in Memphis. In the early seventies, there were two kings in Memphis—Elvis, of course, and Jerry "The King" Lawler, who was blazing a trail of destruction through every smoky warehouse, arena, and state fair in the Mid-South. And in his wake came Jerry Jarrett, Tojo Yamamoto, and the feared but fallen Masked Executioners. Lipksy smiled when he imagined Lawler in the ring, his arms wrapped around the tree trunk belly of Plowboy Frazier, who wore nothing but a pair of overalls.

There was no loud music, no pyrotechnics back then, just bare strength and a metal turnbuckle in each corner stained with scalp blood. The bell would ring, two wrestlers would bounce on the mat, and the ass whooping began.

Of course, every now and then, a metal chair came into play. Or a chain appeared, wrapped tight on a fist. And when things got serious—Lipsky took a deep breath and closed his eyes when he thought of this—they stepped inside for the steel cage match, a totally enclosed chain-linked chamber of mayhem with Ric Flair and Austin Idol climbing the walls like animals.

In those days, when he was off duty as a rookie police officer, Lipsky would buy tickets to at least one match every month. And when he couldn't attend, Lance Russell and Dave Brown brought the action live on Channel Thirteen. It was through Saturday morning television that Lipsky first introduced the sport to his four-year-old son. That was before his wife packed up the car in a rage and left town with the boy to go live with her mother in Oklahoma.

Lipsky stood by the ring and wrapped both hands around one of the ropes. The sheath of leather over the rope was old and dry and cracked, but it felt good pressed into the detective's palms. Lipsky tugged on the rope, gave it a quick shake, and watched the wave travel through all four sides. Putting all his weight on the rope, he flipped his left leg up and onto the mat. His foot made it but his shoe caught the edge and he lurched forward, logrolling across the mat's surface.

As if he were Jerry Lawler himself bounding from the locker room, Lipsky sprang to his feet and bounced along the edge of the ring, fists thrust high in the air as though he'd just annihilated the Masked Executioners.

Above the creak of rusty springs, Lipsky heard applause. A two-fingered whistle blended in with his wrestling fantasy. He stopped.

Off to the corner, light from an open corridor illuminated the silhouettes of his fans—two police officers enjoying the show.

One yelled, "Looking good, boss."

Lipsky waited for the final ripples in the mat to subside. He leaned on the ropes as the officers approached.

The more senior officer commented, "Always thought you looked like a wrestler."

The younger officer joined in, "Are you winning up there?"

"Yeah, yeah," Lipsky said. "Just help me down, will you."

They eased him under the ropes and he jumped to the floor, smacking flat-footed on concrete. Lipsky tucked his shirt back in and said, "Lead the way."

They left the small arena and walked through a concrete corridor decorated with posters of the giants in the history of professional wrestling. The corridor opened to a foyer with empty concession stands and a ticket window. Along the wall, a series of arrows and signs with "Smoking" in red capitals directed them outside. They were greeted with a breath of hot air laced with stale cigarette smoke. A smoking hut the size of a one-car garage had been constructed on the outdoor concrete patio. Motion-sensing sliding glass doors parted as they approached. Lipsky thought of all the smoke-filled wrestling matches he had attended as a child. How times changed. Now smokers had a separate house of their own equipped with a wheelchair-accessible door. Nice.

The room held two rows of picnic tables, four on each side. Metal pails filled with sand sat on top of each table. Ashtrays. In the back, a soft drink machine stood against the wall next to an automatic coffee dispenser that squirted stale cappuccino into a paper cup for ninety-five cents.

In the back next to these machines, a body hunched over a picnic table. She was seated on the bench, her upper half sprawled face down across the tabletop. Her arms stretched out in front, fingers lapping the far edge of the table as though reaching for something, or someone.

The lingering smell of tobacco smoke permeated the room. Lipsky moved closer. The victim wore jeans and a brown leather vest. She was of stocky build, arms full and muscular, fair skin with a cracked heart tattoo on her left bicep. A recent sunburn was fading somewhat in death. She was older than what Lipsky considered average for a wrestling fan. Could have been someone's grandmother.

"Who found her?" Lipsky directed his question to McCormick, the senior officer. Twenty years on the force afforded him an accurate detection of experience.

"Cleaning crew," McCormick said. Then he corrected himself. "I say crew. Really, just one old man here early to empty the ashtrays. Called nine-one-one when he saw the body."

"From a cell phone?"

"Yeah, think so."

Lipsky looked at the officer who hadn't said a word. "Them things come in handy, don't they?"

"Yes, sir."

The victim's face was hidden by a tangled mass of reddish-brown hair that fell forward, bathing in a pool of saliva and blood.

Lipsky leaned in close. "What do we know?"

"Turns out, the old man knew her. Said she's a big wrestling fan. Volunteers in the ticket office to promote the matches."

Lipsky removed a pair of latex gloves from his pocket and slipped them on. Gently, he raised the woman's head by pulling back on her hair. Her face was smashed with creases from the hard boards of the table. She appeared to be in her mid- to late fifties but the lines made it hard to tell. The saliva-blood pool had started to thicken and congeal, and a gelatinous bridge ran from her mouth to the table. There were no visible signs of trauma, except that her mouth gaped open. Her jaw was slack, too slack.

Lipsky let the head fall back into place and looked at the ash bucket on the table. It was in the same location as the others, center of the table, a couple of feet from the victim. Instead of showing the butt-end of cigarettes crammed into sand, a white handkerchief covered the metal bucket. Lipsky saw a thick paper card propped against the bucket, similar to the one found by the victim in the cotton warehouse. The card sat slightly askew as if the sides were uneven. The detailed drawing on it made Lipsky wonder what he was about to find. He looked at the younger officer, whose crew cut was so close Lipsky could see his scalp.

"We haven't touched it."

Lipsky reached for the corner of the handkerchief. His stomach drew tight up in his chest.

Beside old cigarette butts, an oval-shaped piece of meat lay on the sand. Smooth on the surface and rounded on one end, it was the size of a four-ounce steak. A jagged cut had severed the other end, and nubbins of tissue, like ligaments, splayed across the sand.

McCormick leaned over the table to get a better look. "What the—?"

"It's her tongue," Lipsky said. The drawing on the thick paper card depicted exactly what Lipsky saw in the bucket.

Crew cut pulled his head back quickly and let out a long grunt. "Her tongue?"

"Yeah." Lipsky pointed at the tissue attachments. "It's been cut way back at the base."

"What the hell's that about?" McCormick asked.

Lipsky said nothing. He thought about the warehouse victim. How a bone from the foot had been cut out and set apart, as if on display. Similar type case. Except this was a female, missing her tongue.

CHAPTER SIXTEEN

At five a.m., Thomas Greenway parked his Mazda on the side street beside Liza's house. Looking west, toward the river, he saw a blue-gray hint of dawn surfacing at the horizon. But among the houses of Victorian Village, night still dominated. Greenway did not ring the doorbell. He didn't knock. Nor did Layla let him in. The chief resident entered Liza's house with a key given to him by its owner. He climbed the stairs to the third-story office, not pausing at the bedroom of Layla, whom he assumed was fast asleep.

The door to Liza's office was cracked open, a faint light from inside. Liza sat at her desk wearing a fleece robe pulled close to her neck. Both hands were wrapped around a cup of coffee, as though it were midwinter and not the middle of a heat wave. She showed no surprise upon seeing him.

"What did you tell them?"

He stepped inside the room and closed the door. "I told them you were a hot piece of ass."

Liza sipped her coffee. "They already knew that. What else?"

"That you liked it when I—"

"Shut up and just tell me."

He sat in a chair in front of her desk. She, the attending surgeon. Him, the resident reporting for duty. He leaned over the desk, arms folded across a thick slab of dark oak.

"I told them the death occurred because of an equipment malfunction. Device failure. 'The robot,'" he put that term in quotation marks, "did not respond to your input, doctor. Isn't that what you told me to say?"

"And their response?"

He shrugged. "They're a bunch of damn lawyers. They just wrote in their yellow notebooks. What did you expect them to say?"

"Do you think they bought it?"

He leaned back in the seat. "Yeah, I think they did."

This seemed to please her. Liza stood. She walked to the front of her desk and sat sideways with one foot on the floor, one foot dangling. Her robe parted up to her hip. "Did you tell them what else I liked?"

His eyes followed the curve of her thigh until it was obvious the robe was all she had on. She twisted, raised her foot off the floor until it rested in his lap. Using the tips of his thumbs, he kneaded the ball of her foot, slow circular motions that made her writhe.

Liza pressed the tips of her fingers into her lower abdomen and straightened her back, took a few shallow breaths through pursed lips.

"What's wrong?" he asked.

Liza relaxed her shoulders and exhaled. "I've had a few sharp pains."

"You should have it checked out."

"I did," she said. "I had Brenner do an ultrasound in the clinic." She rubbed a spot at her waistline and smiled. "Everybody's fine."

Liza continued to smile at him.

"What?"

"You're worried about us."

"Look, Liza. I'm glad for you. I really am. But for me, it was a business transaction. Nothing more. You wanted this. I agreed to help."

"To help? I think you did more than help."

"I don't want to be involved. That was the agreement."

Liza rolled her eyes. "So technical. Agreements. Transactions." She ran her foot down the side of his leg. "To use *your* terminology, our little merger was not only successful—but fantastic as well."

Greenway gently replaced her foot on the floor and stood. "I have to see your patients on rounds, remember?"

She put her foot back on his knee. "They'll wait for you."

He pushed her leg off. "No, they won't."

Before leaving through the office door, he motioned to the robotic console. "I'm sure he will keep you company."

CHAPTER SEVENTEEN

Blues City Café sits near the corner of Second and Beale in downtown Memphis. Known for its rustic interior, cold beer, and barbecue to die for, Blues City is a favorite of locals and tourists alike.

Liza French sat in a corner booth. She had not yet removed a pair of dark sunglasses. Eli slid into the booth seat across from her.

"Doctor."

Eli greeted her the same way.

"So, is robotic surgery the next big thing?" Liza asked.

Eli took in the room. A little early yet for the lunch crowd. Only two other tables were occupied. The foot traffic on Beale was picking up. A couple peered through the front door, indecisive about their lunch destination.

"It's another excuse for surgeons to keep their hands out of the abdomen." Eli smiled. "Just my opinion."

"Your hands are better than a million-dollar robot?"

Eli uncurled his fists, palms up. Two fingers on his left hand did not follow the others and remained bent like a claw. "They *used* to be pretty damn good."

Liza slid her hands under Eli's and closed them like a book. "I remember those hands very well," she said, kicking him beneath the table.

Eli wasn't ready to revisit that part of their past. He pulled his hands away.

A waitress came to their table. Eli ordered a pulled pork barbecue sandwich. Liza a glass of unsweetened iced tea.

"What do you know about the CEO Bass and his company of robots?"

"He believes in his company, I know that," she said.

"You trust him?"

Liza pulled her shades down. "I don't trust anyone anymore."

"But he supports your robotic surgery program?"

"He did. There is no program of robotic surgery anymore." Liza leaned a little closer, lowered her voice. "I had to meet with the chief of staff, the hospital attorney, and the president of the university."

"Tall company you keep."

"It was a party, let me tell you."

"They're pulling your program, I take it?"

"I thought that was the worst that could happen."

"What do you mean?"

"There's a criminal investigation."

Eli knew this already. He had spoken personally with the federal agents. And after what he had seen at the company's workshop, he agreed an investigation was necessary.

"They're cracking down on biomedical device companies," Eli told her. "Regulation has been much too loose."

Liza raised her voice. "I'm not talking about the damn company, Eli." She changed to a softer tone. "The criminal charges are against me."

The waitress served Eli's sandwich and Liza's tea. The barbeque was piled high on the sandwich. She took a drink. Eli's mouth watered. But it didn't seem the appropriate time for a mouthful. He wondered whether Liza expected him to help her in a criminal investigation. The only assistance he could offer was what he knew about the company. And what might have happened in the operating room.

"Do you still think the cause was device failure?"

"Yes, it had to be. We were practically finished with the operation. An aberrant signal must have activated the robotic arm and caused the vascular injury." Liza picked up her tea, then set the glass down without drinking. "Don't you believe me?"

Eli answered indirectly. "There was an interesting occurrence during the robotic conference."

"Occurrence?"

"During the simulation, one of the trocars slipped. Tore the gallbladder. If that had occurred in a real patient, it would have been disastrous."

Liza nodded, replying only when Eli finished the description. "That's exactly what happened in the operation, Eli. Exactly. What did Bass do?"

"He blew it off, moved on to the next simulation."

"There must be a defect in their robotic system. A fatal defect. They won't let me near the equipment or the company any longer. You have to help me prove they're at fault."

"And how would I do that?"

Liza was quick with an answer. "The company keeps a log of the robotic functions."

"A log?"

"The computer records each robotic movement. They use the data for training and quality control."

Eli understood. "Fewer and more precise movements," he said, "increase the efficiency of the operation."

"Exactly. I review the records on all my operations. The company wants to record the data routinely, on all operations using their robotic instruments."

"So," Eli said, "let's assume the data were recorded during the operation."

"Then there's a record of every movement I made," she said.

"And?"

"The complication occurred after I stopped using the robot. If there were additional movements recorded, then the device was at fault, not me."

"But the robot doesn't move on its own, Liza. Human initiation is always required."

"Is it?"

"Unless you're in the movies."

Liza smirked. "Funny, Mr. Spielberg. But consider this." Liza wiggled her butt and scooted closer to the table. "The robot is run by computer, right."

"Yeah?"

"What happens if a virus infects the computer?"

"The system goes haywire."

"Exactly. If that happens on your home or office computer, you might lose some files. No big deal. But what if a virus infects the computer that happens to run your surgical robot?"

Eli imagined the destructive chaos that might erupt. But he wasn't ready to buy into Liza's theory just yet.

"What if there is a record?" Eli said, using finger quotations for emphasis. "You think they're going to hand that over with a little bow on top?"

Liza shook her head. "Not to me, they won't." She winked at him and then said, "I'm sorry I let your sandwich get cold."

Eli assumed their discussion was over. He looked down at his plate.

"There's something else I want you to know."

Eli didn't like the personal tone of her words.

With her fingers, Liza brushed her hair behind her ears, as if preparing herself. "After our internship, I took a year off. Remember?"

"Sure, I remember."

"Did you ever wonder why?"

Eli looked across the room at no one in particular. "The intern year was hell on all of us."

"It was more than that."

"Liza, I don't—"

She grabbed his hand. "Yes, I need to tell you." She eased back into the booth seat. "I was pregnant."

Eli stared at her. "You had a child after our internship?"

"No. I lost the baby, first trimester."

Eli didn't know what to say. "Why are you telling me this?"

Liza kept her focus on Eli and waited.

"No," Eli said. "There's no way."

"The baby was yours, Eli."

"We were together one time, Liza."

She flashed her bedroom eyes. "Once was enough."

"Why didn't you tell me then?"

"I was going to, but I didn't want to ruin your life, too."

"So you decided to do that now?"

"That was the only time I've been able to get pregnant, Eli. I know people think I'm a cold, hard bitch, but all I really want is another chance to have a baby."

Eli stood. He looked down at the uneaten pile of barbeque. All of a sudden, he was no longer hungry.

"I'm sorry, Eli, but I've wanted to tell you for a long time."

He placed a twenty dollar bill on the table. "I've got to go."

CHAPTER EIGHTEEN

Outside the restaurant, in the blaring midday sun, Eli squinted to see the number on his cell phone. The number looked vaguely familiar. The kind you hope is just an old friend you haven't spoken to in a while. The kind you answer hesitantly, then realize answering is a mistake.

"Dr. Branch? This is Detective Lipsky, Memphis Police Department."

Eli said nothing. The last time he had seen or heard from Nate Lipsky, Eli was in intensive care with a fresh wound on his neck and a left hand he could barely feel. He had all but forgotten about the detective. Until now.

"How are you, my friend?"

"I'm making it."

"Good," Lipsky said. "That's good. Look, I need some medical advice."

Eli relaxed a little. Medical advice usually meant one of a few possibilities: seeking antibiotics that won't help a lingering viral respiratory illness, an "ask your doctor" question about some new drug advertised on TV, or something legitimate, like a sick relative needing a referral. Eli could handle anything but police procedural crap. He prepared to take care of this quickly and send the detective on his way.

"What?" Eli asked. "You catch the drip from a lady friend?"

"No," Lipsky snickered. "I haven't been that lucky."

More silence.

"I need you to look at some pictures for me."

"Pictures?"

"A couple of homicides got me stumped."

There was that word again, Eli thought. Homicide. Why do I keep getting pulled into murder investigations?

"I'm a surgeon, remember? We prefer to keep people alive. Homicide is your business."

"Thanks for clearing that up for me."

Eli tried to wait him out but it didn't work. "And you need a surgeon to look at these pictures because?"

"I think you could help," Lipsky said. "Someone's been operating without a license."

Lipsky was already seated at a booth in CK's coffee shop when Eli arrived. To hide his disability, Eli kept his hand hidden at his side as he walked in. He stopped near the cashier and located the detective. Lipsky extended his hand, and Eli returned a strong grip with his right.

"Have a seat," Lipsky said.

Eli slid into the booth just as their waitress appeared.

"What can I get you fellas?"

She was large and out of breath, sweat gathered in creases on her forehead.

"Cup of coffee," Lipsky said. "Black."

She turned to Eli.

"Coldest Coke you got, please."

The waitress left and Eli noticed that Lipsky was staring at his neck. No matter what shirt he wore, the tip of his scar from the neck injury was visible just above his collar. He had to leave a bit of razor stubble on both sides of the raised incision.

"Healed pretty well," Lipsky said.

"Makes shaving a lot of fun."

"I bet. Back in the OR yet?"

Eli raised his left arm, kept all his fingers curled for the effect. "With this hand?"

Lipsky nodded. "Guess not. No one wants a surgeon who can't wipe his own ass."

Eli smiled. "Got a way with words, don't you, Lipsky?"

"I get the Word of the Day sent to my computer. Know what today's is?"

"Please tell me."

"Pu-tre-fac-tion." Lipsky said it slowly, syllable by syllable. "Apropos, don't you think?"

Eli thought of the peculiar timing of this word that summarized the state of the city. Garbage festering, maggots multiplying, heat-bloated bodies yet to be found.

"Apropos?"

"Last week's word."

Eli nodded. "Should have known."

Without picking it up, Lipsky slid the first of two large photographs across the table.

Eli glanced at the close-up image of a bare ankle, a gashed out hole on top of the foot.

The waitress brought Lipsky's coffee and a glass full of ice. She held Eli's can of Coke under her arm, a little too close to her armpit. She popped the top, filled his glass, and returned to the kitchen.

Eli gave the photo back to Lipsky without saying a word.

Lipsky pushed another one in front of him. This image showed the lower half of a face, dried blood in the corner of the mouth. The detective gave him a few moments, then asked, "What do you make of this?"

Eli looked up. "Both photos the same person?"

"Two different victims." He held up the first glossy print. "Two days ago." He pointed to the one in Eli's hand. "Yesterday."

"Cause of death?"

"Both bodies are in the morgue. Examiner's a tad backed up, what with all the heat deaths."

Lipsky pulled two more photos from his front pocket. Eli took them willingly this time, his curiosity piqued. One showed a close-up of the bone from the first victim's foot. The other revealed the reason for blood on the mouth—the victim's tongue.

Eli tried to hide any reaction to the photos. He knew Lipsky was watching his face closely for any hint that he might help him. Eli found himself squinting to see details within the picture so he tried to relax. He took another glance at both photos and placed them face down in front of Lipsky.

"It's odd, I agree," Eli said. "But then again, this is Memphis."

Lipsky waited for Eli to say more. The doctor remained silent. "What if I told you the first victim was an anal-theist?"

Confused, Eli said, "Come again?"

"You know, one of those assistant anal-theso-tologists."

Eli smiled. "You mean anesthetist?"

"Yeah, that's it."

"So?"

"And the other victim, she was a nurse. Two deaths, two days, both of them medical types."

"Where were they found?"

"Downtown. The first in an abandoned warehouse. The woman, at an old wrestling arena."

"I don't know what to tell you, Lipsky. World's a dangerous place."

Lipsky reached into his front pocket again. "One other thing before you go, doc." He handed Eli the pieces of sketched canvas found at the two crime scenes.

Eli looked at the first one, then switched to the second, each piece the size of a plastic CD case. He didn't have to look back at the photos to appreciate an exact rendering of the foot bone and tongue.

"Nice work," Eli told him. "You have quite an artist down at the police station."

Lipsky shook his head. "Not our work. Whoever killed these people left these cards at the crime scene."

Eli studied the pieces again. At the bottom of each, the letters H.C. were inscribed.

"HC?" he asked.

"Beats me," Lipsky said. "Mean anything to you?"

Eli gave the cards back to the detective. "Not a thing."

"Anything else about the photos?" Lipsky asked, turning both of them face up. The crease on Eli's forehead reappeared.

"No, not really."

"Okay," Lipsky said, standing to leave. "Good to see you again, doc."

"Let me see those pieces of canvas again," Eli requested.

Lipsky complied and remained standing while Eli examined them. Moments later, Eli returned only the sketch of the tongue to the detective.

"Let me keep this one," Eli said, holding onto the illustration of the foot bone.

Lipsky laughed. "No way, doc. That's evidence from a murder scene. Are you kidding?"

Eli handed the sketch back. "Okay, I just thought you wanted my help."

Lipsky looked at the card without taking it. "If you lose that, they'll have my ass."

"Trust me," Eli said. "I'm a doctor."

"Yeah, right. Sometimes I wonder."

Before Lipsky walked away, Eli asked, "Did the bodies go to the medical center?"

This made Lipsky smile, as though the exact question he hoped to hear.

"Yeah, both of them should be there," Lipsky said. Then, using his hands, the detective mimed the outline of a curvaceous figure. "Hanging out in the morgue with your lady friend."

CHAPTER NINETEEN

Like most temporary hotels for the dead, the morgue was located in the basement. Lately, freezer space at the University of the Mid-South Medical Center had been choked full of ripening summer kill, and an additional cool room had been constructed to keep the mounting bodies just below the temperature of decay. The forensic pathologist had triaged the bodies, stacking those who had died from heat-related causes in the cool room while reserving prime freezer space for suspected homicides. Two bodies in particular, both with odd wounds, had risen to the top of an overbooked autopsy schedule.

Eli had not entered the autopsy suite in over a month. He needed a reason to return, and now that Lipsky had shown him the photos, he had more than enough reason.

But Eli's real need to be there was pathologist Meg Daily. After the heat of the previous investigation had cooled down, so had their relationship. Following Eli's release from the hospital after an emergent operation to repair his injuries, the yachting trip they had planned fell through when Meg's diabetic daughter became ill again. It was all fantasy anyway. Even though the trip was a gift from one of Eli's wealthy patients, neither Eli nor his pathologist companion would have taken off work and sailed the ocean for two weeks. After the cancelled trip, a week turned into two. Then six weeks passed, and they had not spoken a word to each other.

Eli pushed open the doors to the Pathology Suite. As though she'd been waiting for him, the receptionist, Miss Conch, sat at her desk, arms folded over her first of several stomach rolls.

"You've got some nerve coming through those doors."

Eli expected this. Conch had been the gatekeeper for the autopsy suite for nearly two decades, a position equivalent to the grand hostess at a cadaver ball.

Fat, fifty, and far from married, Miss Conch guarded her roost like a pissed-off mother hen. And now the rooster had come to peck at her favorite chick, Meg Daily.

"Hi, Miss Conch."

"No, no. Don't try to smooth talk me. We've been working our tails off down here and you haven't even called her. Not once. Just like every man I've ever known."

Eli held up his hands in surrender. He wondered how many men that could have been. "Is she back there?"

"Maybe she is and maybe she ain't."

He tried to think of an appropriate response to this straight-from-elementary-school answer. He went for a direct approach.

"I need to see her."

Miss Conch stared him down. "She's had a hard month. Margaret's been sick." She pointed a stubby finger. "You be especially nice." With the same finger, she pushed the button on the intercom. "Dr. Daily. Got a surgeon here wants to see you."

After a few moments of silence, Eli heard static, then, "Let him back only if he's carrying an autopsy knife."

Miss Conch stopped Eli before he pushed through the autopsy door. "Remember. Extra nice."

Meg was in the same position as when he'd first met her, bent over a dead body split stem to stern. She wore a mask, gown, and gloves. Her hair was pulled back and tucked into a surgical cap, though a few errant strands escaped and fell toward her face. So sexy, those unruly strands. For the moment, with so much of her covered, the essence of Meg Daily poured out of intense brown eyes.

She looked up from her work but said nothing.

Eli knew the drill. He removed a plastic gown from the corner table and slipped it over his clothes.

Hard-angled stainless steel on dingy tile floors formed the autopsy room. A single table in the room's center efficiently removed body fluids, its corners sloping into drains like pockets on a pool table. Even the floor sloped toward a center drain hole. The continuous sound of running water came from a black hose on the autopsy table and another hose that curled like a snake on the floor. Always a drip-drip-drip that made your skin crawl.

The body on the table was that of an obese male, skin mottled bluish-gray. The breastplate had been removed through a Y incision that extended down the middle of the abdomen. Meg stood on a stool that lifted her over the protuberant belly. She struggled with a pair of heavy Mayo scissors.

"Hand me that big Richardson." Meg pointed at the instrument table without looking up.

Eli slipped on a pair of gloves and removed the right-angled retractor from the instrument set. But rather than give it to her, he stood on the opposite side of the table, inserted the retractor into the incision, and pulled to provide the exposure Meg needed. He immediately saw the problem. Adhesions from a previous operation prevented Meg from eviscerating the abdominal contents, a feat normally accomplished with a few targeted snips.

With the abdominal wall retracted, Meg could visualize the appropriate plane of dissection, and she quickly removed loops of small intestine and colon. Versed in the sequence of evisceration, the two physicians worked in silence, Eli with gentle pressure on the tip of the spleen, then rotating positions with Meg, both hands on the liver, giving, taking, lost in the void they created, until it was done.

"Looks like your hand's much better," Meg said as she placed the liver in the cradle of a hanging scale.

"Works well enough for dead people, I suppose."

Meg replaced the liver with the spleen, recorded the weight, kept moving.

"I hear Margaret's been sick." Eli felt odd asking about Meg's five-year-old daughter, a lame way to reacquaint himself.

"Yes, Eli, she's sick. Hasn't been well a day in her life, really."

"I'm sorry."

To calm herself, Meg stopped and put both hands on the bench in front of her. Then she turned to face Eli. "I haven't heard a word from you in over two months." She gestured over her shoulder at the day's work. "I've got six autopsies on the schedule and I'm already behind."

"Six weeks," Eli said, interrupting her.

"What?"

"It's been only six weeks."

"What do you want, Eli?"

"I need your help."

"With what, may I ask?"

Eli motioned to the bank of freezers. "I know things have been crazy, you may not have examined them yet."

Eli watched her pull out a freezer drawer on the bottom row. As the drawer opened, the feet presented first and Eli immediately recognized the extremity wound he had seen in Lipsky's photo.

"This who you're looking for?"

The horizontal incision across the foot had dried but the missing bone was obvious. Eli looked over the rest of the body. There was no obvious trauma on the anterior half of the nude male.

"How did you know?" Eli asked.

"Only two bodies have been interesting, one male, one female. There have been a lot of heat-related deaths, two straightforward gunshot wounds, a stabbing, one strangling—you know, the usual stuff." Meg pointed to the foot wound. "But not this."

Eli stepped closer to the body.

"What do you know about this?" Meg asked.

Eli shook his head. "They're dead."

Meg glanced at him as though peering above eyeglasses. "Damn. You must have gone to one of those Ivy League medical schools."

"No. I was lucky to be accepted here in Memphis. Lots of dead patients to work with."

"Anything else about these patients," Meg asked, "that a ditchdigger couldn't figure out?"

"No, not much. Detective Lipsky asked me to look at the photos. He thought these were a weird combination of wounds, and the fact they were both medical personnel."

"Medical?"

"Yeah. The guy's an anesthetist and the female victim you refer to is a nurse."

"That is strange," Meg agreed. "What did you tell him?"

"I didn't tell him anything. He thought there might be some connection between the two victims."

"And?"

"And what?"

"Is there a connection?"

"Hell if I know. Why is it that all of a sudden I know what makes people kill each other?"

Meg closed the drawer and returned to the autopsy Eli had interrupted.

"I'm sorry," he said, following her.

"Something made you come here, Eli," Meg said, facing him now. "Something about those deaths, I presume." She grabbed the hem of her protective gown and curtsied. "Or maybe you just wanted to see me in my new yellow dress?" She bellied up to the head of the autopsy patient.

Eli didn't know how to start. Why exactly the sequence of foot bone, then tongue removal, bothered him. Before he could speak, Meg pressed the Stryker saw into the man's scalp, and the high-pitched circular saw spit a line of bone on the table. She finished the 360-degree cut and pulled the skull off by the hair.

"What was the cause of death?"

Meg laid the saw on the table. "I'm running behind in the autopsy schedule so I haven't started on the first victim yet, but I did find an external wound that is telling."

Eli knew it had to be a finding other than the foot wound; that insult alone would not kill a person. "Telling for what?"

Meg placed her hand at the back of the victim's neck. "A single hole, tiny, like an ice pick." Meg pointed to another body drawer, yet to be opened. "Same with this one. Whoever did this knows their anatomy."

Eli reacted by cupping the back of his neck with his hand. "Speaking of anatomy," he said, "the bone from the foot, was it the navicular?"

Meg turned and stared at him. "Yes, as a matter of fact, the excised bone was the navicular."

Eli felt the room turn cold. He knew what she was thinking. The navicular is one of many bones in the foot, and not the only one that could have been removed through the wound.

"You've got a reason for asking that, don't you, Eli?" She pointed a blood-stained finger at him. "Now, tell me what the hell is going on."

"Can I see the next victim, the woman?"

"Sure," Meg said. She maneuvered herself away from the table and pulled out the top drawer. "Would you like fries with that?"

The drawer rolled forward easily to reveal the body. Eli had been so focused on examining the first victim's foot, he had not even glanced at the man's face. With the second victim, he would focus his initial exam on the victim's face and the absence of her tongue.

Meg folded back the sheet. Eli stepped toward the head and froze. The corpse's mouth was swollen, old blood smeared across her lips like a bad lipstick application. Her tongue lay beside her head in a transparent plastic bag.

The possibility that he would know the victim had not occurred to him. Her mouth was contorted; perhaps her jaw had been broken during the assault. But her identity was unmistaken. He stared at the face of Virginia Brewer, a respected operating room nurse who had been at Gates Memorial Hospital for years.

As a medical student, he had known her a decade ago. He saw flashes of her helping him through that awkward time of learning to gown and glove when he scrubbed in for his first operation. And just six weeks ago, she had welcomed him back to the hospital in the midst of a gory operation that had begun the spectacular derailing of his career. Now, he looked upon her in death, less of a colleague, more as a mother figure.

Eli was paralyzed by the memories of this gentle nurse. "I knew her," he said. He couldn't quit staring at her disfigured face. "She was an OR nurse."

Lipsky had told him her body was found in an old wrestling arena. He thought that was odd, a portion of her life he knew nothing about.

Meg said, "I'm sorry." Then, she pulled the sheet, slowly this time, until the body of nurse Virginia Brewer was covered.

CHAPTER TWENTY

Liza French cut her course short of the usual three miles. It was too damn hot and she was too fatigued after a near-sleepless night. When she returned from her early evening run, Liza found medical student Cate Canavan waiting for her in the living room. Layla sat beside Cate, trying to console her with a cup of tea. Cate was too upset to drink.

Liza was not surprised to see Cate. As her mentor, Liza knew the death of any patient could be traumatic for health care providers, even when it is expected. But no one, especially not a medical student, is prepared for the death of an otherwise healthy woman on the operating room table. Cate had witnessed the event firsthand. The blood, the shouting, the chaos as robotic instruments were frantically removed and the patient's abdomen sliced open.

As attending surgeon, Liza did not have a chance to speak with Cate after the operation. At least not in a consoling way. Liza remembered yelling at the resident, the nurses, even Cate, trying to determine what had gone so horribly wrong.

Cate stood when Liza entered the room. Her eyes were puffy and red.

"Dr. French, I'm so sorry to bother you."

"I'm glad you're here, Cate. Please, sit down."

Liza asked Layla to bring her a bottle of water. Sweat continued to run down her back as she sat beside Cate.

"What happened in the operating room," Cate said, "I can't quit thinking about it."

"I know. It was a terrible complication. I'm sorry you had to see it."

"But everything was going so well. We were almost finished."

Layla brought the water. Liza held the bottle without opening it.

"I know, Cate. I thought the same thing."

Cate shook her head. "I feel like I should have done something to stop it. I just stood there. Paralyzed."

"There was nothing you could have done. And that's a normal reaction at first, to feel paralyzed."

Merely talking about the case, Liza felt the empty pit return to her stomach. She had pored over the facts of the case, each step, each movement of the operation. But now, the emotional response returned. She too had felt paralyzed, as if the blood had drained from her as well.

"Panic in the OR," Liza said. "That hurt us." She stood and took several gulps of water. "In your own practice—" Liza put her hand to her mouth, belched. "You'll find that experience keeps you calm and allows you to act."

Cate shook her head. "I can't do it."

"What do you mean, you can't do it?"

"Be a surgeon, like you. I don't think I can do it anymore."

Liza knelt in front of Cate. "Sure you can, I've seen you. You're wonderful with the patients, Cate. And your technical skill will come naturally during your fellowship."

Cate took a sip of tea.

Liza stood again.

"Come. I want to show you something."

Cate followed Liza up the spiral staircase. They stopped on the second floor landing.

"Remember the robotic simulator I told you about?"

Cate turned to see Layla several steps below them. "The one the company donated to your program?"

Liza continued up the stairs to the single room on the third floor.

"Wasn't it supposed to go to the OB Department?" Cate asked.

Liza looked over her shoulder. "I had them drop it off here, first." She smiled. "On a trial basis."

The upper staircase ended at a single door. Liza opened it and motioned for Cate to enter.

CHAPTER TWENTY-ONE

Cate stopped just inside the door. An operating table occupied the center of what appeared to be an office. Bookcases lined the dark-paneled room. A large wooden desk sat beneath the room's single window. And off to the side, near the far corner, a sleek gray robotic console looked completely out of place.

Liza put her hand on top of the console and stroked the smooth surface as if it were the hood of a Mercedes-Benz. The front of the console was cut out to accommodate a screen, robotic hand controls, and a bucket seat.

"This simulator is like the real thing, Cate. I want you to come here and practice on it any time you wish."

Cate approached the machine. Not because she wanted to, but because her mentor insisted. She looked at a pair of leather straps that crossed the operating table. In this room, the simulator looked more like a device for torture than a means to save lives.

"I can't believe you have all this in your house," Cate said.

"It doesn't exactly fit with the Victorian décor, does it?" Liza laughed. "So I keep all the high-tech stuff in this third-story office. Here," she said, pointing to the console, "have a seat."

Standing between the console and the operating table, Cate had a flashback from the operation. How she'd glanced at Dr. French when the anesthesiologist announced the plummeting blood pressure. How the video screen had filled with the image of spurting blood.

Cate took a seat inside the console. Cold sweat beaded on her forehead. Her hands shook as Dr. French told her to take the controls.

"I want you to feel comfortable with the instruments."

Cate felt Liza lean over her shoulder.

"By the time you start residency, you will be well above your peers."

Cate sensed the delicate positioning of the hand controls, felt Liza's breath on her hair, smelled the sweat soaked into her teacher's running clothes.

Cate wanted to be the good medical student, to show her utmost appreciation and dedication to what Dr. French was offering her. She knew this opportunity was afforded to few students. But her pulse was pounding, and for the first time in her life she felt claustrophobic. Cate stepped out of the console and bumped into Liza, knocking her back. She crossed the room and opened the door to the staircase.

"I'm sorry." Cate tried to slow her rapid breathing. "It's too soon. I'm just not ready."

Liza followed her down the stairs. "It's okay. I shouldn't have shown you this yet. It was inconsiderate of me."

Layla met them in the parlor. "What's wrong, darling?"

"Nothing. I just need some fresh air," she said. "Thank you, Dr. French."

"You will overcome this, Cate," Liza called from the doorway. "You will be a fine surgeon. I hope you know that."

Cate ran from the house down the walkway. Relieved, she took in a full breath of the humid night. She looked back at her mentor's stately mansion. The front door was closed, the porch light already turned off.

CHAPTER TWENTY-TWO

Secret Lives of Doctors.

The newest in reality-based television shows. The premise: What former lives had doctors given up to pursue a career in medicine? World-class cellist, Broadway actress, pitcher in triple-A minor league baseball, lingerie model?

The doctors chosen for each episode of this show were in their first years of training for specialties such as OB/GYN and surgery. Only a few years before, each had faced the decision to pursue the professional life of an artist, an athlete, or the profession of medicine. One more performance, another competition, could have pushed them into celebrity status.

So what happened?

Do they still hold to these dreams once pursued through obsessive hours of practice and training? Or did the stress and demands of medical school and residency force them to drop their preoccupying desires? Or had they simply replaced these activities with something less admirable? A vice, perhaps?

This is what the producers were hoping for. The hook. The dirty laundry. They were looking for someone like Thomas Greenway. The man was six foot three, had the body of a swimmer: broad shoulders, trim waist. In fact, he was a swimmer, spent his evenings and weekends, when he wasn't on call for OB/GYN service, training for triathlons. He had been paying his way through college and medical school working as a model for magazine ads.

He was handsome enough, but his main attribute had not been

captured through facial photography. That was part of the deal. No pictures of his face. He thought he would never get into medical school if his identity in the pictures was known. The photos that had paid for an expensive medical education were pure torso shots. He had a rolling set of abs that led the eyes below the waist. What started as advertisements for men's boxer shorts soon went to men's briefs, and then the Speedo-like mini briefs in which his abdominal muscles were not the only prominent organ displayed.

The modeling gigs paid good money for a while, but gradually the work opportunities became more infrequent. He faced big-time debt to get through four years of medical school. Then another modeling opportunity came to him. This time no underwear was required. The magazine wanted not only full frontal but a head shot as well. He refused to put his anonymity at risk. The magazine editor compromised by allowing him to wear a surgical mask that at least partially hid his face. This seemed to work.

After a year of this, Greenway left the modeling world behind him. Now two things consumed his life: training to be an OB/GYN, and training for the triathlon. He had replaced showing his body with training his body—and for one of the most grueling competitions known to the individual athlete. The Annual Memphis Wolfpack Triathlon was only three weeks away.

Then a girlfriend found a proof of one of the photos in his apartment. She could see beyond the mask—and more. She liked the idea of dating a male model. And she promised not to tell anyone. Except one of her medical school girlfriends. Then everyone knew. Including the producers of *Secret Lives of Doctors*. Greenway refused to meet with them. So they went to him.

Shelby Farms is an expansive park in the center of Shelby County. More than four thousand acres, it is the largest urban park in the United States. In the mid-1990s, the farm supported prisoners from the county penal system who grew their own food and sold the surplus. The park boasts activities such as riding horses, taking aim at a pistol and rifle range, or windsurfing on sixty-acre Patriot Lake. With a 10K cross-country running course, Shelby Farms provides a superb environment to train for marathons and triathlons.

After unsuccessful attempts to arrange any interviews on the medical school campus, the staff at *Secret Lives* went looking for Thomas Greenway. They asked his fellow residents where he spent his off hours. All answers were the same, and the staff found him swimming laps in the brownish-gray water of Patriot Lake. Without his permission, they filmed his lean body cutting the water, and then waited for him on the shore.

Dressed in a dark suit and looking hot in both meanings of the word, Carol Baylor, the show's executive producer, smiled at Greenway when he emerged from the lake. Rivulets of water streamed down his tanned, firm abdominals and dripped from a body-tight pair of swimming briefs. She said to her cameraman, "This is going to be good."

Greenway reached into his bag, removed a shirt, and slipped it over his head. The shirt fit tight on his wet skin and he had to inch it over his chest.

The producer of the newest medical reality show watched every move. "I'm Carol Baylor from *The Secret Lives of Doctors*."

Greenway knew that a television show had been conducting interviews at the medical center. He pulled a pair of running shorts over his Speedo. "I know who you are."

"How's the water?"

He looked back at the lake. "Muddy."

"We'd like to interview you about your training. A doctor who does triathlons would interest our viewers."

"A lot of doctors do triathlons." He picked up his bag, started to walk off. "I know what you're after, and I'm not interested."

She followed. "Look, I know what you're thinking. We'll only film your training and a few shots at the hospital."

The look he gave her was pure skepticism.

"That's all," she added. "Nothing from the past."

"And why should I agree to do this?"

"There's good money in it for you. Enough for a year's worth of rent."

"How do you know I rent?"

"We've done our homework."

He shrugged. "Good for you."

"And a Cervello racing bike."

This got his attention.

"A Cervello?"

"We know that you train with an old bike. We'll give you a brand new P3 Carbon. It's top of the line."

"I know it's top of the line."

Then she went for the kill. "And a year's membership at David's Gym. Have you ever worked out there?"

Any serious athlete in Memphis knew that David's was the best-equipped, most exclusive gym in the city.

"No, I haven't."

"It will put you in top form for the triathlon."

She extended her hand. "Deal?"

He shook her hand.

"And," she added, with a wink, "you can keep all your clothes on."

CHAPTER TWENTY-THREE

A throng of darkly dressed adults stood on the steps of Madison Avenue Episcopal Church and slowly inched their way inside. Across the street, Eli stood beside his Bronco and watched. The two-o'clock sun seemed to melt asphalt and metal. Eli felt his shirt begin to cling to skin beneath his black suit.

He had not been to a funeral since his father's, two years ago. Elizer Branch had not wanted a church funeral. Instead, a sterile memorial service was held at a sterile funeral home. Only a handful of people traveled to Elmwood Cemetery for brief graveside remarks before Eli's father was buried beside his mother.

Eli crossed the street. The small crowd had entered the church. He wanted to slip in, take a seat in the back row, and pay his respects to a woman he had known ten years ago, and more recently during intense moments at Gates Memorial Hospital.

Organ music filled the church as he entered and slipped past the ushers to find an empty space in the back. The church was not full, but those attending were positioned such that the sanctuary appeared occupied. When his eyes adjusted to the darker room, he began to recognize a few of the people in attendance. Robert Largo, Gates Memorial's Chief of Staff, sat near the front. Next to him, Eli recognized the director of nursing and the nursing supervisor from the OR. They stared at the closed casket as the organist continued to play. Across the aisle, a few pews up, a young nurse whom Eli recognized from the OR turned and looked at him. She smiled briefly and then looked away. The music stopped and the priest addressed the congregation.

As words blurred into liturgy and ritual, Eli wondered why he had come to Virginia Brewer's funeral. He tried to convince himself that he was there as a friend of a woman who had been somewhat like a mother to him. But his mind flashed to her death and the death before her, and he became aware that the real reason he was in this church was to attempt to make sense of the two murders with which somehow he'd become involved.

The first two pews, where the family sat, had been sectioned off with gold rope. A man, who Eli assumed was Virginia's husband, sat by an older woman with thin gray hair. Beside her were a young man and woman, both in their mid-twenties, likely Virginia's children.

When the service was over, Eli stayed behind in his seat until most of the gathering had filed out down the center aisle. He had no desire to speak with Robert Largo, the administrator who had signed the papers that officially suspended Eli's clinical privileges at Gates Memorial. Nor did he care to see any of the nurses or other hospital personnel whom he'd recognized during the service. He wanted to talk with no one, a plan that backfired as he left the church a few minutes later.

"Dr. Branch?"

A stocky man with red, swollen eyes walked up the steps and shook Eli's hand. It was the man Eli had seen in the front pew, Virginia's husband.

"Thank you for coming," he said. "Virginia spoke of you often. She thought the world of you."

Unprepared for this confrontation, Eli searched for the right words. "Your wife was a special lady, and an incredible nurse."

Long, awkward moments of silence followed. The small group of family members stood by cars lined up behind the hearse. The funeral attendants stood with hands clasped in front of them, watching Eli and beckoning the husband so that the procession could depart.

Virginia's husband lingered, as if he had more to say.

"My wife had been upset about the death in the hospital. She was there that day, working as a nurse in the operating room." He shook his head. "She even talked about quitting her job. It was so unlike her. And now this. Someone took her life. There's no sense to it."

Eli took the man's hand, held it with both of his own. "I'm so sorry."

The man remained there another moment, searching Eli's eyes as if hoping Eli had some information that would ease his pain. When Eli said nothing, the man descended the steps toward the waiting hearse.

CHAPTER TWENTY-FOUR

Liza French entered the basement corridor of Gates Memorial Hospital. She looked each way before fully stepping from the stairwell into the hallway. A sheen of moisture glistened from the concrete flooring. She considered it appropriate that the basement was reserved for pathologists and other personnel who attended the dead—the precise reason she never ventured to the basement. She had no reason to. Until now.

She wandered through a maze of halls until she found a solitary MORGUE sign with a thick black arrow pointing the way. She passed a janitor, stepping around his mop, which jutted from a bucket of brown water, and soon reached a set of double glass doors. PATHOLOGY was printed on the left door, SUITE on the right.

Inside, she found a heavyset woman sitting behind a desk, looking at her over the top of a pair of horn-rimmed glasses. She adjusted her eyewear and gazed at Liza's leopard skin skirt, her high heel pumps.

"This ain't Macy's," Ms. Conch told her. "You lost, sweetheart?"

"Is this where I can sign a death certificate?"

"Death certificate? You might find that here. Who's asking?"

"I'm Dr. French. Liza French."

Ms. Conch stood, which raised her up only a foot or so, a portion of that gained from the thick soles of her shoes, part business pump, part army boot. She took in a full view of the female chief of OB/GYN. "Well, I'll be."

"I'm here to sign the death certificate on—"

"I know which one," Ms. Conch said, interrupting her. "Everybody and their dog knows about that death."

"Gee, thanks. Can you just get it for me?"

"Sure." Ms. Conch continued to stare at Liza's shoes. "Just like they say."

"What?"

"You are quite a sight."

Liza snapped her fingers. "The certificate, please."

Ms. Conch turned, waddled toward a filing cabinet, and returned with a thin stack of papers.

"Death certificate's on top, autopsy reports on the bottom." Ms. Conch pointed at the papers in Liza's hand. "Might want to read the report, so you put the correct cause of death."

Liza smirked. "I've done this before."

"So I hear."

Liza thumbed through the pages until she found the autopsy summary page.

Ms. Conch sat at her desk pretending to work at her computer until Liza interrupted the silence.

"That bitch."

"Scuze me?" the Conch said.

Liza riffled through the pages again. "Where is this doctorrrr—Daily?

"She's not in at the moment. Something I can help you with?"

"This report, it's screwed up."

"Screwed up?" Ms. Conch asked, her furry eyebrows scrunched toward her nose, as though she was actually concerned. "You must be mistaken. Screwed up best describes what happened in the OR."

"Get her out here," Liza demanded.

"Something wrong with those ears? I said she's not here."

From the autopsy room rang the sharp clang of steel on steel.

They both looked toward the door.

Then at each other.

"Sometimes," Ms. Conch said, "they're not as dead as we think."

Liza made a quick move toward the autopsy suite.

Ms. Conch tried to block the way but succeeded only in knocking over her chair. "You can't go back—"

But Liza was already through the swinging doors. "You've got to change this report," she said, shaking the papers in the air.

Ms. Conch was right behind her. "I told her she couldn't come back here, Dr. Daily."

Meg stood behind a table of instruments. She continued to wipe an autopsy knife with a towel, linear crimson stripes staining the cloth.

"Your description," Liza said, "is all wrong."

Meg stepped from behind the table, wiping her gloved hands on the dirty towel.

"Dr. Daily calls it as she sees it, Frenchie."

Meg held up one hand. "I've got this, Ms. Conch."

The bulky receptionist turned to leave, then glanced back at Liza French. "Hope Formalin seeps into that leopard skirt and you stink to high heaven." She let the double doors swing freely behind her.

Meg stood not three feet from Liza. "You've got a problem with my autopsy report?"

"Reading this," Liza said, waving the report in Meg's face, "you make it sound like I practically killed the woman."

"The patient's aorta was skewered with a long instrument," Meg declared. "I just report what I find."

"What I found," Liza said, inching closer to Meg's face, "as her doctor, was a diseased, bleeding uterus. That's what caused her death."

"Are you suggesting I change my report?"

"Not suggesting," Liza said, slapping the papers against Meg's chest. "Ordering."

Meg glanced down at Liza's hand, felt the pressure of Liza trying to push her backward. Then Meg swiped the bloody towel across Liza's face.

Ms. Conch banged through the doors. "I've called security on her, Dr. Daily."

Liza wiped her face and spit in the direction of Ms. Conch. "I'll take care of this myself," she said, and flattened the death certificate against the wall. She filled in the cause of death and signed it. As she left the autopsy suite, she threw the papers at the battle-ready shoes of Ms. Conch.

CHAPTER TWENTY-FIVE

Eli felt a gradual sense of relief as he departed Memphis. The heat intensified a degree or two as he traveled south on Interstate 55 through northern Mississippi. Abandoned warehouses and low-income housing changed to flat, rich Delta farmland. The toll taken by the drought and scorching heat was evident. Whole fields of soybeans curled their leaves trying to hide from the sun. Even King Cotton, normally resistant and thriving in such conditions, had this year made only hard white knots of fruit.

After discussing the two murders with Meg, and seeing the bodies firsthand, Eli now had postmortem confirmation of the sequence of removed body parts—bone, and then muscle—a sequence he hoped could be interpreted by an old professor and colleague in Oxford.

It wasn't the mere detail of a bone removed that had triggered his trip from the Bluff City. It was Meg's confirming identification of the bone as the navicular. The sleek bones of the femur or humerus, prone to fracture during sporting events or motor vehicle accidents, and commonly splinted in a plaster cast, served as models for display and illustration of the entire bone family. The navicular bone, however, was a small, oddly shaped, underappreciated bone in the foot named for its resemblance to a boat. From his comparative anatomy course at University College London, Eli remembered that the navicular was an important bone in the horse, located in the hoof just behind the coffin bone. But in humans, it was just one of a handful of bones in the foot. Of all the ways to mutilate a body, to show the conquest of murderer over victim, why take the time to locate, dissect, and remove the entire navicular bone?

Eli had developed his appreciation for anatomical detail as a young boy from his father, an anatomist at the medical school, who emphasized the importance of proper nomenclature and precise details of origin and insertion of muscle into bone. When it came time for Eli to enroll in college, his father arranged for him to study under Dr. Aldous Salyer at the University of Mississippi in Oxford. A scholar in the history of anatomical dissection and anatomical art, Dr. Salyer had served on the faculty at the medical school in Jackson for nearly twenty years, when his personal habits began to interfere with his teaching. He'd been asked to leave. He landed in the history department at the undergraduate campus in Oxford.

At Ole Miss, Dr. Salyer's classes soon became legendary for their full-scale productions, including detailed drawings of historical dissections projected on the wall. To the delight of his students, Salyer brought the dissections to life by contorting his own body, arching his back, and twisting his neck sideways, imitating anatomical art.

The students laughed the first time Salyer performed his demonstrations, until they realized that it was no joke, that he was absolutely serious. A thin man with a wiry, muscular build, Salyer used his physique to illustrate the location of a muscle or even demonstrate its function, lifting his pants leg to show the gastrocnemius, rolling his sleeve and locking his triceps, showing too much skin at times around his protruding hip bone.

Always one to make class interesting, Salyer had each student examine his or her own body before the course was over. The snuffbox, for example. Open the palm of your hand like you're about to shake hands with someone. Then rotate your hand back against your wrist. A small pocket develops between the base of your thumb and wrist, just big enough for a pinch of salt, or a dip of snuff.

As the son of Elizer Branch, professor of anatomy at the University of the Mid-South Medical School, Eli was already known to Salyer before he attended Ole Miss. At Ole Miss, Eli was drawn to Salyer's passionate study of anatomy and anatomical dissection and he enrolled in the professor's class as a sophomore. He would have enrolled his first year except that freshmen were not allowed to take the class.

Salyer became his mentor and Eli his graduate student, assembling scholarly papers—even substituting for him in class when Salyer's absences became more frequent. Although Eli always credited his father, it was upon Salyer's urging that Eli applied for and was accepted in a prestigious comparative anatomy fellowship and year abroad at University College London, a crucial step in his path to becoming a surgeon.

On Highway 78 toward Holly Springs, Mississippi, he passed the town of Byhalia. Just off the highway, he looked for a double-wide trailer at the edge of a parking lot. The rural medical clinic appeared the same as when Eli was a second-year medical student and worked there one summer, providing hypertension and diabetes care for the underprivileged. The only improvement was a new sign over the cinderblock steps that announced the Byhalia Free Clinic.

Past Holly Springs, on Highway 7, as the miles flowed behind him, so did past decades. Ahead of him, the Mississippi landscape unfolded and a crossroads came into view, a grove of trees stood on one side, a green Dumpster on the other, paper trash scattered between. Beside the Dumpster on the two-lane road, a man sat on a discarded recliner. He leaned forward, smoking a cigarette, and watched cars pass while his dog sniffed and scratched in the rubble. Beside him sat a lonely straight-backed chair as if recently vacated by a lost companion.

This image of the man and the dog and the empty chair stayed with Eli as he neared the town of Oxford. He wondered how he would find Professor Salyer or if he even still lived in Oxford. It had been over ten years since Eli last saw the man. The professor would be well into his late sixties now, if not seventies. Salyer could be retired, in a nursing home, or dead, for all he knew. *It's not as if someone would have called to tell me if the old man died.* Salyer had no family that Eli knew of. He'd probably pissed them off at some point. He could be dead and no one would care.

On the outskirts of Oxford, Eli passed St. Peter's Cemetery. He liked to enter Oxford by the cemetery where the creator of Yoknapatawpha County was buried. Traveling this route, with its representative literary history, seemed to ground him. He stopped at the roadside across from the historical marker that told of Faulkner's Nobel Prize. The author's gray headstone lay a few paces away.

The smell of cut grass lingered in sunlight that reflected off grave markers scattered on the rolling hillside. Across the road, newly constructed condominiums revealed progress for Oxford, Eli guessed. He pulled his car forward slowly, past the gravesites, and wondered what Faulkner would think about his hometown of Oxford today, new condos beside his grave. Eli zigzagged over to Lamar and gained speed toward downtown. Oaks and magnolias prayed over the sidewalks in front of magnificent homes with wraparound porches and spacious yards.

He circled Oxford Square with the majestic old courthouse as centerpiece. Tidy shops lined the streets with antiques and fine women's apparel, a bookstore on the corner so inviting Eli had to resist temptation to saunter in and browse. Second-story balconies with open railings beckoned for sipping coffee or stiff cocktails while the lazy flow of traffic circled the square.

At the edge of the Ole Miss campus, he crossed the deep gorge with its train track at the bottom, transportation for students of the university in the early 1900s. He entered the Ole Miss campus and passed the Grove, a small stand of trees in the center of campus that was transformed each fall into an outdoor cocktail party with fancy hors d'oeuvres, tabletop candelabras, and women decked out in formal attire. Tailgating in the Grove—an occasion to be interrupted only by a fleeting game of football with their beloved Rebels.

Eli felt homesick for a simpler time, before the long nights of hospital call and constant pressure to excel as a surgeon. A time before his father's integrity was in question, before Eli had fallen, somehow, toward the dark side of medicine.

Near the entrance to the Circle, he stopped at the newly restored Confederate monument, the slender white stone base supporting a young, saluting soldier at its peak. Only a few students walked the campus in mid-summer, likely student athletes or grad students taking summer semester classes. Eli parked in front of Ventress Hall, its Gothic design and central tower unique among buildings on campus. Salyer was one of the few faculty members who'd been assigned an academic office there. The administration might have believed they could keep a closer watch on him if he were under their noses.

Little did they know.

He remembered Salyer's office to be on the second floor, with a long window facing the Circle. It was noon now and if the old man was still alive, he would be departing for his daily excursion. Salyer's routine was to walk to the downtown square most every day and take a long lunch, leaving Eli behind to work on a paper or prepare the professor's notes for class. During Salyer's absence, Eli not only had a great view of the coeds through the professor's window as they sunned on the lawn, but he could also see Salyer ambling down the sidewalk on his way back from town, so that he could appear studious when the professor walked through the door.

Since his graduation, the campus had been landscaped and several academic buildings restored. He climbed the stairwell to the second floor of Ventress Hall, wondering if any semblance of the professor remained there. Narrow hallways led past a series of closed office doors. Eli was relieved to see "A. Salyer" stamped on the professor's door. It was cracked open and Eli gave it a gentle push.

The office was just as Eli remembered it—a mess. Papers were stacked on the desk in haphazard piles, books strewn about the place, many lay open faced and probably hadn't been moved in months. At the long window, a young man looked out. Eli paused as if seeing a younger version of himself.

"Hello," Eli said.

Startled, as though he had missed the professor's return, the student turned, obviously relieved to see someone other than Professor Salyer standing at the door.

"Is Salyer in?" Eli asked, knowing full well he was not.

"No. He stepped out for a while."

Eli smiled. The same old drill. Have a graduate student cover so Salyer could frequent the square each day. He approached the student, shook his hand, and they both stood looking out the window. No students were currently on the lawn, just the Confederate monument baking in the sun.

"Does he still pose the dissections?"

Surprised, the student glanced at Eli, then back out the window. "Oh, yeah."

"How about salt in the snuffbox?"

"That's everyone's favorite."

"Still with the little shot glasses of tequila?"

The student nodded.

Eli pictured the students pouring salt on their wrists. Taking it to their mouths. Then shooting the tequila from their personal shot glass which Salyer handed out at the beginning of the course. Back then, most students were of legal drinking age. Not so today.

"How does he get away with it?"

"The students would never tell. His class is the best-kept secret on campus. There's always a waiting list."

It was so Salyer. The renegade. What the Ole Miss administration didn't know.

"What year were you here?" the student asked Eli.

"Early nineties."

Eli looked at a door near the corner of the room. A heavy wire screen covered the top, a faint light emanating from behind it. Eli knew the door was always locked. Salyer checked it frequently.

"Does he still go to Magnolia's?"

"No, that place closed a few years back." The student didn't offer more information. That was one responsibility of the position, protecting the professor while he took his lunch.

"It's okay," Eli told him. "I had this job a few years ago."

"He'll be at the Rebel Yell. He walks there. But I always pick him up at one fifteen."

Eli decided to walk to the square, reminiscing on the familiar sites as he went. He stopped on the bridge over the gorge with the railroad track nearly one hundred feet below. Kudzu covered both sides. Amid all the brown and dying grass rampant across the Mid-South during the drought, kudzu seemed to thrive, crawling the bank on either side like

a green carpeted monster. Eli looked at the railroad track deep below
and imagined students arriving for the winter semester by train adorned
in long woolen coats befitting the time.

When Eli arrived five minutes later, the square in downtown Oxford
was roasting hot. No air moved nor were many people present. A pickup
truck with a busted muffler circled the stately courthouse. A sleek gray
Range Rover followed impatiently behind, an Ole Miss alum sticker on
the bumper. In an odd sort of way, this contrast between social classes
endeared Oxford to Eli.

On a side street off the northwest corner of the square, Eli stopped
at the entrance to the Rebel Yell. Part bar and part new southern cuisine
restaurant, the Yell's door was painted with a fresh coat of rebel red. Inside, however, the lights were cut low against a dark wood interior. Only
a few of the tables were occupied. No waiter greeted him. Eli walked
straight to the saloon-length bar that lined the back wall. A pyramid of
liquor bottles effaced a floor-to-ceiling mirror.

Professor Salyer sat at the bar, dead center, arms resting on the
counter. All the other spots were empty. The bartender stood at the opposite end reading a copy of the day's *Oxford Eagle*.

Salyer wore a tan-colored suit, the hem of his jacket hung over the
bar stool. In the mirror, Eli saw the old man's reflection. His graying hair
seemed longer, unruly, as he leaned over a bowl of soup. Salyer noticed
Eli's movement in the mirror, studied it for a moment, then picked up a
glass half-full with brown liquor. As if the image deceived him, he shook
his head at the glass, then took another drink.

Eli took a seat on the bar stool next to him. Without turning his
head, the professor launched into soliloquy: "Eli Branch, 1991 to 1993,
first author on the seminal paper 'Function of the Platysma Muscle in
Equinus: Comparison to Homo Sapiens,' accepted for fellowship in
comparative anatomy at University College London—"

Eli began to smile. This was classic Salyer, recounting historical aspects of a person before properly greeting them. It was charming, even
if Salyer was slurring a few words.

"To medical school, surgical residency, teaching awards, research awards—" his voice trailed off. He admired the glass again, tipped it sideways to unsettle the ice. "A guy like that doesn't just walk into a bar, middle of the day," he said, and took another drink.

Eli continued to watch him, intrigued by the way his mentor chose to scold him for his absence all those years.

Salyer held the glass rim against his lips as if talking into a microphone. "Not so much as a phone call." He drained the glass.

Eli put his hand on the man's shoulders. "It's good to see you again, Professor."

At this, Salyer summoned the barkeep from his daily paper. "Would you kindly pour me another," he said, pushing the empty glass to the bar's edge. "And one for my friend, Dr. Branch, if you don't mind."

"No, I'm fine," Eli said, trying to wave off the bartender. But the man had already tipped a bottle of George Dickel, a smooth swirl of liquor filling one glass, then the second.

Salyer picked up his glass, turned to Eli. "The water of life, my friend."

Eli recognized this as both acknowledgment of his presence and the origin of a toast. Their drinks met in a gentle push, the deep clank of thick glass ringing pure.

"To Tennessee," Salyer said, his glass held at face level. "Coffee County in fact. Maple charcoal and oak barrels," Salyer added, referring to the distillation of distinct Tennessee whiskeys.

This defines Salyer, Eli thought. His creed, in fact. If something was worth knowing about, it should be appreciated in fine detail, whether distinctive whiskey distillates or the sixteenth century description of human anatomy.

"You ever been there?"

"Where, sir?"

"To the George Dickel distillery, of course. What do you think we're talking about here?"

"No sir, I've never been."

Salyer looked astounded. "All those years in Nashville and you didn't make it down to Tullahoma?"

Eli shook his head.

"To Cascade Hollow," Salyer said as he lifted his glass. "That place is fantastic." He took a sip in commemoration.

"Eli," Salyer said, as if they had been reunited for hours now, "do you know the difference between bourbon and whiskey?"

Just like old times, Eli thought. Ever the teacher. "No sir, I can't remember."

Salyer thought a moment. "Hell, neither can I, but I prefer the latter."

The bartender settled down with his newspaper again. A few lunch guests filtered into the Rebel Yell. In an awkward transition, Salyer expressed sympathy to Eli for the loss of his father. *He was a good man. One of the best.*

Eli sipped his liquor and listened to a recounting of the friendship the two men had cherished, a relationship dating back to when they'd been graduate students together at Emory.

When Salyer spoke of how he and his father shared appreciation for Vesalius and the classical anatomists, Eli took the opportunity and stopped him.

"That's the reason I'm here, professor. The *Fabrica*."

Now he had Salyer's full attention.

CHAPTER TWENTY-SIX

"What about the *Fabrica*?" Salyer asked, already turned square on his bar stool to face Eli.

"It's still in your possession, I presume?"

With a skeptic's gaze, Salyer proclaimed, "I would never part with it, you know that."

Eli did know that. For a scholar in the history of anatomy, the *Fabrica* is considered the most important scientific work in the discipline.

In the sixteenth century, the understanding of human anatomy was largely based on the teachings of Galen. As the leader in medicine around 100 A.D., Galen acquired his knowledge of anatomy based largely on the dissection of dogs. And the canine dissections needed to obtain this knowledge were performed by a prosector while Galen himself watched from a perch above, and described to his audience of students what he observed. No intimate contact occurred between the anatomist and his subject.

That was about to change.

At the dawn of the Renaissance, a man from Brussels named Andreas Vesalius grasped the future of human anatomy and medicine in his hands, literally.

In 1543, Vesalius published his illustrated tome of anatomy based on his personal dissections of the dead: *De Humani Corporis Fabrica*—The Fabric of the Human Body.

The sixteenth-century manuscript, composed of seven books, is thought to be one of the most important medical works in print. Few well-preserved first editions of the *Fabrica* remained in existence, one of which Salyer possessed. Based on its age and rarity, Eli had always assumed the manuscript to be very valuable. And Salyer protected the document as if national security were at risk. For Salyer, the mere mention of Vesalius's masterpiece was more than enough to cut through the whiskey.

Before Eli could explain why he was asking about the rare work, they were interrupted.

"Are you ready, Professor?"

Eli glanced at the clock behind the bar.

One fifteen.

Salyer's graduate student was right on time.

Even though Salyer was distracted, he waited for Eli to continue.

"I need to look at Vesalius's first illustration, Book One."

"Are you going to tell me what this is about?"

"Yes." Eli gestured to help Salyer off his bar stool. "In your office."

CHAPTER TWENTY-SEVEN

Detective Lipsky drove an unmarked squad car south on I-55. He had just crossed the state line into Mississippi and felt relieved at the geographic transition. Maybe it was the magnolias painted on the state welcome sign. Maybe it was getting the hell out of the garbage-ridden, flesh-melting pothole of Memphis for the afternoon.

So what if he was en route to investigate another strange death. More body parts on display. At least it was not in his downtown. Lipsky planned just to take a look and assess any possible relation to the recent murders. Then he would let the local crew clean up the mess.

He settled back, found an oldies station, and the song took his mind back to a high school dance and a particular grinding with Mary Elizabeth Delbechio. Smack in the middle of a slow dance with Mary 'Lizbeth, his radio crackled to life.

"Detective Lipsky, what's your twenty?"

He shook his head. "Damn, Basetti. I had her all the way back under the bleachers."

"Who's that, boss?"

"Never mind. What do you want?"

"Where you headed?"

"Do you have to know every time I take a piss?"

"No. Just in the interesting places. Heard you were going to Tunica."

"If you already knew, why you asking me?"

"Strange time of day to go down and shoot craps. You got a gambling problem?"

"No, I got a Basetti problem. And I feel like shooting *him*."

"Just thought you'd want to know about our pro wrestling fan."

"Who?"

"You know, tongue lady."

"Oh yeah, what about her?"

"Happens that she was a nurse. Another Gates Memorial employee, dead."

Casinos and high-rise hotels in Tunica sprout from the Mississippi delta like bastard offspring from Las Vegas. With over a dozen casinos, Tunica boasts America's third largest gambling destination, all in the midst of flat cotton fields and a stone's throw from the mighty Mississippi.

Lipsky turned into the entrance of Spankin' Rich, the latest member of an ever-branching family tree of Tunica-based gambling establishments. The parking lot was smoking hot, wavy lines warping his view of the casino as though in a mirage. He parked next to a Nissan Altima with Lafayette County tags. Retirees over from Oxford, he thought, in for some mid-morning blackjack.

Off to the right, well away from the entrance, a couple of Tunica County police cars sandwiched an ambulance. Apparently, casino management wanted to keep this debacle as low key as possible so as not to disturb the customers. Dead bodies tended to slow down action at the slots.

A security guard greeted him at the entrance. Lipsky flashed his badge. The guard shifted his eyes side to side without moving his head. Lipsky knew he was reveling in this brush with violent crime, hungry for more than just escorting tipsy gamblers back to their rooms. The guard cocked his right arm and his hand came to rest on the holstered pistol.

"Follow me, detective," he instructed Lipsky. "Best keep your profile low."

Lipsky splayed his hands out to emphasize his pudgy five-foot-six frame. He cocked a grin. "I'll do my best."

Inside the cool casino, they wove through a maze of slots, blackjack tables, and roulette wheels. Waitresses in short skirts carried trays full of multicolored cocktails.

From the main floor, Lipsky noticed a man in a tan-colored suit watching them through a full-length second-story window. The security guard took Lipsky up one flight and the man met them at the elevator.

"I'm Alex Dalhauser." He extended his hand. "I manage the casino. Glad you could come so quickly. Follow me."

Dalhauser led them past conference rooms until the carpeted hallway ended at the health spa. After nights of drinking and draining your bank account, it's nice to know a treadmill's close by to whip you back in shape.

Entering the spa, Lipsky was introduced to the Tunica County police chief and his deputy, a man named Weaver. In the foyer, gilded molding surrounded a central reception desk. Above the desk, a heavy chain dropped from the ceiling, an electrical cord woven inside it, typical for a chandelier except that a black plastic bag had been draped over the light fixture, completely covering it.

"We'll come back to this," the police chief said.

They moved en masse to follow the manager of Spankin' Rich. Behind the reception desk, the room opened to an indoor pool with a Jacuzzi off to one side. Lipsky knew immediately that was where the victim had been found.

The man was dark-skinned, of Indian descent, and overweight. Very overweight. His back lay against the edge of the tub, both arms out, apparently resting in a position of comfort. His head was back, eyes open, staring at the ceiling. The Jacuzzi jets were still on, churning the blood-stained water, red waves lapping over the sides.

Lipsky looked at the chief of police, who answered his question without his having to ask it.

"The Jacuzzi was on when we got here, so we've been resetting the timer, trying to preserve the crime scene as close as possible."

This never happens, Lipsky thought. The locals always disrupt the scene. He tried to imagine the deputy resetting the timer every fifteen minutes.

"How do we know it's a crime scene?" Lipsky asked, just to challenge them. "Maybe his hemorrhoids exploded and he bled out." Lipsky gave a quick laugh but the others didn't follow the humor.

"Turn off the jets," the police chief said.

The turbulent water calmed, air bubbles evaporated, and the fluid leveled out until the tub looked like it was filled with Hawaiian Punch.

"How the hell we getting him out of there?" Lipsky asked.

The deputy and the security guard stepped forward.

"Weaver already lifted him," the chief said.

The guard chimed in. "Part way."

"So you have been in there?" Lipsky asked.

"Just enough to see what we're dealing with," Weaver admitted.

Like a game show host, Lipsky motioned toward the victim. "Okay, let's see what we have."

Both the deputy and the security guard put on a pair of gloves and approached the body, their shoes sloshing through a layer of bloody water covering the floor tiles. They grabbed the man under his shoulders and hoisted him until his butt came to rest on the side of the tub. It was easy to see where all the blood had come from. The man's abdomen was split down the middle and his intestines coiled out like loops of spaghetti.

"What the hell?" Lipsky said.

The officers turned the man sideways, pulled his legs out of the water, and laid him flat.

Lipsky crouched down to examine the wound. The incision made a clean cut from his breastbone, around his navel, and stopped just short of his crotch. The wound was remarkable by how straight and precise its maker had been. Not a knife jab and an uppercut. Moreover, none of the intestines appeared to be damaged, even though the coiling mass was displaced from its abdominal home.

The manager of the casino cleared his throat. "This is very distressing for our casino."

Lipsky nodded. "Yeah, for him, too." He searched the area for a calling card such as was left at the previous two scenes. Finding none, he felt relieved for some reason. He asked, "Did any of you find a card next to the body?" Lipsky made a square with his hands to demonstrate.

"Yes," the deputy said. "In the reception area."

They turned away from the tub, and Lipsky followed them back to the health spa's entrance.

Behind the reception desk, Lipsky noticed a pool of blood that had coagulated on the floor. Above it, the police chief reached up and removed the black plastic bag from the light fixture. Suspended from the chandelier was a glistening piece of pale-colored meat. It was oblong and round, forming a tube.

"They cut his damn stomach out," Lipsky said.

Then the deputy spoke, again. "I've seen a lot of crazy things but this beats all."

Lipsky thought about what the deputy might have seen out here in the Delta. Dead cows bloating in the road, someone stealing a tractor. At most, a nice clean bar fight turned homicide, if the deputy was lucky.

Lipsky moved closer, but not under the line of dripping blood. *I'm the one who sees crazy things. That should've been my line.* But Lipsky had to admit, piece of a man's gut cut out and hung from a chandelier was weird as hell.

He looked at the reception desk. There it was, leaning against the lamppost. From where he stood, Lipsky could make out the sketch of a stomach on the card he had asked about.

"Is someone usually sitting there?" he asked. "Maybe they would have noticed their work space being adorned with human organs."

The casino manager stepped forward, reluctantly. "There's an attendant on duty from ten a.m. to ten p.m., Dalhauser said. "But after hours, a guest can enter with a room key."

Lipsky thought about that. "So potentially, if no one else chooses to spa in the middle of the night, the killer could have taken his time carving up his artwork."

Dalhauser cleared his throat. "A guest came in at six this morning to use the treadmill and found Dr. Singh."

Lipsky caught the prefix. "Doctor?"

The manager left the reception foyer and returned to the body. Lipsky and the others followed him.

"He was a regular here," Dalhauser said. "Dr. Singh was one of our best customers."

"How regular?" Lipsky asked.

"Drove down from Memphis once a week. Took off from his medical practice. Very faithful."

Lipsky thought faithful was an interesting way to describe a gambling habit. "What kind of doc was he?"

"Anesthesiologist, I believe."

Lipsky looked down at the body. "He's put his last patient to sleep, that's for sure."

"He was well-liked around here," the manager said. "Very generous with his money."

"I guess that will boost one's popularity at a casino," Lipsky said. "Wife? Anyone come down with him?"

"No, he came alone but usually ended up with a friend here."

"Friend?"

The casino manager looked at the police chief who looked away. "A lady friend. Let's leave it at that."

Lipsky turned to face the manager. "We got a dead body and I need to talk to the last person who saw him alive."

Dalhauser remained silent.

Lipsky told the police chief, "You need to get a crime-scene tech in here. Start taking samples."

The police chief glanced at his deputy who just shrugged his shoulders. "Our tech quit a few weeks back," the police chief said. "The guy who's supposed to replace him is not answering our calls."

Lipsky punched numbers into his cell phone. A few seconds later, "Basetti, I need you down here in Las Vegas South." Lipsky turned away from the others. "Got some more twisted shit. Bring your camera."

CHAPTER TWENTY-EIGHT

Salyer's student's car had been parked in front of the Rebel Yell for only five minutes and already the vinyl seats were too hot to touch. Salyer climbed in the backseat and lay down on it long ways. He said nothing during the short drive back to his office. Eli didn't know if he was hiding, trying to nap, or what. When they arrived, Salyer told the graduate student to take the afternoon off. Eli followed the professor into Ventress Hall. He was surprised by how easily the man took the stairs after several midday drinks. Once inside his office, Salyer locked the door behind them. Then, he removed a key from the back of his desk drawer and opened the closet he'd converted into a shrine to the sixteenth century anatomist.

During his college year abroad in London, Eli learned the history of Vesalius, anatomist from Brussels, author of *De Humani Corporis Fabrica Librim Septum*, the fabric of the human body. Little did Eli know that a series of murders would bring him back to Vasalius's work.

The renegade, Renaissance anatomist had published the seven books that comprised the *Fabrica* in 1543, the same year Copernicus published his heliocentric theory *De Revolutionibus Orbium Coelestium*, on the revolutions of the celestial spheres. Just as Copernicus had proven that the sun, not the earth, was the center of the universe, Eli learned that Vesalius had proved Galen wrong in many aspects of anatomical dissection. He knew that Galen's anatomical teachings were based on his observed dissections in dogs and monkeys, for instance, whereas Vesalius performed the dissections on humans, often executed criminals he pulled from the gallows himself.

Centuries later, the *Fabrica's* woodcut illustrations were considered works of art. And Salyer's passion. Eli knew the anatomist-turned-history-professor never missed a chance to lecture. As though giving a confessional, Salyer faced the iron-gated door and spoke of just these Vesalian details.

Standing behind Salyer, Eli glanced at his watch. He was scheduled to work a graveyard shift in the ER and hoped to return to Memphis a few hours before it started. At this rate, that would not happen. Finally, Salyer unlocked the door.

The tiny room allowed Eli to enter only a couple of steps, more step-in closet than walk-in. The *Fabrica* rested on a podium of sorts that slanted forward to display the over four-hundred-year-old masterpiece, which was measured at least three times larger than a dictionary and twice as thick. Salyer turned on an overhead light that illuminated the book's magnificent cover. Tiny illustrated scenes, each no larger than a postage stamp, were carved into tanned vellum. Eli squinted to see the details, one scene showing a priest kneeling and ministering to the sick.

Salyer had pulled on a pair of white cotton gloves. He opened the cover to the title page, a magnificently detailed rendering of Vesalius at a public dissection. The drawing showed the anatomist in the center of an outdoor theatre framed by a semicircle of Corinthian columns. A host of onlookers surrounded him: scholars, students, and rogues who had ventured in to see the spectacle. Next to the depiction of Vesalius lay a female, nude, her abdomen open, organs on display for the pleasure of the audience.

Salyer's voice pulled Eli out of the mesmerizing picture. "Tell me why you must view the *Fabrica*."

"I'm not quite sure myself," Eli said. He reached in, bare-handed, and Salyer slapped his wrist. Eli slipped on a glove provided by his professor and then gently turned the pages of the Latin text to the illustration on Plate 4. At the bottom of the page, an oval, boat-shaped bone was displayed. The bone was cut through the middle and cracked open to reveal the spongy marrow inside.

Eli swept his index finger over the bone's image as though touching the fabric would make a full confirmation. He could sense Salyer's growing unease. The professor didn't allow anyone to touch the pages of the

Fabrica, even if latex should block the transfer of noxious oils from human skin.

"That's amazing," Eli said. The resemblance to Lipsky's photo was striking. The killer had reproduced the image perfectly.

"Yes, it's all quite amazing," Salyer said, distracted.

"The photo was exactly like that."

"What photo, Eli? What the hell is this about?"

Eli owed his professor an explanation. He was deciding where to begin when his cell phone rang. He had a beeping ringtone, no pop music melody or angry rap. But the electronic tone in this small chambered room, with its ancient holding, seemed absurd. Eli answered quickly to stop the intrusion.

Lipsky's voice grumbled and cracked. "Sorry to interrupt your golf game, Doc."

To avoid Lipsky's joke, Eli snapped, "What do you want?"

"I'm down in Tunica—"

Before he could continue, Eli interrupted the detective. "How are the slots going? Your pockets full of quarters?"

"Good one, doc. I'll tell you what, though. We're both taking a gamble."

Eli watched Salyer, his white gloves gently turning the *Fabrica's* pages in admiration of the text.

"Someone's a bit displeased with your profession."

"What else is new?" Eli responded, as Salyer passed through the *Fabrica's* second book. He caught a glimpse of the tongue illustration, a thick slab-like muscle splayed across the page, identical to Lipsky's photo of the killer's drawing, and to the specimen Meg had showed him in the morgue. Eli motioned for Salyer to linger on that page. The detail of the drawing was exquisite, down to the ligamentous attachments, little horns retracted against the meat of the tongue.

Lipsky went on.

"Got a dead doctor down here. Had a little mishap in a hot tub."

Salyer moved on to the third book—*The Vascular System*. Eli thought of arteries and veins, delicate, tubular channels that Vesalius had dissected and displayed so elegantly. If the killer, for some reason, followed the order of Vesalius, a bone from the first victim, muscle from the second, then the vascular system would be next. Something superficial, easy to remove.

"Someone cut out this guy's—"

"Veins?" Eli asked, interrupting Lipsky. "Stripped the veins out of his leg?"

Salyer shot a glance at Eli and turned the pages of the *Fabrica* to the illustrations of the venous system.

"Sorry, doc," Lipsky said. "I'm not too good with the blood and guts, that's your department."

Salyer closed the book and was removing his gloves. He motioned for Eli to step back. The small space was too cramped and they both wanted out. Just before Salyer locked the door, Eli looked again at the *Fabrica*. Three deaths in three days. If the pattern of deaths could be predicted by the seven books of this ancient anatomy text, there would be four more killings. Four more unsuspecting doctors or nurses or take your pick of healthcare workers.

"Did you say veins?" Lipsky asked. He didn't wait for an answer. "I'm no genius, but I think this guy's missing his stomach."

Salyer had returned to his desk. He opened the bottom drawer and placed a half-empty bottle of George Dickel on the desktop.

Eli repeated what he heard. "Stomach?"

Salyer filled a shot glass.

The stomach, an abdominal organ, did not fit the pattern. Organs of the abdominal cavity were addressed in Vesalius's fifth book. At once, Eli felt the whole thing was preposterous. This was police business. Murder, no less. *What was he doing in the middle of it?*

Salyer appeared irritated at Eli's prolonged phone conversation. In unison with swirling his glass, he shook his head.

"Lipsky, I'm in Oxford. Just an hour or so east of you."

"I remember," Lipsky said. "You're an Ole Miss boy. I probably disturbed your reunion. Old fraternity buddies back in for a throw down."

Eli ignored all this. "I want to see the body. Can you wait for me?"

"Sure, Doc. I've got time. Might just visit those slots after all."

CHAPTER TWENTY-NINE

Eli told Salyer all he knew about the three murders. The professor sat behind his heavy oak desk and listened. He didn't interrupt with history lessons or other professorial words of wisdom. When Eli told him of the photos and the odd resemblance to Vesalius and the *Fabrica*, Salyer filled another shot glass, turned it up, and filled it again.

A glazed expression gradually took over Salyer's face, and it became progressively stone-like after each glass until Eli lost count and departed for Tunica, the besotted professor still sitting at his desk.

Lipsky wasn't at the slots. Eli found him at the crap table, and from the looks of his stack of chips he'd done pretty well.

"Thought you had to stay at the crime scene."

Lipsky looked up. "That's the beauty of deputies, doc. You know about that, don't you? Hierarchy? Hell, I thought surgeons invented that shit."

Lipsky's cursing was definitely for the benefit of his onlookers. A small group of retirees had gathered to watch a consistent winner play. They enjoyed the detective's banter, but two younger women, dressed in short, tight skirts and sipping umbrella drinks, got bored and turned to leave.

As if their lost interest were his cue, Lipsky collected his chips and said, "Got to go."

He led Eli through the casino and into the spa, where two officers guarded the entrance. They moved aside when Lipsky flashed his badge. Inside the yellow tape, Eli saw Basetti bent over the body, collecting samples. Eli recognized the Memphis crime technician's ankle-high black sneakers crimped at the toes just inches from the obese body lying flat and nude on the tile floor. The water in the hot tub was still pink, with frothy bubbles along the edge. Eli crossed under the yellow tape and stood over the body.

"Well, if it ain't Doc Branch," Basetti said, like Festus in an episode of *Gunsmoke.*

To Eli, Basetti looked like he should be in college. But with his youth, Eli guessed, came technical craftiness, in a television forensics sort of way. Basetti ran a Q-tip inside the victim's mouth. Eli doubted the importance of this step to the investigation, especially when the lethal abdominal wound was so obvious.

Lipsky approached with more evidence, a glistening tubular-shaped organ held in his gloved hand. From twenty feet, Eli could see that it was the man's stomach. On closer examination, he noted that the dissection was intricate and precise, the proximal cut made smooth at the junction of the esophagus, the distal transection line just below the muscular pylorus where food empties into the small intestine.

"Ain't no hack job, is it, doc?"

Eli shook his head, part answer, part disbelief. "Whoever did this knows what he's doing."

But exactly what is he doing? Three victims, each with a specific organ removed in its entirety, without damage. He imagined the drawings in the *Fabrica,* how the sequence of bone to muscle to stomach no longer fit the sequence of Vesalius's manuscript.

"On the phone, you guessed that veins were removed from the victim." Lipsky emphasized the question by rotating the stomach resting in his hands. "What did you mean by that?"

"Nothing," Eli conceded. "It was nothing."

Basetti announced he was finished taking samples. He held open a plastic specimen container and Lipsky dropped the stomach inside, the image of a steak marinating in a freezer bag. Lipsky and Basetti stared at Eli as though he held the answer.

"What?"

Lipsky laid out the prompts. "Over the past three days, we got two doctors and a nurse murdered. Each of them with different body parts cut out, displayed, and sketched on paper."

Lipsky waited. Eli said nothing.

"I been in this business about twenty years now. Seen people gutted, heads cut off, seen one guy doubled over kissing his own ass."

Basetti snickered, cleared his throat.

"Difference is, Doc, those homicides were all from plain meanness, your everyday I'm-pissed-gonna-hack-somebody rage." Lipsky regarded the victim again. "This is different. There's some kind of pattern here."

"Damn straight," Basetti said, amen-like, agreeing with the preacher.

"And frankly, I ain't got a clue."

Basetti agreed. "Damn straight."

"Shut up and collect your Baggies, will you," Lipsky snapped.

Basetti held the bag to the light, acted like he was reading a message. "There's got to be some connection, don't you think? A doctor and two nurses? Maybe they're friends or work at the same hospital. Or maybe—" Basetti became animated, "it's a ménage à trois." He did his best charade to demonstrate. "That's when three people do it together."

Lipsky turned to Eli. "He's an expert on that sort of thing. Except he has to inflate his partners with an air hose."

Eli checked his watch. His ER shift started in one hour. And here he was, listening to this crap.

"I am a little curious, though, Doc." Lipsky stroked his bare chin. "How come you happened to be so close to Tunica when I called?"

When Eli didn't respond, Lipsky went on.

"And you didn't seem very surprised to hear about another death."

Eli decided it was time to spill what he knew. *Or thought he knew.* Maybe Lipsky could use the information and make the whole thing go away.

"Do you remember the federal agents who visited me in the hospital a couple of months ago?"

Lipsky nodded. "Yeah, I remember the suits. Said they may be calling on you again for another investigation once your wounds heal."

"They called."

Lipsky paced a few steps as if considering the implications. "Okay, Mr. Investigator. Want to bring me up to speed?"

"The first victim had a bone removed," Eli began. "The second, her tongue cut out." He stopped, knowing the explanation to Lipsky and Basetti would be difficult to comprehend.

Check that.

Damn near impossible.

"And?" Lipsky asked.

Basetti raised both hands in the air. "The tongue wasn't just cut out," the crime technician said. "It was dissected, the way an anatomist would do it." Basetti looked at Lipsky. "His dad was an anatomy professor."

"I know that, Sherlock," Lipsky said. "Let him finish."

"The specific bone removed, called the navicular, is the same bone, of all the bones in the foot, illustrated separately in a classical text on human anatomy. Even the way the bone was cut open."

"Doc, we know you went to medical school," Lipsky said. "Studied hard, fell in love with your textbooks—"

Eli interrupted him. "I'm not talking about a modern text. This one was written in the sixteenth century. The first two books of the manuscript describe the bones and muscles, in that order."

"Bones and muscles," Lipsky repeated. "But the second victim had her tongue cut out."

Basetti interrupted. "The tongue is a muscle."

Lipsky ignored him, turned to Eli for confirmation.

"He's right."

Basetti stuck his tongue out at Lipsky. Flicked it up and down.

"Okay," Lipsky said, trying to piece it together. "The killer gets his ideas from some book."

"Not just any book," Eli corrected him. "This one was written in the year fifteen forty-three."

One by one, Basetti flipped up four fingers. "Makes it over four hundred years old."

"You said the first two books. I'm betting there's more," Lipsky said.

"There are seven books in all," Eli informed him. "But the third book is on the vascular system, veins and arteries. The sequence fit, until now."

Eli pointed to the victim. "The stomach is part of the abdomen. That's book five."

"Maybe he's skipping around," Lipsky said, laughing at his own next thought. "Maybe he likes to read ahead."

"Or maybe this anatomy book theory is a bunch of shit," Basetti said. He must have realized he was out of line so he started collecting the specimen bags.

Lipsky held up seven fingers. "If the doc's right—" He folded down three fingers. "And if my third-grade math serves me, there are four more deaths on the way."

CHAPTER THIRTY

She had completed the last autopsy of the day. A few moments of dusk light crept through the door as she left the pathology building and walked toward her car.

"Dr. Daily?"

A young man approached her. He wore a black, collared shirt, somewhat unusual for this heat. In his hand, he carried a pen and a piece of paper and held them up as though a peace offering, obviously aware that dark parking lots in Memphis were alarming places, especially for women.

"Are you Dr. Meg Daily?"

Meg knew what he wanted. She had been through this drill before. Reporters were always looking for the inside story on a homicide. A single murder put them on the scent. But a string of murders? They'd circle like wolves. Interviewing a forensic pathologist was a good place to start.

It was no use trying to deny her identity. The reporter knew who she was already. A couple of prior interviews on prime-time news and she could no longer hide.

"Promise to make this brief," Meg said, "and I'll answer your questions."

Surprised, he waited as if to confirm her offer.

"I've got to get home to my daughter."

He put pen to paper. "The two recent murders. Did you examine the bodies?"

"Yes, I performed the autopsies."

He scribbled away. "Can you confirm that the killer left some type of card with drawings at each of the crime scenes?"

"No. Any evidence at the crime scene, you'll have to talk with police."

He looked disappointed.

"I only said I would answer your questions. She glanced at her watch. "Clock's ticking."

"Can you confirm that bodily organs were removed from the victims?"

Meg nodded. "During the organ recital, I remove all the organs from the body, systematically."

He stopped writing.

"Did you say organ recital?"

Organ recital was the term her pathology mentor had used in medical school during his autopsy demonstrations, when he would methodically put each organ on display. She liked the term and had adapted it as her own. But she felt regret now for using it.

"Yes, the autopsy—organ recital."

He wrote that down, underlined it.

"But were specific organs removed by the killer?"

"Yes."

He looked up, eyes wide. "Which organs were removed?"

"I can't tell you that."

He winced as though he had just been turned down for a date.

"You've got time for one more question."

He thought a moment, as though running through a list. "Do you think there will be more murders?"

Meg smiled. "How long have you lived here?"

"About, six months."

Meg opened the door to her car. "Been busy?"

The young man rolled his eyes. "Yeah."

"There's your answer."

CHAPTER THIRTY-ONE

At night, Victorian Village is illuminated only by the yellow glow of a few window lamps. The footpaths are dark and anyone can pass through from the medical center to downtown without being seen—unless the moon is full, when the century-old oak trees cast thick shadows.

Through the parlor window, Layla watched a young man walk back and forth on the sidewalk. She saw him look toward the other houses, as if checking that he had the right one. Liza had told her students of a unique feature to look for—a single third-story window with a Japanese lantern on the ledge.

There. He saw it, turning with a brisk step up the walk.

Damn, he's young, Layla thought. The medical students were getting younger or she was getting older. *Probably a first-year.* She would know soon enough, cadaver Formalin sweating from his clothes. New to the city, alone, not daring to ignore the request of an attending surgeon who would soon be determining his grade. They all gave the same line after knocking on the door, as though a password.

"Dr. French told me to come for extra tutoring."

Layla smiled.

Extra tutoring.

They were all so cute, so innocent. She let him stand outside a few moments. Waited until his eyes drifted down to her leather skirt, black leggings, knee-high boots.

"Tutoring? Have you not been studying enough?"

"No ma'am. I guess not."

"Well, now, let's see if we can fix you up." Layla extended her arm. "Dr. French is waiting for you in her study."

Layla led him up the spiral staircase, twitch-twitching her leather skirt at the level of his eyes, warming him up.

Dr. French sat at her desk, reading glasses on, studying a medical journal, or at least pretending to. When the student entered the room, she took off her glasses, leaned back in her chair, and studied him.

He thanked her for inviting him, his eyes darting across the room, trying to comprehend the operating table in the center of the room, a modular console in the corner, surgical instruments scattered on a table in between.

"Have you ever been in an operating room before?"

"Once, in college," he said, eyes still searching the room, "but not like this."

He looked confused, trying to piece all of it together. Deep wooden bookcases lining the wall, the stainless steel table to finish the décor. Hospital-inspired interior decorating.

Layla came up behind him, placed her hands on his shoulders. He winced as if he had forgotten she was in the room.

"So tense, my dear," she said, messaging his back.

Liza wore a hooded sweatshirt with a front zipper and no shirt underneath. Green scrub pants. She walked toward him.

"This is where I practice my skills," Liza said. "Surgical simulation."

"Have you ever been simulated?" Layla asked, moving her hands closer to his hips.

"You can learn how to operate here, get a leg up on your classmates."

Layla wrapped her leg around his. "Yeah, a leg up."

Liza handed him a long pencil-thin telescopic grasper, one that would be placed through small ports during laparoscopic surgery. The grasper had a finger hole grip at one end, fine pincers at the other.

He held the instrument, worked the grip, watched the pincers open and close.

"Very good," Liza said. "You're ahead of the curve already."

He smiled.

She pulled the instrument toward her until the tip nearly touched the zipper on her sweatshirt.

"Open," she instructed him.

He complied.

"Now, close."

The instrument grabbed the zipper.

He looked at her for the next set of instructions.

She waited.

Using the instrument, he inched the zipper up, toward her neck.

"No," she said. "Wrong way."

With her index finger, Liza pushed the shaft of the instrument down.

With more of her skin exposed, the student's hand began to shake and the grip of the instrument released the zipper.

Liza shook her finger. "We'll have to work on that tremor before you operate on real patients."

Layla pulled his arms behind him, slowly, and held his hands as though cuffed. "Needs a bit more practice, does he, Dr. French?"

"A lot more practice."

Layla tugged his hands, pulling him backward, step-by-step, until he was at the edge of the operating table.

"Do you know what empathy means?" Liza asked.

The student looked behind him at the table, glanced at Layla, then back at Liza. "Empathy?"

"Yes, what does it mean?"

"It's . . . it's when you understand how another person feels."

"That's right," Liza said. She pressed down on his shoulders until he met the table, leaning on the edge with his feet on the floor, unwilling to commit.

"Before you become a physician—a surgeon, certainly—you have to know how the patient feels."

From the other side of the table, Layla pulled him back, gradually, until his head rested on the hard surface. Liza lifted his feet, rotating the lower half of his body until he was completely supine.

Layla moved to the head of the table, taking the position of surrogate anesthesiologist. She leaned over him to reach the leather strap, her full chest covering his face.

As Layla secured the strap over the student's waist, Liza asked, "Do you want to know how it feels?"

His voice full with fear and excitement, he whispered, "Yes."

CHAPTER THIRTY-TWO

Eli reported for his ER call shift in Whitehaven at seven p.m. The off-call doc gave him a report on patients waiting for test results. Routine blood work on a diabetic patient with a toe infection, urinalysis on a nursing home patient with mental status changes, and a head CT on a seventy-year-old man who lived alone and was found unconscious next to his porch swing by his neighbors—but who was now only complaining that the nurses had stolen his clothes. Nothing too exciting, which suited him fine because he'd brought along some homework that he desperately needed to complete. All the awaited test results came back within the hour, and after Eli treated an additional case of noncardiac chest pain, he retreated to the call room with a stale but hot cup of coffee.

His homework consisted of two texts.

The first was *Andreas Vesalius of Brussels*, the definitive biography of the master anatomist by O'Malley. The second, an account of Vesalius's first public anatomy dissection at Bologna in 1540.

If the killer was so intent on imitating the work of Vesalius, Eli felt he needed to know more about the anatomist himself.

Vesalius was born in 1514 and died in 1564. During those fifty years, he brought an era of enlightenment to the study of anatomy, as he refuted the teachings of Galen whose knowledge of anatomy was largely based on dissections of animals a century before. Vesalius brought a literal hands-on approach to anatomical dissection. Rather than orate his observations after delegating the cutting to a prosector, Vesalius took his place beside the body and became the center of attention. And the center of attention he was.

Vesalius's public dissections became legendary. Often, he performed them outdoors on a makeshift stage constructed for the purpose of hosting an audience. A visual collage of this audience is depicted in the title page of the *Fabrica*. The elaborate sketch shows a motley crew of townspeople: politicians, scholars, and curious onlookers lusting after a gruesome sight. At the center lies the body, abdomen opened, with Vesalius not only performing the dissection himself, but also teaching the spectators, their necks craning for a better view.

The voices of a couple of nurses talking in the hallway drifted through the door. Eli assumed they were about to summon him with a knock on the door. Their voices faded. He continued to read.

Obtaining a body for these dissections was far from easy, it seemed. Vesalius had no cadaver donation program, so beneficial to medical schools today. If he wanted to dissect a body, he had to find it and steal it himself. The most ready source were the bodies of executed criminals. At night he went in search of a gibbet, the inverted L-shaped structure on which the bodies of the executed were hung.

While in Paris, Vesalius traveled to Montfaucon, passing the Cemetery of the Innocents, where multitudes of plague victims were interred. At Montfaucon, a gibbet had stood on the mound since the twelfth century. Near it was a charnel house, its colonnade of thirty-foot-high stone pillars joined by wooden beams, where the executed bodies hung until arrangements for their disposal were completed. Crows and outcast dogs held vigil nearby, waiting for a chance at the rotting meat.

When robbing a gibbet, timing was important. For both dissector and audience, a fresh body was preferable to one in which organ decay had begun. This made a public anatomy a spur-of-the-moment event, announcement spreading by word of mouth, spectators scrambling for position near a recently erected stage.

Eli tried to imagine the scene. The crowd gathered around Vesalius on makeshift bleachers waiting for the renegade anatomist to make the first cut, demonstrating layers of soft tissue before working inward. *How different the teaching of anatomy is today*, Eli thought. Emphasis is placed on predissected specimens, fixed and mounted in glass for use year after year, or on virtual specimens presented by computer that can be rotated in a three-dimensional space and viewed at any time. The change in medical school study of anatomy reflected the current direction of medicine as a whole, emphasizing technological intervention rather than hands-on interaction with the patient. Eli was surprised that robotic surgery came to mind so easily, but it fit this theme perfectly. For all its purported advantages, robotic innovation detached the surgeon, the ultimate hands-on practitioner of medicine, from the patient.

In the call room, reclining on the bed, Eli drifted off in a swirling dream of bodies being stolen by robotic machines. Three sharp knocks on his door brought him upright in bed.

"Dr. Branch? Got a patient for you."

Scenes of sixteenth-century body procurement melded with a bright bedside lamp and an open book across his chest.

"Be right there," he yelled.

"Your private patient is here to see you." He heard the nurses snicker, then sneak away.

Private patient?

Eli pulled himself off the bed into the bright hallway. Three nurses waited for him at the central desk and each pointed to bed three, enclosed in a curtain.

For confirmation, Eli pointed. "I'll take curtain number three," he said, playing along with the classic game show.

They smiled. "Yes," the charge nurse said, "I guess you will."

Eli pulled the curtain open to see a familiar face. And stocking cap. Tobogganhead.

"Mr. Felts, how are you?"

Eli's patient sat up straight on the gurney. "Doctor Branch, I am wonderful."

Voluntarily, he removed his toboggan. The nurse in the room, not Janice, who'd been on duty Eli's previous call night, stood aghast at the sight of heaped up raw tissue on top of Mr. Felt's head.

Eli stepped closer for a better look. The top of Tobogganhead's scalp was blood raw, but clean. Not a maggot in sight.

"Very good, Mr. Felts. You have tended this well."

"You're the one killed all the creepy crawlies, Dr. Branch."

An immediate visual of maggots crawling across the ER floor flashed in Eli's mind.

"Creepy crawlies?" the nurse asked. She looked nauseated.

Eli waved her off. "Don't ask."

Eager to talk, Tobogganhead described the event. "Dr. Branch blew maggots off my head with a WaterPik."

Nurse Nausea cupped her hand over her mouth.

"We did have a blast," Eli said. "No pun intended."

Mr. Felts laughed, replaced the toboggan on his head, and reached into the pocket of his ill-fitting trousers. He produced an expensive-appearing cellular phone, flipped it open, and asked the nurse, "Would you take a picture of me and my doctor?"

As though it was covered in blood, the nurse reluctantly took the phone in two fingers. "Sure," she said.

Eli put his arm around Tobogganhead; he put his arm around Dr. Branch.

"You two make quite a pair," she said, moving in closer for the shot. She snapped the picture and handed the phone back with the screen facing them. "There you are."

Tobogganhead beamed with pride. "Is there anyone you'd like to send it to, doctor? My new phone does e-mail."

Eli glanced at the picture. "No, let's not send it to anyone."

While Tobogganhead held the phone, it rang. An angry rap ringtone. He hit the end button quickly, before another explicit lyric played. "I haven't figured out how to change that yet."

Surprised by the ring tone, Eli asked, "Who is calling you?"

Tobogganhead snapped the phone closed. "Wrong number. It's always the wrong number."

CHAPTER THIRTY-THREE

Cate Canavan and Mary, the self-appointed nurse from the Poplar Avenue Free Clinic, ascended the elevator to the fourth floor of Gates Memorial Hospital. They stopped at the nurse's desk and asked for the young girl's room number. The ward clerk pointed to Deanna's room but told them that the newborn was in the nursery. They decided to go there first.

Cate entered the nursery like she was the pediatrician there to do a newborn exam. She made sure her student ID badge was appropriately displayed and she began to search for their patient.

Mary followed her through the maze of plastic cribs, nice little bundled wads lying in each one. She just couldn't help herself. She reached out and tickled the pink toes of a sleeping infant.

Cate saw her and whispered, emphatically, "Don't touch them."

"I was just—"

"Shhhh."

They both stopped by the bassinette labeled "Baby Boy Deanna Rogers." That was the first they were aware of Deanna's last name.

"He is adorable."

Mary was correct. The baby had curly black hair and bright eyes. His toes peeked out from under the blanket. Mary reached out to touch them but stopped herself and gasped.

"Somebody put a string on his toe."

Next to the fifth toe on his left foot was a blue nub, a constricting suture tied at the base.

Cate smiled and tried to calm Mary. "He has an extra digit. They're tying it off."

"What?" Mary counted. "Crack baby's got six toes?"

"It's okay Mary. The extra toe will slough off and no one will ever know."

A nurse approached them.

Cate spoke before Mary had the chance.

"I'm a medical student here to take the baby to her mother."

The nurse glanced at a clock on the wall. "I guess it is time." She gave Mary a skeptical look. "Make sure you sign the baby out."

After Cate signed the form, and another nurse checked the baby's wrist band again, they located Deanna's room. Mary entered the room first, followed by Cate who carried the baby. Deanna was watching television, as if nothing different had happened in her life. She looked at them, her eyes shifting to the infant, briefly, and then back at the screen.

A nurse followed them into the room and informed Deanna that she was being discharged.

When Cate offered to take the girl home, the nurse left the room.

"Fine," Deanna said. "Get me out of here."

Cate and Mary convinced the young mother to hold her baby as they passed the nurse's station and down the elevator. In the hospital parking lot, Cate pulled a thin blanket over the baby's face to protect him from the scorching sun. Deanna walked across the asphalt in a daze. She held the baby low, near her waist, keeping him a few inches from her dress, so that he would not touch her.

Mary followed beside Deanna and then moved in front of her. She was afraid the teenage girl would drop the newborn on the pavement.

"Hold the baby close to you." Mary cradled her arms, rocked them side to side to show her how.

Deanna made a face. "I don't want it near me."

Mary went on the offensive. "This is your baby boy. He needs you to mother him." Mary began to push the infant closer to Deanna.

Cate intervened.

"We'll help you get the baby home. Then your mother can help you take care of him."

Deanna stopped. "Mother? What Mother? My mother's dead."

Cate said, "I'm sorry. Who do you live with?"

"I stay at my aunt's house. But she's not there most of the time."

The baby started crying. Mary told Deanna, "Rock him real easy. That'll calm him."

But Deanna held the baby farther away from her. When Mary reached to help, Deanna said, "Here, you calm him," and she handed the child to Mary.

"In fact," Deanna said, after she had taken a few steps back, "You can keep that baby." She started to cry. "I don't want him."

Cate tried to stop her, but the young girl turned and ran across the parking lot.

Then Cate heard singing. Mary had the baby cradled close to her. She sang a lullaby. A rap lullaby, of sorts.

"Hush little baby, don't you cry. Your mother ran away. Say bye-bye."

CHAPTER THIRTY-FOUR

Meg leaned forward in a swivel chair typing on her computer. Eli stood behind her. He had brought her a fresh copy of *The Commercial Appeal* and had it rolled in a tight column in his hand.

Lipsky is right, he thought. *There has to be some connection between the victims.* Although a social link was possible, a professional relationship seemed more likely.

To search for the connection, Eli chose medical records and personnel files as a starting point. Since these files were electronic, and protected, and Eli no longer had access to the Gates Hospital computer system, he convinced Meg to log on for him.

While they waited for the computer to boot up, Eli's eyes wandered to Meg's hair and how it touched the olive-toned skin of her neck.

"You realize I could lose my hospital privileges for doing this."

Eli did not respond. He took one step back and admired Meg's arched-back posture, her scrub pants pulled tight.

"They check who accesses records and files. If you don't have a reason to be there, they can fire you."

"I know what that's like," Eli said, a knee-jerk response to the word *fired*.

Eli imagined if he were sitting there, Meg in his lap. Swiveling, swiveling—

"Eli?"

He placed the newspaper on her desk, put his hands on Meg's shoulders, and began to knead with his thumbs. She was tense as a board.

"There's no way they can check every file accessed. Besides, you can blame it on me. Tell them I stole your password."

Meg drew her shoulders, pulled away from him. "By the way, that surgeon bitch didn't quite agree with my autopsy findings."

"You talked to French?"

"Oh, yeah. We had a little postmortem tea party down here yesterday."

"What do you mean, she didn't agree?"

"I told her the patient died from an aortic injury. She didn't like that."

Eli nodded. "I bet she didn't."

Meg handed him the papers. "Take a look at how she signed the death certificate."

Eli read the three short lines where Liza described the woman's symptoms and illness.

The third line, reserved for "Immediate Cause of Death," he read aloud.

"Acute Uterine Hemorrhage."

Eli looked at Meg. "She's blaming it on the patient?"

"Damn right she is."

Eli read the certificate again. He shook his head. "As though she's not in enough trouble already, now she's falsifying medical-legal documents."

"I've notified the hospital's legal department," Meg said.

"And?"

"Let's just say they weren't amused."

Meg logged on and the University of the Mid-South Medical Center home page covered the screen.

"What now?" she asked.

"We know that the first victim, the nurse anesthetist, worked at Gates Memorial." Eli said, "Go to the Department of Nursing. See if we can bring up his file."

Meg shook her head as she typed. "The crap you get me into."

A brief profile of the murdered anesthetist appeared. There was no picture.

Nursing School: University of Arkansas
Certified Registered Nurse Anesthetist program:

University of Arkansas
Years at Mid-South Center: Two

The next line listed his affiliation with a specific type of surgery.

Primary Nurse Anesthetist assignment:
General Surgery and OB/GYN

After Eli read the basic information, he asked, "Is that all?"

"What did you expect, a biography?"

Eli ignored this. "While we're here, put in the second nurse, Virginia Brewer."

"Our wrestling fan?"

"Yes."

After a moment's delay, a message appeared on the screen.

No File Matches That Name

"This makes no sense," Eli muttered. "Virginia was an employee at Gates. I'm sure of that."

Meg waited, impatiently. "I feel like that guy on *Star Trek*, you know, always in front of a screen punching in Captain Kirk's orders."

"You mean, Chekhov?"

"Yeah, Chekhov. That's me."

"No way, you're much prettier."

"Gee, thanks."

"Go to Anesthesia. Let's look up the doctor, Singh."

"Aye, aye, Captain."

Moments later, a similar profile appeared for the anesthesiologist found in the casino in Tunica.

Professor of Anesthesiology and Obstetrics/Gynecology
Specialty / Research Interest: Epidural anesthesia techniques
in OB/GYN

Meg turned to Eli. "So, two of the three victims were Gates Memorial employees."

"The file on Virginia Brewer must be a mistake."

"Then let's say all three worked at Gates."

"Not much to go on, is it?" Eli admitted. "We don't know if the nurse anesthetist and the anesthesiologist even knew each other."

"Maybe there is no connection between the victims," Meg offered. "Maybe the killer's just after healthcare professionals. He wants to show power over them, so he not only kills but also takes the risk of lingering at the scene and removing body parts."

"So how does this killer select them?"

"Could be random," Meg said. "Any doctor or nurse who presents an opportunity."

"If it's random," Eli said, not wanting to accept the possibility, "there's no way to stop him."

Eli hoped Meg would refute this, but she didn't.

"Even if we do find a connection between the victims," she said, pointing at the computer screen, "there may be more deaths no matter what we do."

Eli retrieved the copy of the morning paper from her desk. He read the headline from page one.

The Organist Claims Another Victim:
Death Count Rising

Meg reached for the paper, but Eli took a step back and kept reading.

"Dr. Meg Daily performed the autopsies. During these organ recitals, she found that specific bodily organs had been removed from the victims. When asked if she believed The Organist would kill again, she answered affirmatively."

"That son of a bitch."

Eli lowered the paper below eye level. "The Organist?"

"I never said that."

"But you said organ recital."

"Well, yeah."

Eli folded the paper and laid it on her desk.

"Organ recital. The Organist." He smiled, raised his eyebrows. "Congratulations. You've given our killer a name."

CHAPTER THIRTY-FIVE

The long summer days allowed Greenway to train on weeknights. If he could leave the hospital by six thirty and get to Shelby Farms by seven, he could put in a half hour each of biking, swimming, and running and be finished by dusk at eight thirty. If he had the weekend off and started at dawn, he could train for three, maybe four hours straight before the heat became prohibitive. Even with in-hospital call every third night, he could train at least four times a week, often five. That left very little time for a social life. But the Wolfpack Triathlon was a short-term goal, held once a year in late August. After, Greenway would focus on finding a job. Who needed friends anyway?

With less than a year left of his residency, he knew the prime OB/GYN positions would fill early, especially in coveted locations like Vail and Aspen or Breckenridge, where he could ski in winter and hike and mountain bike during the warmer months.

In the park's pavilion, he changed from hospital scrubs into a light-weight pair of drip-dry shorts. Dedicated, goal-oriented, he was right on target with his training. With just a week to go before the Wolfpack, he knew he'd have to push it during the final few days. He found the idea of a television crew stopping by at any time to film him distracting. As he stepped out of the pavilion, the distraction became reality.

"What's your first event today?"

At least she had gotten rid of the suit and was dressed more appropriately this time. Someone had given Carol Baylor a dark orange T-shirt from The Rendezvous Restaurant. She had taken the front of the shirt and tied it in a knot just above her navel. That and a snug pair of white shorts and she didn't look half bad.

"Event?" Greenway asked.

"You know what I mean. Biking or swimming, or—?"

"Swimming," he said, cutting her off. "Always the lake first. Then the bike. Then running. Same order as the triathlon. Always."

She gave him a salute. "Got it."

He walked toward the lake.

A guy holding a heavy camera hoisted it onto his shoulder and began to film.

Greenway turned toward them. "I do some warm-ups first, stretching, stuff like that."

"Don't change anything for us," Baylor said. "We want your normal routine."

After a period of abbreviated stretching, he waded out into the cloudy lake, then cut into the water, his shoulders slicing the still surface.

They filmed until he was out of sight. Then they took a position by his bike and waited.

He emerged from the water fingering his stopwatch and he ran toward Baylor and the cameraman. He slipped on a pair of cross trainers, mounted the bike, and without a word to either of them, took off on the path, a trail of lake water dripping behind him. Over the next half hour, he passed them four times. On the last pass, he parked the bike, set his watch, and tilted a bottle of water in preparation for the day's run. The evening temperature had dropped from 101 to 99. Baylor waited for him to swallow.

"Does training take your mind off it?"

He screwed the cap on. "Off what?"

"Work."

He shrugged and pulled his foot behind him in a stretch to his mid-back. "I guess."

"After what happened, I can only imagine."

He was surprised she knew, but he kept stretching.

"What is it like to lose a patient?"

Looking directly at her, he said, "It sucks."

She had no response to that.

Greenway walked toward the race path.

Baylor and her cameraman followed. "The newspapers report that an investigation at the hospital is underway. Are the doctors at fault?"

"As opposed to whom, Ms. Baylor? The patient?"

She waited a moment. "Tell me about Liza French."

He turned around. "What about her?"

"The newspapers are not very complimentary to her."

"She can take care of herself."

Baylor nodded. "Do you take care of her?"

"What is that supposed to mean?"

"Seems your relationship with her goes beyond the professional."

"I thought this was about my training for a triathlon?"

"This is about you, Thomas. And it appears that 'you,'" she mimed quotation marks with her fingers, "include Dr. Liza French."

Thomas Greenway pressed the tiny buttons on his stopwatch.

"She is quite attractive," Baylor continued. "You two would make a spectacular couple."

He glared at her. "We're through for today." He took off in a dead sprint.

Baylor and the cameraman were gone when he finished the route. Greenway entered the pavilion to change clothes. The park closed at dusk and with only a faint orange horizon remaining, he was pushing it. The parking lot was empty except for his Jeep Cherokee.

Just as he entered the changing room, the flash of a camera surprised him. Someone ran past him and out the door. He ran after the photographer, yelling for them to stop. But outside, he saw no one.

CHAPTER THIRTY-SIX

No fingerprints were identified on any of the pieces of canvas found at each crime scene. The Organist obviously wanted the anatomical sketches to be found, but not traced. Basetti had taken them to the forensics lab. He told Lipsky and Eli that he had a series of sophisticated tests to perform. Basetti was able to identify the type of ink and the canvas structure. But neither the ink nor the type of canvas were unique, both commonly used by artists in a variety of settings, from introductory college courses to sophisticated galleries in New York and Paris.

Eli hoped that Basetti's work might lead them to a particular artist, or at least narrow the field down from any artist proficient at sketching on canvas. This dead end prompted Eli to delve into highly sophisticated research and investigative work.

In the phone book, Eli found three art supply businesses. He hoped that one of the stores sold the type of canvas found at the crime scenes. Of the three, Dekko's Art Emporium on South Main caught his attention. The store was in the heart of the Arts District, where aspiring artists were buying up loft space at semiaffordable prices above art galleries that might eventually display their work.

The Memphis Arts District is a trendy new development south of Beale Street, with boutique shops, coffee houses, and apartments. A historic district once home to depots and tracks for the city's train station, the Arts District represents nouveau chic juxtaposed with the leading edge of urban decay.

Eli passed the Lorraine Hotel on Mulberry Street, now home to the National Civil Rights Museum. He crossed over to South Main and parked in front of Dekko's. Neon tube lighting adorned the entrance.

Two large murals hung on either side of the door, a profile of a young Elvis in a leather jacket on one side, BB King embracing Lucille on the other. Wind chimes sang as Eli entered. A middle-aged woman with gray hair stood behind the counter.

"I'm looking for canvas cloth," Eli told her, wondering if that was correct artistic terminology.

The woman nodded. "What size and weight do you need?"

Eli showed her the piece of canvas that Lipsky had reluctantly let him keep. He flipped it over so the sketch of the navicular bone faced down. The woman pushed her glasses up onto the bridge of her nose, rubbed the canvas between her fingers.

"This is high quality canvas. I do believe we carry it."

Eli followed her down an aisle lined by shelves filled with easels, canvasses, and large tablets of specialized art paper specifically for charcoal or watercolor. They passed a stack of bristol board. Eli had no idea what that was.

"Let me see the paper again."

Eli gave it to her. But this time while examining it, the woman flipped the paper over. She stared at the illustration. Kept staring.

"What's wrong?" Eli asked.

"Oh, nothing. It's just—Did you draw this?"

"No," Eli told her. "I found it."

She admired the sketch again. "There was an artist who came into the store a couple of times. She did sketches like this."

"What do you mean, like this?"

"Detailed anatomical drawings. Skeletons, bones. Her work was beautiful, but sort of odd." She handed the canvas back to Eli and asked, "Do you know the artist?"

The question surprised Eli. "No, I was going to ask you the same question."

"Where did you find the sketch?"

"I bought it, actually. At an estate sale. Sold for five dollars. Can you imagine that?" Eli couldn't believe how easily he had taken up lying.

The woman began to search through her stack of canvas again.

"But I'm trying to find the artist. I want to buy more of her work."

That statement seemed to grab the woman's starving-artist sensibility.

"She orders a lot of canvas from us. Has it delivered directly to her place." The saleswoman hesitated, as if trying to decide whether to divulge any more information.

"I'm a collector of sorts," Eli added, hoping to up the ante. "I'd be willing to pay her good money if only I could contact her."

This was enough.

"Let me see what I can find."

Back at the counter, the woman began thumbing through a thick register. "Here it is. She has a loft studio just down the street."

Eli leaned over to see the address.

The woman turned the register toward him.

This allowed Eli to read the artist's name.

Helen Claire.

CHAPTER THIRTY-SEVEN

Eli climbed a dimly lit stairwell to the third floor loft while he thought about the name.

Helen Claire.

H.C.

The initials on each crime scene sketch.

That was all.

Eli thought about calling Lipsky before climbing this stairwell. He knew that he should. But it was just an art studio. And he was right in front of it already. He would simply take a quick look. If he found anything, or anybody, Lipsky would be the first person he called.

Pastel green paint peeled off in curls from the stairwell's ceiling and from its walls along the baseboard. Ironic, paint peeling in a painter's studio. He found the door that matched the sales log of the art store. The door was closed but not flush with the frame, as though it had swelled and would not latch. Eli knocked, softly at first, then when no one answered, harder. He pushed against the door. It was wedged tight. He pushed with his shoulder and bumped it a couple of times until the door gave way. He looked behind him. Seeing no one, Eli entered the studio.

A musty draft pushed against him. A single window on the far side of the room had been left open. Through a skylight, slants of sun captured a floating cloud of paint flecks and dust. White sheets hung from loops of wire and swirled rhythmically in the breeze, dividing the loft into shifting rooms.

Within each room sat an easel. Paint brushes had dried against palettes and sketching tools lay scattered about as though the artist had left at an inopportune moment.

Eli passed by the undulating sheets to find more and more easels occupying the space. Each canvas was filled with sketches and paintings of the human form in fine anatomical detail. The easel closest to him displayed a brilliant reproduction of the skeletal man. On the easel adjacent to it, a skull, the zigzagging fissures drawn to perfection. Eli raised an easel that had fallen over and set it upright. An exquisite rendering of the muscle man greeted him with an outstretched hand, suspended effortlessly. Eli felt an intimate familiarity with each of these sketches.

Vesalius.

Brilliant reproductions of the Renaissance anatomist filled the entire loft. He recognized a plate from the *Fabrica*, the long bone of the leg and the foot. At the bottom, a square block was cut out of the canvas. From his pocket, he extracted an envelope containing the card left at the first crime scene. He removed the sketch of the navicular bone. The fabric of the canvas was an exact match and its shape was an exact fit for the missing corner of the original canvas. Eli's heart raced.

He called Lipsky on his cell phone and told him where he was, what he had found. Eli wanted to search the loft alone, to continue examining these fantastic sketches, but at least it would be several minutes before Lipsky arrived when he'd have to explain the anatomical art to the detective.

He crossed the wooden floor of the loft to close the window. As he reached for the high, open sash, a pigeon rousted from its perch at the loft's apex, swooped down, and took off through the opening. Eli watched the bird fly across the alley before he pulled the window shut and latched it.

With the draft calmed, the flowing sheets collapsed like sails withdrawn at harbor. Visible now in the center of the loft, he saw sheets of black plastic spread out like a tent from a single point near the ceiling. Eli circled the wide base of the plastic tent and searched for an opening. Whatever was contained inside must have been more valuable to the painter than the smaller easel works. He circled the structure again and found a slit in the plastic that he had missed on the first pass.

Protected by the tent, a large mural-like painting rested on the floor, supported by thick wooden beams behind it and to the sides. The painting was at least ten feet high and equally as wide. A fold-out ladder was parked at the center of the painting.

The painting showed exquisite detail. Eli stepped closer to the marvelous reproduction of the *Fabrica*'s title page. Numerous times, he had seen a page-sized reproduction of the marvelous illustration. But he had never seen one as a life-sized rendering.

Centered at the top of the composition, a crest featured three small animals stacked vertically above an ornate nameplate that announced, in Latin, the leading man—Andreae Vesalii. Stately Corinthian columns provided backdrop for the ragged audience who gathered for the public anatomy. The ladder obscured his appreciation of the central figures in the painting, so he pushed it aside to view the female subject of dissection, her abdomen open for Vesalius to inspect her uterus.

In contrast to the black-and-white original of the *Fabrica*'s actual title page, this oversized reproduction of the scene of public dissection came to life on canvas with the vivid colors used by the artist.

Although the painting at first appeared complete, Eli realized that its central figure was missing. Vesalius had yet to be painted, the entire piece suspended in time with a captive audience awaiting the anatomist's arrival.

Eli stared at the vacant spot on the canvas and imagined Vesalius there imprinted on the background, his face turned toward the viewer, hands displaying the intimate details of his subject. Moments later, the vision disappeared and he was left wondering why the painting had been abandoned. Why had the artist not started with Vesalius and worked outward toward the periphery? But these questions were merely a prelude to the larger puzzle.

Who was Vesalius's modern day successor?

And why must he kill?

Eli heard the door to the loft open, a subtle creak of hinges. He felt the draft, less now because the window was closed, but enough movement of air to lift the edge of the sheet beside him. Perhaps he had left the door cracked—a breeze through the lofty old warehouse had simply pushed the door open. Or maybe Lipsky had arrived and was casing the place before making himself known? No. Not enough time had passed for him to travel from the police station. Then the door closed. Hems of the sheets deflated once again. He knew he was no longer alone.

Eli listened to slow footsteps along the edge of the loft. Most likely this was the artist returning to her work. He was about to meet Helen Claire. He started to call out.

The footsteps stopped.

Then the footsteps were heavier, faster, someone was running behind him. He heard the crash of easels and turned to see the large mural falling toward him. The bulky wooden frame struck his shoulder and knocked him to the floor where he landed on his injured arm. Eli scrambled from under the frame and saw the sharp corner of an easel inches from his face. The blow from it knocked him on his back. Eli pressed the gash on his forehead, blood oozing between his fingers into his eyes.

A blurry figure stood over him, winding up for another blow. Before it could be delivered, Eli straight kicked his assailant in the knee causing him to stumble backward. On his feet again, Eli took two steps before a blow to the back of his head took him down again.

This time, he did not get up.

CHAPTER THIRTY-EIGHT

"How many fingers?"

Eli blinked. Drying blood had glued one lid closed. He could see light and an object in front of his face.

"How many fingers, doc?"

Eli tried to raise his head. The room was spinning. He felt like throwing up.

"Just count them for me."

Eli recognized Lipsky's voice, more irritating than ever.

"Isn't this how you test for brain damage? With a finger count?"

Gradually, Eli remembered where he was. The loft. The paintings. Someone beating his head in with a folded easel. He felt the cut on his forehead, rubbed the blood from his eyes. He knew he should be grateful to be alive, but right now he just wanted Lipsky to shut the hell up.

"I learned this from one of those medical documentaries on TV. Here," Lipsky offered, "what if I hold them closer?"

Eli cleared his throat. "I see your chubby paw. Okay? Help me up."

Lipsky pulled Eli's shoulders until he was in a sitting position. Eli kept his eyes closed.

"I'd stick to hospital work if I were you, doc. You suck at self-defense."

"What happened?"

"You called me, remember. So I came. When I was climbing the steps, heard a big crash. Come in here and yelled 'Police' and saw a man running toward the window. Saw you lying on the floor. Whoever it was, he jumped out like Batman and was gone. I called for backup, but they won't find him."

Eli rubbed the back of his head.

"Someone was trying to beat your brains out." Lipsky pointed to the bloody easel on the floor. "Never seen one of those used as a weapon. What did you do, tell the artist his paintings were crap?"

Eli told Lipsky how the assailant had entered after he was already inside the loft.

"What did he look like?"

Eli didn't feel like answering any questions. "I don't know—big, tall, strong."

"Handsome too, I bet."

Typical, compassionate Lipsky.

"Hard to see details," Eli said, "with a block of wood in your eye."

Lipsky leaned over for a better look at Eli's head. "I see what you mean. Looks like that needs a needle and some thread."

"I'll live."

Lipsky walked through the loft, admired a few sketches, found the card from the first crime scene and brought it back to Eli. "So this is where these cards came from?"

Eli nodded. Big mistake. His head throbbed. He closed his eyes and pointed. "That piece matches the canvas used here. I found the sketch where it had been cut from."

Eli listened to Lipsky's footsteps as he weaved through the easels.

"So, this guy sketches away during the day, kills at night, and leaves his work behind as a memento. How nice."

"The artist's name is Helen Claire. But she is not the killer."

"How do you know?" Lipsky asked.

"Whoever beat the shit out of me is not a woman. I'm sure of that."

CHAPTER THIRTY-NINE

When Eli returned to his apartment in South Memphis, a phone message was waiting for him. A nurse had called from Green Hills State Home where his brother lived. Henry's nightmares and panic attacks were becoming more frequent. His caretakers had injected him with sedatives to keep him from hurting himself or the other residents. This time, the nurse warned, they had to physically restrain his brother.

As Eli listened to the message, he pictured the decrepit conditions at "The Home," as it was called. When he visited, it was not unusual for him to find dead bugs matted in Henry's sheets and pools of urine on the floor in the bathroom. Eli wondered what their version of restraints might be. He envisioned Henry fighting against a straitjacket.

Eli was not surprised by the call. A pattern had become predictable. Each year, a few days before the anniversary of their mother's death, Henry changed from calm and cooperative to agitated and downright belligerent. The day their mother died in August was the only day Henry circled on the bedside calendar Eli gave him every Christmas. The nursing staff could inject Henry with sedatives, but Eli knew that only one thing would satisfy his brother—a visit to their mother's grave.

Historic Elmwood Cemetery dates back to the pre-Civil War era. Resting place of Civil War generals and politicians and prostitutes, Elmwood is a visual sanctuary. Civil War historian Shelby Foote is buried there, as is E. H. "Boss" Crump, the Memphis politician so important in the city's history, as is the wife of an obscure anatomist, who was buried there at the base of a hill on a sweltering afternoon ten years earlier. And every year, on the same day in August, her two sons visit the site of her modest headstone.

Eli drove south on Dudley Street, took a quick left onto E. H. Crump Boulevard, then zigzagged back onto Dudley. His Bronco passed old warehouses and open lots where the grass was long dead and the ground lay bare and dusty.

Henry rode in the backseat. As a child, whenever their mother took the boys for a ride, Henry rode in the back of the car. Not one for changing routines, he was not changing now, no matter how much Eli urged him to ride up front.

Dudley Street came to a dead end at the entrance to Elmwood Cemetery. The street narrowed to a single lane bridge that arched over a gorge, a train track lay below. Eli glanced at a sign to the left that announced visiting hours: 8–4:30 daily. By the time Eli had convinced the staff at Green Hills State Home to release Henry to him for a few hours, their trip to the cemetery started late. It was almost four o'clock. If they missed their annual visit, Henry would be unable to cope.

A high fence surrounded the bridge on both sides. Eli drove onto the bridge and stopped midway. A train passed slowly under the bridge a few feet below them. Henry had always been fascinated by trains. He leaned close to the window.

They waited until the short train passed before continuing across the bridge, then drove past the cemetery manager's office, which doubled as a visitor center. The road branched into three paths. Eli chose the middle path and they followed it as it curved at the bottom of a hill before ascending the hill's western side. Eli considered this hill the heart of Elmwood because at its crest lay the centerpiece of the cemetery, a five-column stone colonnade elevated on a platform and modeled after ancient Roman architecture.

Eli parked along the side of the paved path. He removed Henry's wheelchair, unfolded it, and pushed it to the side of the car. Able-bodied Henry climbed out of the back and plopped into the chair, leaning forward, ready for the ride.

Henry must have sensed that it was late in the day. He bucked against the chair, trying to move it along while Eli retrieved the box holding the grass clippers, the scrub brush, the liquid soap.

"Hold on buddy," Eli said. "We're going."

Eli glanced at his watch. In a half hour, the grounds would be closed to visitors.

The attendant on duty, a young man named Jason, met them on the path.

"Hello, Branches."

Jason called everyone by their last name, knowledge he gained by watching family members at their respective gravesites. He knew the tombstone of each family member and the exact path they would take to get there.

Eli greeted him with a single nod, "Jason." He kept pushing the wheelchair.

Henry did not acknowledge Jason's presence. He would not make eye contact with anyone other than Eli, and even then, no longer than necessary.

"We're closing in a half hour," Jason told them.

Eli said nothing. He pushed Henry toward their mother's grave. Henry insisted on using the wheelchair in the cemetery even though he did not need it now. Eli had pushed him in a wheelchair during their mother's funeral ten years earlier. Every year, on the anniversary of her death, the two brothers reenacted the same ritual using this same wheelchair on the concrete paths to her grave.

Sunlight reflected at a slant off stone-encased mausoleums that projected from the ground like shrines. A deftly crafted cherub kept watch as time covered her in a skin of green moss. They passed tombstones that presided over bankers, and lawmakers, and harlots; a refuge in the midst of the city where some inhabitants lived larger in death than life.

Henry leaned forward, engine-humming his way to a faster trip. An older couple passed arm-in-arm and Eli steered off the path to give them way.

Eli wondered how different their own lives would be had their mother lived. Henry would be with her, sharing home-cooked meals, a clean bed to sleep in each night. Eli had been a poor substitute for Henry's mother, as every annual visit to her grave reminded him. Over the years, his twice-monthly visits to Henry's facility had dropped to every other month. But they always had this date, a time when the memory of their mother bonded them as brothers.

Henry watched for the landmarks that led to their mother's site. He pushed forward, harder, as the colonnade on top of the hill came into view. Arranged in a semicircle, the five Corinthian columns stood on a stone platform, a stage awaiting the cast of a Greek tragedy.

There was no traveling troupe present, rather a father and his young daughter sharing a late lunch on the stone steps. Staring over the graves, the man halved an apple and ate it, while the girl skipped in and out of the columns, a streaming blue ribbon in her hair trying to keep up.

Eli was reminded, by contrast, of his father, who had died two years before. How in the years before his death, Elizer Branch never visited his wife's grave, at least, not with his sons. For that matter, he never visited Henry, either.

Henry was distracted by the girl and her father. Eli guessed that Henry was wondering what had happened to the mother, and why she wasn't there to see her daughter at play. Eli pushed off the main path closer to the stone columns. Because Henry rarely showed interest in other people, Eli felt obligated to foster any opportunity. When the girl saw the wheelchair, she ran out to them against the warnings of her father. She stopped in front of Henry. She held a tattered, wilting bouquet of wildflowers garnished with weeds and grass.

"What's your name?" she asked.

Henry looked down at her feet.

"What happened to your legs?" she asked. "Why can't you walk?"

After a few moments of silence, Eli intervened.

"He's sad today. Doesn't want to talk."

The girl bent with hands on her knees, trying her best to make eye contact. "My mother died. We come here a lot."

Henry rocked against the chair, eager to leave the little girl and her questions. She reached for his hands, which Henry allowed to open, and into them she placed the flowers. She closed his hands around the bouquet and skipped back to the safety of her father. The rest of the way, Henry held the flowers protectively suspended over his lap.

Many visitors were attracted to Elmwood each year by the craftsmanship of the headstones, combined with the history of those buried there. A photographer's haven. Eli felt at times that the cemetery was more tourist attraction than resting place. However, in these last few minutes of visitation, only a few family members were making their way back to their cars.

Eli and Henry approached the grave of Naomi Branch. Henry jumped from the wheelchair before Eli fully stopped. He rushed to the headstone and knelt in front of it. Eli saw the reason for Henry's agitation. Weeds sprouted at the base of the stone and a vine climbed across their mother's engraved name. The sun had baked on a layer of grime.

Henry ripped up the vine, wrapping it over and over around his hand until he had enough purchase to dislodge it. He flung it to the side, grabbed the brush and soap from the box, and began to scrub the limestone. Eli clipped the weeds at the base of the stone.

Fifteen minutes later, Henry stood, took a step back and examined their work. Satisfied with the appearance, he placed a single peach-colored rose on top of the headstone, as was their custom. Then he collected the girl's bouquet of wildflowers from the seat of his wheelchair and sprinkled them at the base of his mother's grave.

CHAPTER FORTY

A car crept along the paved road at the bottom of the hill. Visiting hours were over, but by the looks of the spotless black sedan, the occupants were not here to visit the dead. The car stopped behind Eli's Bronco. Eli continued to push Henry in his wheelchair until two men wearing dark suits got out of the sedan and began walking toward them. At first, Eli thought they might be undertakers or some other representatives for the cemetery.

Not quite.

"Dr. Branch, may we have a word with you, sir?"

As they came closer, Eli recognized the federal agents that had approached him a few days ago at the hospital. He kept pushing Henry, who was already becoming anxious to leave.

The big agent flashed his badge as though that would make Eli stop. It didn't.

"I know who you are," Eli said.

"We need an update on the investigation," Moustache said.

"Now's not the time. We're in a cemetery, in case you didn't notice."

The agent looked over a few plots. "They won't mind, trust me."

"Maybe I don't know anything."

"Yes you do."

"Why's that?"

"Because you know this isn't right. That something happened in that OR. Something bad."

"Yeah, a patient died. That's pretty bad."

"You know what we mean. You can't turn your back on this."

Henry pushed at the wheels, trying to move them along.

"I've got enough to take care of on my own," Eli said and gestured to Henry. "I don't need this mess."

"But this 'mess' started years ago, didn't it, Dr. Branch?"

Henry was becoming impatient with the slow progress. He started rolling the wheelchair himself.

"What exactly happened that night, doctor? When you and a much younger Liza French were on call together." Using his fingers, Moustache smoothed the hair on his lips. "A certain patient needed your assistance—emergency, life-saving assistance—but the two of you seemed preoccupied, unable to respond to desperate calls on your beepers."

Eli reached his car and opened the back door for Henry, who climbed in without assistance.

"Or so the nurse said in her incident report. She said she saw both you and Dr. French come out of a linen closet while a prominent Nashville politician was taking his last breath. Seems the two of you were quite breathless as well."

Eli folded Henry's wheelchair and placed it in the back.

The agent continued. "That incident happened over a decade ago and it just faded away. You would like to keep it that way, wouldn't you, Doctor?"

CHAPTER FORTY-ONE

Eli's cell phone rang as they were leaving the cemetery.

"I found some information on Nurse Tongue."

"Nice name, Meg," Eli said. "Shows sensitivity to the victim."

"Sorry, I forgot that you knew her. Do you want to hear it or not?"

"Sure I do."

Meg said nothing for a few moments. Made him wait.

Eli drove across the cemetery bridge. In the backseat, Henry craned his neck to look at the empty train track below.

"Meg?"

"She worked at Presbyterian Hospital."

"Presby? That doesn't fit." As he said this, Eli knew Meg was giving him only bits and pieces. He accelerated on Dudley Street, as though going faster would coax the information out of her.

"But get this, she was hired there only a couple of days ago after transferring from . . ." She hesitated long enough for Eli to fill in the blank.

"Gates Memorial."

"Where she worked for eleven years," Meg continued, "in the operating room."

On Interstate 240, Eli merged behind an eighteen-wheeler, felt the turbulent air shake his Bronco until he fell in behind the truck's draft.

"Of course, because I knew her as an operating room nurse. But how did you find out she was working at the other hospital?"

"There's a citywide nursing data base you can access online."

Eli considered the source. "First, it was the Gates doctors' files, now city nursing. What's next, Meg? Classified federal information?"

"You put me on this trail, Eli. Once I get a whiff, I can't stop."

"Did you have a password to get in?"

"Yeah, as a matter of fact. Miss Conch gave it to me."

"Miss Conch?"

"She's been around longer than antibiotics. She knows everything."

Eli pictured the woman squatting behind her desk, glow of a computer screen in her glasses. "I'm curious, Meg. What surgical specialty did the nurse cover other than general surgery?"

He could hear taps on the keyboard.

"General surgery and—OB/GYN."

Eli set his cruise control near eighty and fell in behind an eighteen-wheeler that cleared their side of the interstate. "If I remember correctly, there's one specialty that all three victims have in common."

Meg was apparently waiting for the answer.

"OB/GYN," Eli said.

"What are you thinking?"

"Maybe that's the connection."

"So they all worked in the same specialty. What of it?"

"I need to get in the OR database," Eli said. "Search for operations they may have had in common."

"Is that separate from the doctors' files?"

"Yes, I think so. I'll be there in less than an hour. Think you can get us in?"

"I can try," Meg said. "If not, I'll find out how from the Conch."

CHAPTER FORTY-TWO

When Eli arrived at the morgue, he found Meg sitting at the computer. She had pulled a white dry-erase board next to her desk, written the names of the three victims, and next to each name their identifying organs:

Bone

Tongue

Stomach

This ID scheme fit with the method used in clinical medicine, referring to the patient by their diseased organ rather than by name: *the gallbladder in room six, pancreatitis in nine.*

Eli turned a chair backward, straddled it, and tilted toward the screen.

Meg greeted him. "Where you been?"

Eli released a pent-up breath. He had driven a straight shot from Henry's institution, staring absently at the road, preoccupied with the series of murders, trying to discern a pattern.

"I went to see my brother."

Meg turned toward Eli. He did not look away from the computer screen.

"How is Henry?"

Eli shook his head. "Not good."

Meg already knew how dedicated Eli was to his brother. Each other's only close family, Eli was Henry's sole financial and emotional support.

"You're doing all you can, Eli. The place may not be pretty, but they will take care of him. They will."

Eli nodded, confirming her words and moving on.

"What are we looking at?"

Meg slid the mouse and advanced to the next screen. "You asked for the OR log files. You got 'em."

"The Conch-inator rocks."

"She has her moments."

Eli studied the web page and pointed to a section of the screen. "Go to Operating Room Register."

The next window presented the search options, by *Specialty*, *Operation*, or *Personnel*.

Under *Personnel*, eight empty fields appeared in which to enter the names of OR personnel.

"What is this database used for?" Meg asked.

"Quality control. Allows you to search outcomes based on different OR teams."

"Outcomes?"

"Say that the infection rate of a certain procedure starts to rise. They can search for common denominators within the teams. Maybe someone who's breaking sterile technique—or carries staph in their nose."

Meg fake gagged. "Hospitals are nasty."

"Yeah," Eli said and turned to the white board. "Enter the three names. See what happens."

Meg started typing. "Any certain order?"

"No, it shouldn't matter. The computer will search for all operations that have those three in common."

After typing the third name, Meg looked at Eli.

"Hit enter."

A prompt appeared asking for dates of inclusion.

"How far back?" Meg asked.

"I don't know, say, six months."

A list of operations filled the screen, listed by date, type of procedure, and surgeon. Meg scrolled to the end of the list. Twenty-three operations in all.

"So what does this mean?"

"It means that these three employees, all of whom are now dead, were assigned to work together on twenty-three operations over the past six months."

They read through the list. Orthopedic operations such as hip replacements and spinal fusions. General surgery cases, mainly laparoscopic cholecystectomies. And gynecologic procedures including cervical biopsy, D and Cs, hysterectomies.

"How does this help, Eli? They worked at the same hospital, with some of the same patients. So what?"

"We're looking for a connection, Meg. You got a better idea?"

She gestured toward the sheet-covered lump lying on her autopsy table. "Yeah, I could take care of my customer. He's been waiting patiently through all this."

"I forgot about him," Eli said. "I guess you never get lonely down here."

"Never."

Eli turned toward the gurney. "Just a few more minutes, sir. She'll be right with you."

Meg turned his face back toward the screen. "Very funny."

Eli grabbed the mouse, clicked at random on one of the operations listed. A spinal fusion.

The screen gave a detailed account of the procedure. The patient's name was listed at the top of the page followed by all the personnel involved. Eli found the names of the anesthesiologist, the anesthetist, and the nurse. Also listed were the circulating nurse, orthopedic resident, medical student, and, of course, the attending surgeon.

"That confirms they worked together," Meg said. "But what does it tell us about why they were murdered?"

"I don't know," Eli said, "we're looking for something unusual." He read information on the screen that included start and end time of the operation, designation of infection risk, and any complications that occurred. The spinal operation lasted one hundred and thirty-four minutes, was a clean case, no complications.

Eli returned to the previous screen and scrolled up to the top of the page Meg had initially displayed.

"Wait a minute."

"Wait a minute, what?" Meg asked.

Eli waved the cursor over the most recent operation and underlined the surgeon's name, Liza French. The operation was marked with a red exclamation point. Eli double-clicked it.

A gray warning box appeared.

> The following report contains sensitive information protected under HIPPA. Are you authorized to access such information?

"No, I'm not," Eli said aloud as he clicked a smaller box marked *Yes*. A second warning box appeared.

"I don't think they want us to be here," Meg said.

> This patient died during the operation. The confidentiality of all patients, including those deceased, is protected. Do you wish to continue?

"Hell, yes. I wish to."

The patient's name and list of personnel were arranged similarly to the previous case. Eli found the name of the most recent victim, nurse Virginia Brewer.

He imagined what must have occurred. The calm of an operation coming to a close. A shift into terror. He saw flashes of the anesthesiologist checking the airway, nurses scrambling, Liza watching from the robotic console, her career crashing in a sea of red.

Meg realized that Eli was staring at the screen. "Eli?"

He refocused. Scrolled down to a section labeled *Comments*:

> *Intraoperative death occurred at one hundred forty-seven minutes. Patient pronounced dead by Dr. French at 10:27 a.m.*

"I should know," Meg said. "I did the autopsy. It was awful."

She had Eli's full attention.

"And Liza French did not agree with my findings or the cause of death."

"Yes, I remember." Eli said. "A vascular injury, right?"

"Aortic laceration. Right at the bifurcation. Likely from a misplaced trocar. They opened her, tried to repair it, but she was gone."

Again, Eli saw flashes of the operating room. He sensed that stomach-to-the-floor feeling of a bad complication. But he'd never had a fatality in the OR. Eli read the names of the victims again. He thought of the other personnel in the operation as survivors. At least for now.

For the first time there seemed to be a link between the three murders and this operative death. Only he could not imagine how.

"Maybe it's just coincidence, Eli. These three people died *and* they happen to work together."

"Not just died, Meg. They were murdered. Bones and tongues cut out, stomachs put on display." Eli realized that he'd raised his voice, was almost shouting. But he kept on. "And not just worked together but were assigned to the same operation during which the patient happened to die."

Meg said nothing while Eli calmed down somewhat. Then she pointed at the screen. "Are we looking at the names of the next victims?"

"Put it this way," Eli said. "I wouldn't want my name written on this page."

They stared at the screen in silence until Meg asked, "What's this?" She pointed to another *Comment* at the bottom of the page.

> This operation was broadcast live on the Internet until the complication occurred, at which time SurgCast terminated the transmission.

"SurgCast?" Meg asked.

Eli knew of operations webcast in real time, but he'd never seen one. *Why didn't Liza tell me about this?*

"That operation was an unfortunate choice to post live on the Internet," Eli said.

"No kidding," Meg agreed. "Why did the hospital do it?"

"Reality surgery on the web. It's great advertising."

"Maybe I'll just start filming my autopsies. I could use some extra cash."

"It's being done, I'm sure."

Meg shook her head. "I could've filmed this woman's autopsy. That way," Meg explained, "the viewers could have seen her die in the OR, then watched her postmortem exam. Bet that hasn't been done."

"Probably not," Eli agreed. "Hang on to that one for sweeps week."

CHAPTER FORTY-THREE

At eight o'clock in the morning, The Poplar Avenue Free Clinic felt like a sauna. By midday, the temperature would be nearly intolerable, with a predicted high of 103. Not a good day for the clinic's single air-conditioning unit to quit.

Cate discovered this when she arrived at seven a.m. to prepare for the day's patients. Out of habit, the first thing she did was turn on the window unit. Straight to high. When she flipped the switch, only an electric hum emanated from the aged machine. The fan did not blow at all. Not even hot air. Cate turned it off, then back on again, stopping at the low setting this time, saying a desperate prayer.

Nothing.

She had run the unit on high each day, nonstop, all summer. Single-handedly she had killed it.

The patients would start showing within the hour. She could open the windows. That would help for a couple of hours. But then—

The care basket of snacks from her brother sat on the table in the break room. She had given most of the goodies away. She reached in the pocket of her white coat and felt for her cell phone tangled up in the rubber tubing of her stethoscope.

She called her brother. He was good at fixing things. Had the touch, as they say. She looked at her chipped fingernails, at a long scratch on the back of her hand that she had clumsily scraped on the counter's edge in her apartment. Funny that *he* was the one born with the hands of a surgeon.

Her brother said he would be there in an hour. Fifty minutes later, he pulled his black Trans Am to the back of the clinic. An air-conditioning unit bulged from the open trunk which was held down with a piece of rope.

Cate was busy dressing a diabetic foot ulcer. By then, Mary and her shopping cart had arrived and she helped with the procedure by opening packages of sterile gauze. When her brother walked in, Cate was so happy to see him she wanted to hug his neck.

He tested the air conditioner with the same dead result. While Cate wrapped the final bandage around the patient's foot, she watched her brother unscrew the bolts on the front panel. He wore a sleeveless black T-shirt.

Mary watched him as well. She approached him as he strained against a rusty bolt, reached over and pinched his flexing bicep.

"Cate, your brother's got rats tattooed on his arm."

He said nothing.

Cate glanced at her brother's tattoo, a crest of three slender animals drawn one on top of the other.

As usual, Mary wouldn't let it go. "Why's he got rats on his arm?"

"They're weasels, okay?" He pulled away from Mary. "And don't touch me again."

Mary backed up. "Sorry." Then under her breath. "Rat man."

He finished removing the panel and returned outside.

When Cate opened the door to call in the next patient, she was surprised to see her brother standing out front near the patients. While he admired Cate's work with the indigent population, he preferred to have no interaction with them. But there he was, talking with Joey the Flicker. By the way her brother motioned with his hands, he seemed to be explaining something to them. Joey took a step back, and for once stopped flicking his lighter, as though surprised himself at the interaction with this man.

Cate closed the door and watched them through the window. By then, Foster and the Meatman had become curious and moved to stand beside Joey. The three men stepped closer. Cate watched her brother open his wallet and hand each man what she thought was a twenty dollar bill. Then he led the men around to the back of the clinic. Cate called in the next patient.

A few minutes later, Cate's brother pulled the air-conditioning unit out of the wall, without the help of the men he'd just hired. Not only does he have good hands, Cate thought, but he's also strong as hell. She wondered why he even paid the men if he wasn't going to use them.

He removed the replacement unit from the back of his car and carried it toward the clinic. Foster, the Meatman, and Joey the Flicker shuffled alongside and held to the side of the unit as though trying to help. They held the unit in place while her brother secured it with screws. He flipped a switch and cool air blew into the clinic. Her brother waved to her and left. The three men returned to the end of the line.

CHAPTER FORTY-FOUR

Nate Lipsky drove his squad car down South Cooper Street and stopped at a light before turning onto Central Avenue. The timing of this homicide call was unusual—4:30 in the afternoon. Lipsky blocked the sun with his hand so he could see the light change. What was most unusual about this call was its location. He looked again at the address for the Zante Repository.

How could someone have been killed in the Zante?

Primarily an attraction for school groups and admirers of odd Southern culture, the Zante held the logical combination of stuffed animals, from anteaters to nutria the size of a small horse, various Native American artifacts, and a historical exhibit on the contribution of the comman American chicken to the Southern way of life. A planetarium brought visitors into the 21st century and allowed gazers to learn about the constellations as tiny lights twinkled against a pitch-black fabric sky.

From the initial call, Lipsky came to a conclusion, or at least an educated guess, about the mode of death. When he heard Zante Repository, he figured someone ambled into the museum from the street in the final throes of heat stroke. But the officer first on the scene had called from the planetarium. He said that in the middle of a shooting star show, a human body part fell from the ceiling, straight through the constellation of Orion.

Lipsky asked him if it was a heavenly body. The young officer didn't get it, but said, "No, it looks more like a heart."

"A heart?"

"And what's weird, we found a drawing of the heart pinned to the victim's clothing. Like a name tag or something."

"Have you found the body?"

"Yeah, stuffed in a closet in the back of the museum."

A few minutes later, Lipsky arrived at the Zante Repository. An ambulance, two squad cars, and a Memphis fire truck were already there. A group of children huddled at the entrance, their adult chaperones reporting frantically into cell phones.

CHAPTER FORTY-FIVE

Before making the call, Eli moved to the far side of the autopsy room with his cell phone, as though he needed privacy.

Meg mouthed the question. "Who you calling?"

Lipsky answered.

"I know who the next victim will be," Eli told him.

"That's good. So you can tell me whose heart this is splattered across the floor."

When he first dialed the phone, Eli had an I'm-calling-too-late feeling. If Lipsky was already at a crime scene, Eli's feeling was valid. What alarmed him most, however, was not that another victim had been killed.

"Did you say *heart?*"

"Looks like it to me, Doc."

Once again, not the pattern of Vesalius and the *Fabrica.* But now Eli had the list of operating room personnel.

"A male or female?"

"Hmm." Lipsky groaned. "I'm pretty good with female anatomy, but I'll be damned if I can look at this piece of meat and call sex. Hold on."

In the background, Eli heard Lipsky ask for the victim's driver's license.

A few seconds later, Lipsky said, "Female. Fifty-eight years old."

"Wait." Eli moved to the computer screen. "Don't tell me the name." He switched the call to speakerphone.

Lipsky hummed an off-key version of the *Jeopardy* theme.

Meg rolled her eyes.

The remaining females on the list were the medical student, attending surgeon Liza French, and the circulating nurse. Both the student and Liza were much younger than fifty-eight.

Eli called out the name and added, "She's a nurse."

"Nnnnnnn," Lipsky buzzed. "Try again."

Lipsky read the name from the license.

"Damn it," Eli whispered. It didn't match with any name on the screen.

"What?" Meg tried to catch up on the conversation.

Eli answered by shaking his head, still listening to Lipsky.

"You did get one part right, though," Lipsky told him. "About her being a nurse. We found a Gates ID badge in her purse."

CHAPTER FORTY-SIX

Eli stepped into the dark sanctuary of Madison Avenue Episcopal Church, a place where he found himself more often during the past few weeks. Sometimes, as he did now, he entered the empty church in the evening, alone, except for an occasional church worker who prepared the sanctuary for the next morning's services, leaving Eli to himself on the back pew, merely nodding to him in affirmation of his need to seek a few moments of refuge. Once, he slipped into a back pew on a Sunday morning. He made it through the entire service, but he preferred his solitary visits in an empty chapel.

Today, another visitor had arrived before him. A few pews in front of him, a dark green blouse covered shoulders that bowed. She rocked slowly forward and back again, meditating.

Eli sat as quietly as he could, not wanting to distract the woman, or not wanting to be known. That was it, he realized. That was why he came here. A place where he was anonymous, shielded by a thick wooden door and stone walls and an expectation of safety. But it wasn't just the violence he had faced in the past few weeks, as disturbing as that was. Eli sought to reexplore where his life had landed—a father who had betrayed him and his family with his secret. The once respected anatomist had ultimately betrayed those who donated their bodies and the families who had taken the safety of their loved ones for granted.

With his parents dead, he was left to fend for his older brother. He had not only failed emotionally with his only sibling, but Eli now feared financial failure as well, his funds to pay rent to Henry's institution dwindling fast.

Eli closed his eyes, felt the silence surround him. He wanted to feel protected, however briefly, from drought and disease and the senseless killings that he knew weren't senseless at all but were a series of calculated deaths in a pattern that he was unable to discern.

He shivered. The ambient temperature must have been in the low sixties. He was surprised that half the city wasn't camped out in this air-conditioned haven. But he knew that for most, the threat of a spiritual reckoning was far greater than the fear of suffocating in the heat. Images of garbage and fire and a corpse in a warehouse melted into one as rational thought slipped drowsily away.

Shuffling past his pew, the woman in the green blouse startled him. He nodded to her, but her gaze remained grounded and she left the sanctuary.

Eli rubbed his eyes and then refocused on a figure standing near the pulpit. The robed priest clasped his hands at his waist and watched Eli. He made his way purposefully down the aisle.

Eli shifted in his seat. He turned and hoped that the woman had returned and was the focus of the priest's attention. As he suspected, they were alone.

The clergyman stopped beside his pew.

"Hello to you, young man."

He was not as old as Eli initially thought. Late fifties, he wore a close-cut beard speckled with grey.

"Hello, Father."

"I am glad that you visit us."

Eli nodded.

"You are welcome any time."

"Thank you."

The priest began to turn toward the pulpit again but he stopped. "May I be of any particular assistance?"

"No. I'm just here to sit a while, if that's okay."

The priest nodded in confirmation, but he wasn't finished. "I recognize you from the newspapers."

Eli realized his anonymity, even here, was not assured.

The priest went on. "I know times have been hard for you."

Eli had not expected this. He had let his guard down, and he tried to harden what must have appeared as a vulnerable shell. But instead, he felt a softening, suddenly aware that no one had acknowledged the life-changing events that plagued him. Eli said, "I'm fine," but he hoped the priest would continue his absolution.

"I knew your father."

Eli assumed his father had not been inside a church in decades. Stunned by the mention of him, Eli stood. "I need to go."

In a surprising gesture, the priest stepped inside the pew to block his exit. "Your father, he struggled. Just as you are now. You should know that."

Eli shook his head. "He didn't struggle enough."

"We all have our demons. Some more than others."

"I can't do this, Father. Not now."

Eli stepped toward the priest, who gave him room. He exited the sanctuary and reentered the sultry world.

CHAPTER FORTY-SEVEN

It happened after a code blue at three in the morning almost ten years ago. They were interns, paged stat to the hospital room of an obese male admitted with a bowel obstruction but found unconscious and pulseless by the night nurse. The room was full of nurses and medical residents barking out orders. Liza and Eli were relegated to doing the chest compressions, alternating positions every few minutes.

Eli started first. After three minutes of compressions, he yelled "switch" and Liza slid a standing stool beside the bed, locked her elbows, and delivered sequential crunches to the man's sternum. It was a difficult position for each of them, leaning past the edge of the bed over the man's rotund chest and abdomen. Liza was determined to deliver effective compressions, her thin frame bucking with each blow. Then Eli took over so Liza could catch her breath. On Liza's next turn, just as she bent over the man, he vomited around the breathing tube, a forceful spray that sent a plume of yellow bile onto Liza's face and scrubs. Eli motioned to switch places, but Liza waved him off. Using her forearm, she wiped the vomit off her face and resumed the compressions, more forceful than before.

Having been a doctor for only two months, Eli knew, even then, that the resuscitation was not going well. Each check of the patient's heart tracing showed no electrical rhythm. A central venous line was inserted, through which multiple rounds of atropine and epinephrine had been infused. A few minutes later Liza stepped away, and Eli took her place. As he leaned over the patient, his scrubs absorbed the pool of vomit that ran off the man's chest. A minute later, he felt the now chilled liquid soaking down to his underwear.

Liza's turn.

She stepped up on the standing stool, but her foot slipped on the viscous secretions. She kicked the stool aside and climbed on the bed, straddling the man's abdomen in some perverse medical-erotic pose, her elbows locked in front as she delivered the final compressions. Eli tried not to stare. He knew the man was dying, or was already dead, and that his thoughts should be focused on the loss of life, not Liza's rhythmic movements.

The chief resident told everyone to stop. They had been running the code for almost a half hour, with no response to heroic maneuvers. He pronounced the man dead. Eli still remembered the time of death—3:36 a.m. And he remembered the image of Liza, in the straddle position, breathing hard as she climbed off the body. Memorable events, both, but the night would become yet more memorable.

Eli wandered out of the patient's room, looking back to see the floor cluttered with syringes, IV tubing, and strips of EKG paper. The patient lay motionless, naked, and newly dead. He died surrounded by a room full of people, but he died alone. His family would receive a call from a tired intern, much like Eli, who'd been assigned the man's care but who actually knew nothing about the patient beyond what was written on the check-out list for his call night.

Eli passed the nurse's desk and opened the door to a linen closet. Inside, he leaned against the door, and felt the need to let it go. Someone needed to mourn the soul in room 203. But he was needed back on the ward. He had already missed at least two pages on his beeper during the code, and he was behind on the admission reports from the emergency room and on the post-op checks that were overdue.

Behind a cart of linens, Eli found a folded pile of fresh scrubs. He pulled off his scrub top, soiled with bile and vegetable matter. He let his bottoms fall to the floor, stepped out of them.

Then someone opened the door.

Expecting to see a nurse, Eli ducked behind the cart. Then he heard someone crying.

Liza.

She had slid down the back of the closed door and sat on the floor, knees to her chest, sobbing.

Eli remained completely still, hidden by the linen cart. Maybe she would leave without seeing him.

He waited.

She stopped crying.

Then she stood and pulled off her top. She threw it down on the floor in disgust. She kicked the garment away and groaned, beating her thighs with her fists. Her top tumbled past the linen cart and landed beside Eli. He picked it up, smelled it. Rank with vomit. But with a lingering smell of Liza.

He peeked around the cart. She had pulled off her pants and stood in her underwear, searching the pile of scrubs. White lace-trimmed bikini panties had inched up her gluteal fold during intense attempts to save a man's life.

Eli stepped from behind the cart.

Liza turned quickly, her breath caught in a wordless gasp. She glanced below his waist, then met his eyes. She stepped past him and reached for a pair of fresh scrubs, fumbling with the stack, searching for the correct size. Eli reached to help, the back of his hand errantly brushing the full cup of her bra.

The kiss was full-mouthed, forceful, and angry, a product of tired bodies pumped full of adrenaline during the code. Neither sought nor willed it to happen, a fact that allowed both of them to rationalize, even forget, or try to forget, that it had ever happened.

They dropped to their knees in the center of the tiny room on the cold concrete floor. She pulled away from his intimate kiss and drew him into her, groping, vying for submission, to gain a competitive edge where competition was foreign. The scent of clean linen swirled and mixed with the smell of vomit and the sweat radiating from their skin. Any effort to be gentle gave way to revenge for countless nights of no sleep and disease and death that had been driven into them, again and again, until the minutes escaped the capture of time and they reclaimed their lives, however brief, together.

When it was over, they dressed quickly, relieved that no one had entered during those forbidden moments. Liza left the closet first. Eli remained another minute or two, trying to process the convergence of death and urgent intimacy. He saw Liza later during their shared night of call. Another code. Chest compressions. CPR. Another death.

But only their gaze met—once.

Daylight finally rescued them, and since that night, they had pushed through life as though their intimacy never happened.

Until now.

CHAPTER FORTY-EIGHT

Eli made a special effort to visit Henry within a couple of days after their annual pilgrimage to Elmwood Cemetery. Each year, after visiting their mother's grave, Henry seemed to withdraw more than usual after returning to Green Hills State Home. Eli had no idea whether his visit to his brother would help, but he felt obligated to check.

He found Henry in his room sitting on the floor, the controls of his favorite video game in hand, his tattered John Deere cap pulled low, close to his eyes. He watched his brother manipulate the control box, a bulky antiquated piece from the early nineties. Eli wondered how Henry would react to the fancy headsets and Wii-type virtual games of today. He would probably hate them, he decided.

Eli listened to the rapid clicks and smooth dexterity of his brother's fingers. Henry was quite skilled at this game. Why couldn't he translate this skill into something more productive? A job, maybe?

There had been failed attempts at jobs. When Henry finished school, as a high school senior functioning as a third grader, their mother arranged a part-time job for him at a grocery store, opening boxes for the stock boys to shelve. He lasted three days, let go when he was found in a supply closet with six open boxes of Cap'n Crunch, crunching away.

Watching Henry push the buttons on the control box, Eli was mesmerized by the rapid movements of his brother's thumb and index finger. It was all about the motivation. If he wanted to accomplish a task, like winning this game, Henry could do it. Take away the motivation, and he preferred to stare at the wall.

As Eli observed his brother manipulating the box, he remembered the robotic surgery demonstration at the Renaissance workshop. How the young technician, who was not a doctor, demonstrated the hand controls, adeptly, just as Henry was doing now. The video game generation.

You can teach a monkey to operate, Eli had heard his mentors say. *But they can't take care of patients.*

Eli reviewed the error that had occurred at the robotic workshop. The mannequin's gallbladder ripped to hell. What would the monkey do then? He thought about the young man called upon by the company's president to demonstrate their prized instrument. A salaried technician with tattoos on his arm. Did he have any idea of the consequence of that errant move for an actual patient?

Was that what happened to Liza French? One false but very deadly move?

Eli removed Henry's cap, kissed him on the top of his head, and put the cap back. He left the room and glanced back at Henry, but his brother did not look up.

CHAPTER FORTY-NINE

Cate's brother showed up unexpected to the free clinic. She knew his visit was calculated for a time when she would be most distracted with her patients. Although his life appeared to have little purpose, drifting from job to job, everything he did was calculated.

"How are you?" Cate wished she hadn't asked him this. His smile annoyed her. That cocky, all-knowing smile.

"Well," he said. "Very well."

"Look, I've got to get back to my patients."

"Always your patients, right Cate?"

She knew her patient care would not appease him. "And I've got my career to think about."

"*Your* career?" He confronted her, face-to-face. "How dare you call it your career. Without me, you would've never even made it into medical school. This is the way it's always been, hasn't it. All about Cate, Cate, Cate, until she needs better scores on her MCAT and then its big brother to the rescue."

Cate remained silent. She knew better than to stop him when he needed to vent. Even though she hated to admit it, everything he said was true.

"Do you know what kind of trouble I'd been in if I got caught taking that test for you?

"We'd both been in trouble."

"No, you would have denied that you even knew me, I'm sure."

Then his rage seemed to abate and Cate feared what he would say next.

"You never even had the guts to tell our mother that the scores were mine."

Cate saw the strain on his face, the way he squinted to hide tears that came whenever he spoke of their mother.

"It's you and me together on this, Cate. We owe it to our mother."

Cate wanted to escape and bury herself in her patients. But her brother always had the last word.

"And you definitely owe me."

CHAPTER FIFTY

Eli drove slowly down Adams Street in the heart of Victorian Village. At dusk, the street lights were beginning to flicker. Exterior lights illuminated the historic homes. Liza's house was a dark silhouette against a fading northern sky. No porch lights, no windows glowing. Even the gas flame by the walkway had been extinguished.

He parked at the curb and waited for a man clutching a brown paper bag to swagger by before opening the door of his car. He approached the house, expecting no response to his knock. But a few seconds later, the door cracked open and Layla stuck her head out.

"She's not here, doctor."

"I need to talk to her. Tell Liza to come out."

"You not hearing me, are you? She left, out of town. One of those medical conventions."

"Where?"

"I just keep her house, Eli. I'm not her secretary."

"I think she's in trouble. Big trouble."

Layla laughed. "She's always in trouble, doctor. Always looking for the edge."

"Yeah? Well, she may fall off this time." Eli walked away, heard the door close behind him. He got in his car. The sky was darker now. But when he looked back at the house, he thought he saw movement behind the curtains in the uppermost window.

CHAPTER FIFTY-ONE

SurgCast.

What an innovation.

Log on at home or work or the library, and watch controlled, sterile violence.

The reality of surgery is all there. The knife, the incision, the blood. It couldn't be more real unless smoke from the cauterized tissue was blown in through the computer's speakers, unless the abdominal organs were projected on a 3-D tactile instrument so the viewer could feel the slippery layer of blood. Maybe next year.

But cutting on the human body does not produce as predictable a result as most reality shows do. Through a technological glitch, the customary fifteen-second delay did not occur and SurgCast broadcast the death of a patient to thousands of viewers. The video made it to a popular Internet site before being yanked due to its graphic nature.

Eli was convinced the answer to the murders lay hidden within the events of that fatal operation, even though the names of the operative personnel did not match the names of the victims.

Liza supposedly had left town and wasn't available for questions. What an odd time to attend a surgical conference. Her absence in the midst of the murders and ongoing investigation was a little too convenient.

If tapes had been made of the operation, Eli thought, that would be better than anyone's recollection of events in the operating room.

Eli looked up the number of SurgCast, listed as a Boston area code. He imagined the woman who answered to be sitting at a reception desk with a bank of blinking phone lines. When Eli identified himself as a physician from Gates Memorial Hospital, he was immediately put on hold. Another female voice answered, identified herself as the company's legal representative. Eli suspected that SurgCast was well prepared for this call. To even the playing field, he decided his advantage lay in posing as a representative of the hospital's legal office.

"Hi. This is Tom Barnes. I represent Gates Memorial Hospital."

After this fabricated introduction, Eli requested the transcription of the audio recording made during the operation. "To facilitate our internal investigation," he added. He assumed the video recording would not be available.

"We've already discussed this," the attorney told him. "The videotapes are sequestered and can—" She stopped. She obviously had not anticipated a request for the written transcript.

Eli didn't give her time to deflect the request. "We need to compare the transcript with the transcribed operative report." He was on a roll, still not used to how easily the lies were coming. "We discussed that, remember? The video recording is sequestered, but disclosure of the transcripts was approved by your company's president."

"Yes, I . . . I know," she stammered, as though she had been left out of the loop. This made her eager to help. "Do you need both transcripts?"

"Both?"

"You know, the latest transcript and the one from the incident six months ago."

The first operative death.

"Yes, both transcripts, of course."

"Okay, I'll fax them to the hospital's legal office."

"Great," Eli said. "But let me give you a different fax number."

"A different fax?"

"I'm working out of my second office today." From a piece of scrap paper in his wallet, he gave her Meg's fax number in the morgue.

CHAPTER FIFTY-TWO

Moonlight reflected off the river, transforming the muddy water into a broad silver lake. As Eli traveled along the shore road to his apartment, he saw a single light from a boat far upstream. The river served as Eli's muse. Throughout medical school and even now, his best critical thinking could be accomplished by simply staring at the rippled brown waves as they pushed incessantly toward the Gulf.

It was close to midnight, no one on the road, and even the mighty Mississippi had not helped him figure out what Liza French was up to. Maybe she was just sickened by the events of the past few days and needed to get away or hide out at home. Maybe she was running. Either way, Eli felt the investigation into the death of her patient was strangled by her absence. Maybe she could release the chokehold—if he could find her.

The road to his apartment ran straight, with only a few dips and curves that Eli took instinctively while he continued to stare at the river. His new living arrangement was nothing like the luxury of his bungalow in Harbor Town where he lived a few weeks ago. His apartment building sat near the edge of a small bluff. Willow trees engulfed the bank that slid down into the muddy water. For all practical purposes, it was modest-rent housing with a view of the river, aptly named Riverview Apartments. Just before turning into the complex, he was startled by the sudden appearance of a man in the middle of the road.

Eli braked to a stop. Facing the river, in a tan-colored raincoat, the man did not move. Eli recognized him and immediately rolled down his window.

"Professor Salyer?"

As though expecting Eli to arrive at that moment, the old man said, "Hypnotic, isn't it?"

"What are you doing here?"

"Twain said the Mississippi River will always have its own way; no engineering skill can persuade it to do otherwise." Salyer turned to face Eli. "Damn son of a bitch was right."

Eli got out and stood between Salyer and the river. There was no car parked nearby, nothing, as though Salyer had materialized from air.

"How did you get here?"

A smile crossed Salyer's face. "I was beginning to think you weren't coming home tonight."

He had a particular knack of answering questions off sequence.

"How long have you been standing here?"

"Had one of my grad students drive me." He motioned to the apartment building. "I didn't know which one of those cubbyholes was yours."

Eli cupped a hand under Salyer's elbow and turned him toward his car. "Get in. I'll show you."

With a firm grip, Salyer grabbed Eli's wrists. "I've come to tell you how the next victim will die."

During the short ride to Eli's apartment, Salyer said nothing more about the murders. Instead, he told of the three people who had stopped driving along the river, each one asking if they could help him. Salyer seemed surprised they were willing to talk to a total stranger at night.

Especially an old man dressed like a flasher, Eli thought.

Salyer had asked each of them to direct him to the home of Dr. Eli Branch, surgeon at the medical center, son of a medical school professor. He emphasized that not one of them had any idea whom he was talking about.

"That's because I've rented here for only a couple of weeks." Eli turned into his driveway. "I don't even know my next door neighbor."

They entered the sparsely furnished one-bedroom apartment.

"I understand," Salyer said. "I've lived in Oxford for almost ten years and barely know my neighbors. They've brought over casseroles and cakes, invited me to church I don't know how many times." Salyer shook his head. "I don't need any of that." He sank deep into Eli's couch.

Eli knocked around in the kitchen. He wanted to offer his former professor a drink but found only one can of beer in the fridge and a warm bottle of Chardonnay one of his patients had given him. He offered both to Salyer.

"Not to worry," Salyer said. He reached into his pocket and produced a bottle of George Dickel. "Grab a couple of glasses."

Eli returned with the smallest water glasses he owned. Salyer poured and offered a toast. "To life on the Mississippi."

They clinked glasses and sipped. Eli liked a cold beer or glass of wine, and he liked margaritas with a rim of salt. But he was less accustomed to straight whiskey. He swirled it around in his mouth and felt his tongue catch fire. Clenching his jaw, he blew out the excess vapor, swallowed, and said, "Tell me about the next killing."

Salyer took another generous swig of whiskey as if it were lemonade. "The next death will occur by removal of the brain. A male brain."

Eli followed Salyer's lead. Took another sip. His tongue was a little numb now and the liquor went down smoothly. "I thought you were going to tell me I was right about Vesalius and the pattern of dissections."

Salyer lifted his glass in another toast. "You were right about Vesalius, my friend. But you had the wrong manuscript."

"Wrong manuscript?"

Salyer leaned forward. He held his glass with both hands, swirled the liquid, inhaled. "At first, it appeared the killer was following the *Fabrica*, using it as a guide. The bone from the first victim, the tongue of the second. But then the pattern changed."

"Or there never was a pattern," Eli offered.

"Oh, but there is a pattern, Eli. I didn't see it either, when you visited me in Oxford. The order of bone, muscle, stomach—definitely not the *Fabrica*." Another swig. "But yesterday, I read in the newspaper about the woman at the planetarium. Bone, muscle, stomach, and then the fourth organ, the *Heart*. That's when I knew."

Eli shook his head, frustrated. "I'm not following you. Knew what?"

Salyer placed his empty glass on Eli's coffee table, stood, and started pacing. Eli saw his persona change to that of teacher.

"Almost the same time the *Fabrica* was published, Vesalius published his *Epitome*, an abbreviated, more reader-friendly version of the *Fabrica*, if you will. It was good for students, those who wished a quicker reference to human anatomy without the minutiae."

"What does this have to do with the killer's pattern?"

Salyer poured another glass and gestured the bottle toward Eli.

Eli let him refill his glass just to keep the man talking.

"As an abbreviated version of the *Fabrica*, the *Epitome* contained only six books, not seven." Salyer pointed to each organ on himself as he called out the order of the books, much as he did in class for his students.

Bone, Muscle, Abdomen.

He next pointed to his chest, then to his head.

Heart. Brain.

"You see, the killer's sequence fits the order of the *Epitome* exactly." Salyer sat down to his glass, took a drink, and said, "Basically Eli, you were correct. The reason I'm here now is to redirect you."

Eli held his glass to his lips but did not drink. If Salyer was correct and the first four deaths had followed the *Epitome*, two more would occur. "You said the next book is the brain, but that makes only five. What's the sixth?"

Salyer smiled, a teacher reveling in the thoughtful question of a student. "Vesalius proposed that Galen had never dissected a human uterus. So, our anatomist saved the best book for last. His specialty of sorts. His desire to know the feminine mystique deeper than any man had ever known."

Salyer dipped his finger in the brown liquid, brought it to his lips.

"The sixth book takes him deep into the sex of a woman."

CHAPTER FIFTY-THREE

The whiskey rolled and so did Salyer. Eli sat back and listened to the professor's history of Andreas Vesalius. Sort of like being in class except Eli was at home with a stiff drink in his hand.

The anatomist's ancestral family came from the town of Wesel near the Rhine River. His forebear, Johnnes de Wesalia, inspired by the town's name, chose three weasels to represent the family's coat of arms.

"Curious animals, those weasels."

Salyer placed his glass on the table, a sure sign of more pantomime to come. He stretched forth his arms as though about to leap.

"The title page of the *Fabrica* shows the Vesalian coat of arms with the little mammals sprawled out as though dignified."

Eli recalled seeing the coat of arms on the mural depiction in the artist's loft. "Those are weasels?"

Salyer chuckled. "Vesalius's biographer described them as coursing greyhounds. By the looks of them, I think that's more accurate."

There was a rare period of silence from Salyer. Eli watched the man as he swirled his drink, measured his thoughts. Eli hoped that whatever was troubling Salyer pertained directly to the recent murders. It did.

"Three years ago, I was called to testify in a trial. An employee at the Mid-South Medical College was accused of desecrating cadavers."

Eli stopped him. "In my father's Anatomy Department?"

"Yes, Eli." Salyer shifted in his seat, tried to get more comfortable. "But he wasn't responsible for these events."

"How's that?"

"You remember the sabbatical your father took? To Europe I believe? This all happened during that six-month period."

"Okay, so my father was away. What happened?"

"The accused was the apprentice of an old colleague of mine, Howard Beezer. He was there during the years you were in Nashville."

"I know who he is," Eli said. "Go ahead."

"Beezer hired the young man to process the bodies and arrange cadavers for the medical students' dissection. He was getting old—hell, Beezer had always been old—and he wanted someone to do his job while he hid out in his office waiting for retirement. He got lucky by hiring this fellow because he had a way with the dead, if you can call that a talent. Seems the young man had some prior training in anatomy, I can't remember, but nonetheless, Beezer allowed him to assist the students. Had him come in at night and complete the dissections for in-class demonstrations. The next morning Beezer would teach from the dissections as though he had done them himself. Ultimately, though, Beezer would regret giving the young man a key to Anatomy Hall."

"Why's that?" Eli asked.

"Weird shit started happening."

Salyer took a long overdue drink, then added, "The bodies were rearranged."

"Rearranged?"

"Propped up, in poses. A cadaver suspended from the ceiling by chains, for instance, arms spread out, much like Da Vinci's man. It appeared harmless at first. The students got a kick out of it, thought it was all a prank by one of their fellow classmates. The students would arrive the next morning to find a cadaver wearing a stethoscope, listening to another cadaver's heart. Then what you might predict next—one cadaver on top of another." Salyer chuckled and elaborated. "Missionary positions of the dead. The students always returned the cadavers to their original positions before the Beezer arrived in the morning. But then it turned sick."

"That's not sick?"

"Still thought to be pranks, Eli. You remember how it was in medical school, anything to relieve the stress. Beezer eventually found out about it and hoped it was a joke by the students, but he came to suspect it was his apprentice. By then, Beezer had a good thing going and wanted to keep it."

His glass of whiskey in hand, Salyer stood. Without taking a drink, he sat the glass back on the table.

"Then the dissections and the poses turned very specific."

Salyer contorted his body, arms arched overhead as though about to dive. With the choreography of a dancer, Salyer took on the poses of Vesalius's skeleton man, then a graceful transition to the muscle man—just as Eli remembered from Salyer's anatomy class, and from the sketches drawn in the artist's loft. He was quite the performance artist. Eli stopped Salyer before he started removing any clothes.

"So?" Eli said. "The students had studied Vesalius, some of his most famous sketches are included in standard anatomy texts. They simply recreated those classical poses with their cadavers."

"You're correct, Dr. Branch." Salyer released his pose. The stoop in his shoulders returned and he retrieved his glass. "Harmless poses are one thing. Desecrating a cadaver is entirely different."

"Desecrating? You haven't described desecration."

Salyer reclined on the worn couch, propping his feet on the coffee table. "Name the foot bone illustrated in plate four of the *Fabrica*."

"The navicular bone."

"Correct. How was the tongue displayed in book two?"

Eli thought a moment. "Completely detached with the ligaments revealed."

"Correct again. Beezer found a series of these dissections, in this order, exquisitely performed."

"Exactly as Vesalius described them?"

Salyer nodded. "Exactly."

"Then he turned his apprentice in?"

"No, Beezer kept quiet. But one of the medical students talked. She claimed she had seen the apprentice enter Anatomy Hall at night and perform the procedures. That prompted an investigation. The dean of the medical school became involved. Beezer's apprentice was charged with a felony."

"And they called you to testify because you're an expert in Vesalius."

Salyer bowed his head. "Yours truly."

CHAPTER FIFTY-FOUR

Lipsky turned onto the grounds of Shelby Farms. He looked at the open space, the trees, the lakes.

What was the word for it?

Pastoral.

That's it, Lipsky thought, proud of his vocabulary.

No grime, no crime, no Dumpsters spilling garbage. He passed two horses loping in a field and wondered why he had never driven out here before. But the answer came quickly. He went where murder called him. Up to now, Shelby Farms had been sheltered from homicide hell.

He passed a field of grazing cows. Morning mist hovered ghostlike in patches a few feet off the ground. As he drove closer, he could see that the animals weren't cows at all. Looked more like buffalo. He had a vague recollection that a herd of bison lived at Shelby Farms. Buffalo, bison, what the hell's the difference?

And why the hell is someone dead out here?

Of all places.

Then he thought of the Zante Repository death. That was weird. The whole damn thing was weird. Whatever happened to the good old Saturday night gunfight? Messing with somebody's woman, a couple of bottles of liquor.

Boom.

Someone takes it in the gut.

Crimes of passion. Got the motive, the weapon, the perpetrator usually too inebriated to get very far. Lipsky had built his career on that stuff.

Now things were too complicated. Doctors and nurses getting killed at random. But it wasn't random, was it? Anything but. These deaths were serial killings. Not that this was his first encounter with a serial killer. He'd done that before, several times.

First time was June of '95. Got the call that a serial killer was possibly headed to Memphis. Joined the national search. One big community. But this current investigation was different. Lipsky had little experience with psychological-pattern killers, although he'd taken a crash course the last few days.

He feared more "experience" was waiting for him when he spotted two Memphis police cars parked beside the pavilion. Officer McCormick was talking to an older man wearing a jogging outfit. Questioning the witness. Lipsky parked alongside the patrol cars, took a deep breath, and pulled himself out of the car.

"What we got, McCormick?

The officer wrote down the man's phone number and dismissed him.

Then he greeted Lipsky. "We got a mess in there."

CHAPTER FIFTY-FIVE

Officer McCormick led Lipsky into the pavilion at Shelby Farms. In the cool, dark foyer, photos of the park's animals hung on the wall. A small herd of bison in a layer of morning fog. Ducks on Patriot Lake. For bird enthusiasts, a brilliant shot of a cardinal perched on a limb. Lipsky didn't look at any of it. He was focused instead on bloody footprints that led down a central hallway.

McCormick opened the door into a changing room. Lipsky nodded to a young police officer he didn't recognize. The officer had stayed there to guard the body. The body wasn't going anywhere.

Two low wooden benches ran the length of the room, between a row of coin-operated clothes lockers along one wall, and on the opposite wall, a toilet stall and two sinks in a countertop. Between the sinks lay a rounded heap of bloody tissue about the size of a cantaloupe.

Lipsky approached the benches first. A young male, well-built, naked except for a towel across his waist, lay on his back on one of the benches. He was positioned so that his head lay at the end of the bench. Directly below on the floor, a tray of surgical instruments lay in disarray. Dried blood coated the instruments, which had apparently been used to perform complicated state park brain surgery. Except, as best Lipsky could tell, the brain was no longer home. The skull lay open and the three law officers stared into its deep, vacant, bloodied bowl.

Lipsky pointed at the head, then at the sinks.

"You got it," McCormick said.

The organ had been placed on a layer of paper towels. A blood-tinged ring of moisture had spread on the paper from whatever fluid oozed from the brain tissue. A cutout sketch of the brain, in the tradition of Vesalius, Lipsky guessed, was tilted against the mirror behind the dissected body part.

Lipsky marveled at the specimen before him. Deep ridges cut into the brain, the surface laced with tiny blood vessels. The whole of a man's knowledge, all of his thoughts, right here.

Other than the expected calling card, the dissection was not the tidy presentation of the earlier scenes. The Organist must have been rushed this time. Blood was splattered about, and his instruments had been left behind. At each of the previous four sites, hardly a trace remained other than a sketch of the organ. He—or she, Lipsky thought, in a rare gender-equal correction—must have gotten spooked. Lipsky looked back at the shoe marks. A blood-stained exit pattern was highly uncharacteristic.

"At least Basetti will have something to work with this time," Lipsky said.

McCormick agreed. "Surely there'll be some prints on those." He pointed to the tray of instruments.

"Did your witness have anything?"

"Yes, he did, actually. Turns out he knew the guy."

"You're kidding."

"Nope. The witness said the victim's name is Thomas Greenway. Says he works out here all the time, training for a triathlon."

"What else?"

"Said the young man worked at the—"

Lipsky cut him off. "Let me guess. He's a doctor at the medical center."

McCormick nodded. "OB/GYN, the witness thought."

"Shit."

"What?"

Lipsky shook his head. "The baby poppers are having a tough week."

"I don't know about that, but there's more to the story."

"Bring it."

"Seems this doc is the star of some TV show," McCormick checked his notebook. "*Secret Lives of Doctors.* Ever hear of it?"

"No. I only watch reruns of *Barney Miller* and *Kojak.*"

"Man. Telly Savalas," McCormick said. "He was the best."

"Total kick-ass," Lipsky agreed.

"Even with those little lollipops."

They took a moment of silence, out of respect, or hero worship.

"Anyway," Lipsky said, snapping out of it, "*Days of Doctors Lives* or what was it?"

"*Secret Lives of Doctors.*"

"Oh, yeah."

"Turns out this guy was a male model."

Before Lipsky could respond to that, his cell phone rang, set to the theme song of *Kojak*.

"You weren't kidding about being a fan," McCormick said.

Lipsky stepped away and flipped open his phone. "Who loves you, baby."

CHAPTER FIFTY-SIX

Eli was ready to leave his house early the next morning before Salyer awoke. They had talked for hours, until nearly dawn. After many glassfuls, the professor eventually lay his head back on the couch and fell asleep mid-sentence. Now, as Eli crept passed him toward the door, he saw Salyer curled in a fetal position, his overcoat pulled about his head.

At seven thirty, after circling the block three times, Eli at last found an empty parking meter at the medical center. How nice it had been a few weeks ago to have access to the Gates's parking garage.

He had planned to arrive at the morgue by seven, before Meg started the day's autopsy barrage. But his head still pounded from the night before and only now could he fully open his eyes.

Miss Conch protested as he passed through the reception area into the autopsy room. Meg hovered over an intact body, knife in hand. He interrupted her.

"I need your help for a few minutes."

"Good morning to you too, and take a number." She pointed to a sheet-covered corpse on a gurney. "He beat you here by just a few minutes."

Eli nodded to the deceased. "I'm sure he'll understand." Then, to Meg, "Log me on. We're about to find out who the next victim is."

Exasperated, Meg dropped the knife on the instrument table. Steel clanging against steel made a statement. She walked toward her desk but stopped short in front of Eli.

"You look like warmed-over shit."

"Thanks, I feel like it."

Meg typed in her passwords. "What are we looking for today, nuclear launch codes?"

Eli leaned closer to the screen. No matter how much death surrounded them, Meg always managed to smell fresh and sexy.

"Go to the OR files like we did before."

A few clicks later she asked, "Do you even know how to type?"

"Yeah, but I like to watch you do it."

She gave him a look, started to say something, then accessed the requested files.

"Now, put in the names of the first three victims plus the latest, the Zante Repository nurse."

Meg copied the names from the white board while Eli wrote the fourth name at the bottom of the list.

"If what I'm thinking is right, by entering these four names, the first operative death will be displayed."

"The first?"

"Yes. We've been trying to connect the murders to the most recent patient who died in the OR. But the real link to the murders is the accidental death that occurred six months ago." Eli pointed at the screen. "This program will match any operation with the personnel assigned to work the case. I'm betting each of these hospital employees was involved in that first, fatal procedure."

When Meg finished entering all the names, an operative report appeared on the screen. It was red-flagged like the other, with a central gray box that warned:

> This patient is dead.
> Do you wish to continue?

Yes we do, thank you very much.

As Eli predicted, all four names were listed, plus the surgeon, Liza French.

Meg leaned back in the chair, kept staring at the screen. "But the three murder victims were all listed as part of the operating team during the most recent OR death, including your nurse friend."

"That's correct," Eli said. "These three personnel were part of the operating team when both deaths occurred. But the fourth name didn't fit. That's because all the murder victims were involved in the first operating room death that occurred six months ago."

Meg nodded once to Eli. "I'm impressed."

"By what?" Eli asked. "Four people have been killed and I can't seem to stop it."

These words pulled them back to the list of six Gates's employees and the four murders.

The anesthetist in the cotton warehouse with a bone cut from his foot.

The scrub nurse without her tongue at the wrestling arena.

The anesthesiologist missing his stomach in Tunica.

And the circulating nurse at the Zante Repository without a heart.

The next name that appeared on the computer screen was that of an OB/GYN resident, Thomas Greenway.

Eli said his name out loud.

"What about your Dr. French?" Meg asked. "Could she be the next victim?"

The way Meg said *French*, her head tilted, her lips pursed, Eli sensed a definite attitude. He wondered if Meg somehow knew about his and Liza's past. He had no time to go there.

"Liza's out of town, oddly enough," Eli said. "I don't know what's going on with her. Maybe she *is* behind the whole thing." He thought that was good cover.

"How could that be?" Meg made a face and wagged her head clearly rejecting that theory.

"I don't know, but someone is killing these medical personnel." Eli pointed at the screen. "And it's all related, somehow, to this operation."

Eli recalled the order of Vesalius's *Epitome*. The fifth book focused on the brain. Through a hungover fog, Eli tried to remember the conversation with Salyer the night before. Salyer predicted that the next organ to be removed would be the brain. A male brain. Eli read the resident's name from the screen. Thomas Greenway. Definitely male.

Eli grabbed Meg's phone, started punching numbers. Meg knew

exactly who he was calling. "Is Detective Lipsky buying all this?"

Eli nodded. "He'd better. This is all he's got."

Meg stood and arched her back in an early morning stretch. "*We're all he's got.*" She spoke in a sarcastic, self-important tone.

On the second ring, Eli heard a voice answer, "Who loves you, baby."

"Lipsky? It's Eli."

"Top of the morning to you, doc."

"Listen, I've got a name for you. We need to find this guy before it's too late. Put some police protection on him."

Complete silence on Lipsky's end.

A wave of dread passed through Eli. "The name's Thomas Green-way."

More silence.

Then Lipsky said, "Oddly enough, I'm looking at someone with that same name."

"Damn it!" Eli drew out the words.

Meg placed the autopsy knife on the table and mouthed, "What?"

"Question for you," Lipsky said. "In that old bastard's book, you know, the one who cuts people open and draws pictures of them, what's the next body organ? I'm just curious."

"The brain, Lipsky. It's the brain."

That old saying, about how silence is deafening—

"I'll hand it to you, doc, you're a smart one."

"Where are you, Lipsky?"

"I'm over at Shelby Farms. Got your Tom Greenway with me. You know, it's true what they say about the brain. It does look like a big, shelled pecan."

CHAPTER FIFTY-SEVEN

"When did you last talk to her?"

Lipsky drove in the outside lane of Poplar Avenue toward downtown. He was tempted to put the blue light on the roof, to take on some real speed, but he didn't yet know where he was going, only that they needed to find Liza French.

Eli rode shotgun in the detective's car. "A few days ago," he answered. "Liza seemed more concerned with the malpractice suit than the fact that two members of her medical team had been murdered."

"Now that number is up to five." Lipsky stopped at a red light. "Maybe she just wanted to change the subject."

"You think she's responsible for all this?"

"Most everyone involved in that botched operation is dead, right? Don't you doctors always cover your tracks?"

Lipsky was correct. Five of the seven personnel from the first botched operation were dead. Eli stared at him, waited for Lipsky to retract that statement. He didn't.

"By killing her surgical team? Is that what you're saying?"

Lipsky accelerated through the intersection. "Somebody's killing these people. And that someone has got to have a reason. In the homicide business, we call that motive."

"Thanks for the lesson."

"And we've got to consider all possibilities."

"Like?"

"Like someone connected to the surgical deaths. Family, friends, business associates who may have lost income or power because of the deaths."

Eli looked at Lipsky with pure skepticism. "Business associates?"

"Sometimes people crack, Eli. Normal, sane, well-meaning people just go off. It's not only postal workers. Respected businessmen, housewives. Take your Dr. French Kiss, for example. She's had two patient deaths in the OR within six months. She's in deep shit. Her career's in jeopardy and she's facing criminal charges. She's thinking her medical team will say she's at fault, the one to blame, negligent." Lipsky turned to Eli. "She's found a way to keep them from talking. Permanently."

As Lipsky said this, Eli shook his head. "She's five foot five, maybe a hundred twenty pounds. Sound like someone who could string a body from a chain?"

Lipsky spoke after a moment. "Had a granny in a wheelchair once. Son-in-law assaulted her granddaughter. You know what I mean?"

Eli lay his head back against the seat. Closed his eyes. He wished he could close his ears.

"She found him, held him at gunpoint, and cut his balls off with a hedge clipper."

Lipsky waited for that to sink in.

"So don't tell me how small your doctor friend is."

Eli had nothing to say to that. He could think only about his testicles and sharp garden tools.

"Besides," Lipsky continued. "I didn't say *how* she could have done it. Maybe she had help. Maybe she used some of that big doctor money and paid someone."

Lipsky was enjoying this. Eli let him roll on.

"Hell, for all I know, she's got you sucked into this."

"Yeah, Lipsky, I'm sneaking around at night killing my colleagues and helping you during the day."

"I've done my research," Lipsky said. "I know you two were an item a few years back." He slapped the dashboard. "Old love dies hard."

CHAPTER FIFTY-EIGHT

Alex's Tavern is a small bar on Jackson Avenue in Midtown. Known for late-night entertainment and friendly bar service, it's a popular hang spot for students from the medical school and undergrads from nearby Rhodes College. Liza French didn't care much for the beer, but she had a deep appreciation for the young male patrons. She scooted her stool closer to the bar. No longer did she have to request a glass of Chardonnay. Joe, the bartender, had it waiting for her on a little square white napkin.

At nine o'clock, it was a little early yet for the late crowd. The musician for the night plugged in his amp and started an awful rendition of guitar tuning that didn't bode well for the music to come.

One couple sat off by themselves near a corner. A booth held three guys wearing team softball jerseys laughing over a pitcher of beer.

How boring, Liza thought. She took a sip of wine and replaced the glass in the exact center of the napkin. A man sat down on the bar stool next to her. Older than the average student, he was in his early thirties maybe, black hair cut short under a baseball cap. Even in the dim light, Liza caught a glimpse of a few gray strands. He ordered a draft beer, and Liza watched bartender Joe fill a mug, cap off the foamy head.

She waited to see if Joe knew him. Joe, of course, knew anyone and everyone who frequented the bar. He pushed the beer to the man and asked if he wanted to start a tab. Definitely not a regular.

"That depends," he said.

Liza felt his gaze upon her.

"On how long this takes."

He raised the mug and took a long gulp. He had a sturdy build and

Liza watched the flex of a tattoo on his arm, three cute little animals in a column. He wiped his mouth on the back of his hand.

Nice. Liza took a sip of wine, handed her napkin to him, and sat her glass down on the bar top.

"Thanks," he said.

Liza raised her glass. "You should try wine. Not quite as messy." Then she ran her tongue across her lips.

After a few minutes of small talk, the man told Joe, "No tab, I'll just pay for these two and we'll be on our way."

Liza watched the headlights of his black Trans Am in her rearview mirror as he followed her into Victorian Village. She hadn't seen a Trans Am in years, the type of car driven by bad boys. She thought the make had disappeared in the early eighties. She remembered now that she liked them. Especially black ones.

She drove around to the back of her house into the garage. He parked on the street. Layla met him at the front door and let him in.

CHAPTER FIFTY-NINE

Lipsky parked on Adams Street several houses away from Liza's. He leaned low across the seat to see her house through Eli's window. A Japanese lantern burned in the uppermost dormer.

"I didn't know anyone actually lived over here," Lipsky said. "In all this Victorian crap." He was still stretched across the seat, too close to Eli. "Used to be a bunch of museums you had to pay to see."

"I'll tell you what's crap," Eli said, pushing Lipsky back to the driver's seat. "All that about Liza being involved. If anything, she's in danger herself. Hell, for all we know, she's already dead."

The car was smothering hot. Lipsky opened the door to get out.

"We're just asking her some questions," he said. "If I like her answers, I'll get police protection all over her. I'm sure she'll like that."

Layla escorted Liza's guest up the spiral staircase. He watched her miniskirt climb above him and lagged behind just enough to see that she wasn't wearing underwear. Halfway up the stairs, he stopped.

"What's wrong?" she asked.

"Where's—you know?"

Layla smiled at him. "You don't even know her name, do you?" She continued to climb and didn't wait for an answer. He followed her without stopping again.

Liza waited for them in her study on the third floor, having climbed the fire escape that zigzagged along the back wall of the house to this room. She took a deep calming breath after scurrying up the three flights of metal stairs. She stood still, admiring all the robotic surgery equipment she'd accumulated, and thought how this was a perfect room for entertaining. This would be the last escapade. Then she and Layla would stop. She would get her life in order. They would move far away and maybe the investigation wouldn't follow her. The possibility of freedom excited her. The door to the study opened and Layla escorted the Trans Am man into the room.

CHAPTER SIXTY

Liza took both of his hands and walked backward, pulling him into the study.

"I wondered where you went," he told her.

"I wanted to get things tidied up for you," she said.

He looked back at Layla. *Two beautiful women in the same room.* "You're coming, too, aren't you?"

Layla stepped closer. "Dr. French and I always work as a team."

He pulled back against Liza and stopped her. "You're a doctor?"

"Yes. And I'm going to show you things you never knew about yourself."

Layla brushed up behind him. He didn't seem the least bit intimidated. "Would you like to play doctor with us?"

He looked at the equipment in the room, especially the table, with its sturdy leather straps and steel arms attached like a kind of new-age exercise equipment.

"Are we going to use all this?"

Liza began unbuttoning his shirt. "We just might."

Layla massaged his neck. When Liza released the last button, she pulled his shirt off, noticed the bulk of muscle around his shoulders. Layla ran her fingers over the tattoos on his arm.

He kept his hands at his side, in submission to whatever they chose to do next.

Layla had reached around his waist and unclasped the top button of his jeans when the doorbell rang.

She stopped and looked at Liza.

Then the doorbell rang again.

"Is there another one of you?" he asked, hopefully.

Neither Liza nor Layla said anything, waiting for whoever was at the door to go away.

"I thought maybe there were three of you." He flicked his eyebrows. "You know, triplets."

By the third chime, it was obvious the visitor wasn't leaving. Liza sent Layla to answer the door and send whoever it was away.

With only the two of them in the room now, the man appeared uncomfortable. "That beer's catching up with me," he told Liza. "Where's your bathroom?"

The bathroom was on the second floor, next to a guest bedroom. Liza pulled him toward the door, still distracted by the interruption. "Come, I'll show you."

"No," he said, stopping her. He ran a finger down the front of Liza's blouse. "I don't want you going anywhere."

CHAPTER SIXTY-ONE

What's keeping Layla?

Liza looked out of her small third-floor window. The black Trans Am was the only car parked on the street. *Whoever came to the door must have walked up. Probably a street person.* Layla had the habit of giving the homeless handouts so they would leave. But she would have sent them away and been back by now. And where was their guest? Men can pee in twenty seconds. They don't have to wipe or wash or anything. She had not even heard the toilet. Apparently, they don't flush either.

Liza began to regret bringing this man to her house. The thrill of the chase had faded. What began as a welcome escape from the troubles of the investigation and lawsuit, the loss of her robotic surgery program and her career, now seemed most irresponsible.

That's what these flings with Layla and the next-available-and-willing male were all about. Total escape. Whenever she and Layla were entertaining, feeling the anticipation in this room and seeing a touch of fear in the eyes of the next conquest made her own problems seem a universe away.

She and Layla did have a great setup, she had to admit. And the game was always the same. Layla would admit their male guest through the front door while Liza waited upstairs. It all fit with the Victorian pattern of secrecy. Layla would lead the man up the stairs to the hidden chamber. There, they would seduce him. It never took much effort, what with Layla dressing and acting like a nymph and Liza controlling the action. Then the surgical equipment came in to play. The table, leather straps, stainless steel.

Tonight, however, her moment of passion had been killed by the doorbell. This was the last time she would bring a stranger home. And she would tell the medical students, those impressionable young men, that she could no longer serve as their extracurricular advisor. It was all too risky.

Liza heard two sets of footsteps coming up the stairs. She tried to feel sexy again. It wasn't happening. The man opened the door and stood there, smiling.

"Did you miss me?"

Something about him had changed. The way he looked at her. He was no longer wanting her or needy. Not in that way. He was confident, as though *he* was now in charge.

"Look who I found."

He moved from the doorway so that Layla could enter. Except it wasn't Layla.

Cate Canavan walked into the room.

CHAPTER SIXTY-TWO

Cate's sudden appearance shocked Liza. She tried to rationalize what was happening. She had invited Cate, as her student, to come to her house and practice on the robotic equipment whenever she wanted. But tonight? At this hour? And where the hell was Layla? Of most concern was the manner in which Cate and this man spoke to each other. It was unmistakable. They knew each other.

"Is it okay if we practice on your equipment?" Cate asked.

The way he and Cate walked slowly toward her made Liza's skin crawl. Did Cate ask can *we* practice?

"I really appreciate your letting me come over like this," Cate said. "Opening up your home."

Liza listened to Cate, but she kept watching this man, who came closer and closer. A few minutes ago she had wanted him. Now, all Liza wanted was for him to get the hell out of her house.

Cate too, for that matter. Something was very different about her. Her language was polite, but her eyes betrayed her. She kept cutting glances at the man, then at Liza, back and forth.

"If you really want me to improve my surgical skills, Dr. French, I need someone to practice on."

They were both too close.

Liza took a step back, called out for Layla. There was no answer.

"She won't be of much help to you anymore," he said.

Liza pointed at him. "Get out of my house." Then to Cate. "Go call the police."

Cate laughed. "I don't think so. We should have called the police six months ago."

Liza looked only at Cate now. Mentor to student. Woman to woman. Hoping to find some answer of what was happening. Their faces mere inches from each other.

"Six months ago?" Liza asked.

The man stepped close and stared at Liza, waiting for her reaction.

"Yes, six months ago," Cate said. "When you killed our mother."

CHAPTER SIXTY-THREE

Liza stared at Cate in disbelief. "Your mother?"

"She trusted you." Cate's eyes glistened with tears. "Said you were the only doctor who could make her better."

What at first made no sense now hit Liza like a wall.

The first patient who died was Cate's mother!

Liza could see the slight resemblance she had not noticed before. How Cate's fair skin, her high cheek bones, were exactly like the face of the woman who for the last six months haunted Liza's dreams.

"Why, Cate? Why didn't you tell me?"

The man stepped in. He pointed a gun at Liza's face.

"Because we wanted you to pay, bitch."

Liza stepped back. Cate had not said *my* mother but rather *our* mother. This man she had picked up at the bar had staged the whole thing. He knew she would be at Alex's Tavern, knew that she was prone to leave with a partner. So he had planted himself next to her at the bar. This man, who was in her face, calling her bitch, was Cate's brother.

He grabbed both of Liza's arms, hands wrapping full around her biceps, and lifted her straight in the air. Liza's feet dangled and she went for his groin with a quick kick, but he anticipated this and blocked her foot with his knee.

Liza could feel his anger building, his fingers tighten even more, pinching her skin. She screamed. Then he slammed her down on the operating table. Her back hit first, then her head whiplashed against the rock-hard surface. She blacked out for a few seconds, enough time for him to bind her to the table. She screamed again when she came to and felt the leather straps pulled tight across her chest.

CHAPTER SIXTY-FOUR

Eli and Lipsky approached Liza's house from the street. Before stepping onto her front walk, Lipsky stopped.

"My mother used to bring me here."

"You had a mother?"

"Yeah, a damn good one, actually. My father was a piece of shit, but my mom was a saint. She wanted me to be cultured so she taught me about all this stuff. How to arrange a place setting at the table with lace doilies. About fancy Victorian furniture. How to dance proper."

"Did you say doilies?"

"Yeah, what about them?"

"Nothing," Eli said. He wanted Lipsky's story to end so they could find Liza.

Lipsky went on.

"She used to drag me in and out of these old houses." He pointed. "We would go on all the tours. I'd have to listen about Victorian antiques, crap like that."

"You loved every bit of it," Eli told him.

Lipsky nodded. "You're right."

Eli kept moving toward the house. Lipsky didn't.

"This old house next door, a shipping merchant owned it. He would stand on top of that balcony up there and watch for his ships floating down the Mississippi. That's pretty damn cool, isn't it?"

Eli tried to maintain forward momentum.

"I've been here several times." Lipsky pointed to the top of Liza's house. "See that upper window, with the light on?"

"Yes, Lipsky, I see it."

"The French maids stayed up there. It was a secret chamber."

As much as he wanted to move on, Eli had to ask. "French maids?"

"Hell, yeah. Know anything about Victorian sex?"

Eli wiped a line of sweat off his forehead. He just wanted to find Liza, talk with her, and leave.

"No, not particularly."

Wrong answer.

"I bought a book on it."

"That's all you got out of this, a book on twisted sex?"

"They liked their secret chambers, know what I mean?"

"Yes I do," Eli said and picked up his pace toward the house.

Lipsky followed him, kept talking. "They would serve tea. I hated tea. But my mother would pack us a lunch and we would eat out on the lawn. She tried to raise me up proper, my mother."

Eli put a hand on his shoulder. "She did a fine job."

"Shut up."

Just as they reached the steps to Liza's house, a scream cut through the stale night air.

CHAPTER SIXTY-FIVE

Fear accelerated Liza's thoughts and brought clarity in the face of chaos. The death of Cate's mother on the operating table was an accident. Even though the robotic equipment was new to Liza and the operative team, the robotic device functioned just fine. The vascular injury occurred during what should have been routine removal of the abdominal trocars. After the fatal event, everything got crazy, fast.

The hospital's attorneys and risk management officers descended, trying to save face for the hospital and everyone involved. Liza tried to contact the patient's family. She was told a daughter was out of town and unavailable. During the urgent meeting with hospital officials, one of the nurses from the operation paged Liza and told her a son was waiting. Liza sent the nurse to talk with him until she could get away. The nurse took the young man to see his mother's body in a makeshift "family" room.

When the meeting with risk management was over, Liza went to find her patient's son. But he'd already left the hospital. The nurse told Liza, "The man was very upset and angry that the main doctor had not come to tell him of his mother's death." There had been no contact with the man or any family since. Until now.

Liza wrenched her body against the leather straps. They didn't budge. He had pulled them so tight she could barely breathe. She tried to kick her feet, but he had bound them as well.

It was clear to her now that the most recent operative death was not an accident. Cate was the medical student who'd scrubbed for the operation. That was no accident either. She and her brother had somehow orchestrated the death of her patient to cause all of Liza's problems.

All of that hardly mattered now. Liza had to convince them that their mother's death was an accident. Otherwise, she knew the next death would be her own.

Cate stood at the side of the table, her arms crossed in front, as if holding herself to stop the shaking.

Liza stopped struggling.

"It was an accident, Cate. You have to believe me," Liza pleaded. "The instrument malfunctioned. I'm so sorry."

"I've heard enough."

The son was back in her face, with the gun.

"Shut the hell up."

Cate took a step back but her brother stopped her. "Inject her with the drugs, Cate. Then I'll take her to her final scene."

Cate removed a syringe from her pocket. She removed the cap from the needle but she was crying now. Her hand shook uncontrollably.

The man grabbed the hem of Liza's capris pants and ripped the fabric to expose the skin of her thigh.

"You can do this, Cate. Think of Mother. How she suffered." His voice grew louder. "How this bitch made her suffer."

Cate stopped crying. Liza watched as her medical student raised the syringe, ready to make the stab.

Liza made herself not scream but she yelled, "Wait!"

Cate pulled the syringe back. She had been trained to obey her attending surgeon.

Liza knew that her next words were her last chance. Her voice quivered, but she said the words clearly.

"I'm pregnant."

CHAPTER SIXTY-SIX

After the second scream, Eli and Lipsky, outside the house, heard a male voice shout from an upper floor, "Shut the hell up."

They found the front door locked, of course. When Eli suggested breaking the windows, Lipsky pushed Eli aside, took a step back, and with a quick kick shattered the door beneath the dead bolt.

"I've been waiting for a chance to do that," he said.

Splintered wood lodged in the frame, but with one more kick Lipsky knocked it completely open.

Eli went through first and immediately found a body face-down on the marble floor. Eli knew it was Layla even before he rolled her over and saw her blood-stained face. He felt for a carotid pulse and confirmed she was dead.

Lipsky sprinted up the spiral staircase with Eli a few steps behind.

Cate held the syringe inches above Liza's skin.

"She's lying, Cate," her brother said. "Don't listen to her. Do it."

"Please, just don't hurt my baby," Liza begged. "Please."

Cate let the syringe drop to the floor. Then she felt the house shake, heard the crash of someone kicking in the front door.

Without hesitation, her brother picked up the syringe and released the leather straps. Cate watched him drag Liza out onto the fire escape. Instinctively, Cate started to wipe the tears off her face, then decided against it. Instead, she tore open the top part of her blouse.

CHAPTER SIXTY-SEVEN

Lipsky held the gun above his head with both hands. Eli followed the detective into the room and was surprised that the only person there was the female medical student who had received publicity for founding the free clinic. He remembered meeting her in the emergency room.

"Cate?"

Lipsky scanned the room and saw the open door at the fire escape. Cate was on her knees, sobbing.

Eli knelt beside her. She appeared physically unharmed but emotionally distraught.

"He was going to kill us," she said. "He was going to kill both of us."

Finding no one on the fire escape, Lipsky reentered the room, his gun lowered at his side.

Eli lifted Cate's chin with his hand. "Where's Liza?"

Cate pointed to the study's back door. "He dragged her out there."

"Who the hell is *he*?" Lipsky asked.

Cate shook her head, still sobbing.

They heard a car squeal away. Lipsky ran to the window to see the taillights of a black Trans Am.

CHAPTER SIXTY-EIGHT

Lipsky raced to his car and called in an APB on a black Trans Am headed in the direction of the medical center.

Eli stayed with Cate for another few minutes though he wanted to follow Lipsky, fearing that the detective might leave without him. But he felt obligated to console Cate. He asked, again, who had done this to her. But she just pulled her torn blouse together at her throat and rocked back and forth in a state of traumatic shock.

Eli glanced around the room at the robotic surgical instruments and the actual operating table in the center. The instrument table was in disarray, the operating table askew, with the top leather strap folded back but the bottom strap locked. When he saw the scalpel on the floor, Eli knew the Organist had captured his final victim. And just as Salyer predicted, he had chosen a female for dissection.

Cate tried to talk. Eli leaned closer to hear.

"Please go—and find Dr. French."

That was the release Eli needed. At the door, he heard Cate again. She was standing now and had stopped crying.

"What Cate?"

She hesitated a moment, then said, "You have to hurry. Dr. French said she was pregnant."

Lipsky pulled away from the curb. Eli ran in front of the car's headlights to stop him. Lipsky slammed on the brakes and Eli jumped in the front.

"Wondered if you were coming." Lipsky made a U-turn in the street.

"I know what he's doing," Eli said, between breaths.

"He being the Organist, I presume?"

"French is pregnant."

Lipsky laughed. "Thought you doctors knew about contraception."

"It's not mine, Lipsky. Will you shut up and listen."

"All ears."

"The final book is the reproductive system, the female organs, the uterus."

Lipsky passed a car in the left lane.

"The title page of Vesalius's work shows a public dissection on a female cadaver. Some scholars believe the woman in the illustration had been accused of a crime and sentenced to death. To avoid this penalty, she claimed she was pregnant."

"And your point is?"

"After the hanging, with a crowd of public officials and townspeople to provide evidence for or against her claim, Vesalius dissected her uterus."

Lipsky shrugged. "You're telling me—"

"Yes, he's going to recreate the scene—with Liza as his subject."

"To cut out her uterus?"

"The Organist is after his last organ," Eli said.

"This is some freaky shit." Lispky shook his head. "French is probably already dead."

"I don't think so, Lipsky. The patient in the operation six months ago was alive when her uterus was removed."

"Come again?"

"I'm talking about the first patient of Dr. French who died. So far, he's killed everyone who was a part of that operation, except Liza. This is his final revenge."

"So why didn't he already kill her?"

"He will—but he wants her to suffer like he thinks the first patient did before she died."

"He's going to remove her uterus while French is still alive?"

"Yes," Eli said. "Question is—where's he taking her?"

CHAPTER SIXTY-NINE

Cate's brother dragged Liza up a hill covered in dead grass. This time, she screamed from pain, not fear, as her hip scraped the corner of a flat tombstone. He stopped and slapped her in the face. The blow numbed her so she merely moaned when he grabbed her hair and kept pulling her up the hill.

When they reached the top, the Organist smiled at what he saw. The men from Cate's clinic had come through for him. *They may be homeless, he thought, but they're damn reliable. Especially when they get a fifth of whiskey and some cash.*

Altogether, he counted seven men sitting on the concrete stage beneath the cemetery's Corinthian columns. He had hoped for ten, but this would do. Foster had brought the dog. It pulled against its leash and tried to greet the others.

"Good," the Organist said. *At least it's close to the scene Vesalius created.* There was no monkey, as in the original illustration, but at least the dog was among the audience, an insult to Galen and his canine-based anatomical knowledge. He thought of his mother's painting of the sixteenth-century public anatomy and how he was recreating the scene in real life.

She would be so proud of me.

If she was still alive.

Sadness turned to rage, a familiar, comforting feeling.

He knelt beside Liza, grabbed her shoulder-length hair and yanked it back. "You're the last one. All the others are dead. They will never, ever, kill another patient. No one else will have to lose a mother, like Cate and I did." He twisted her head toward him. "Do you hear me? I have saved the world from those incompetent nurses and doctors. Now, it's your turn."

Liza struggled against him. "Don't kill my baby."

He released her hair, as though her pregnancy made her toxic.

"You're lying, bitch. There is no baby. But we shall soon see. Like the great anatomist before me, I will cut your womb and see for myself."

He gently rocked Liza's head back to show her the colonnaded stage and the men who waited.

"That's where you die."

CHAPTER SEVENTY

The call came through on Lipsky's radio. He had notified the entire Memphis police force to be on the lookout for a black Trans Am. It didn't take long. A car fitting that description was seen heading south on Dudley Street at a high rate of speed. Problem was the officer who spotted the car was unable to keep up.

Lipsky responded to the call. "Where did they lose him?"

"Last seen at the corner of Dudley and Crump," the dispatcher said.

Dudley and Crump. Eli knew this area well. South side of town. Warehouses. Somewhat deserted. Eli and Henry traveled south on Dudley Street once a year, in August, with a single peach-colored rose, their mother's favorite.

Before Lipsky answered the police dispatch, Eli stopped him. "I know where he's going."

CHAPTER SEVENTY-ONE

Liza began to fight him, her fingernails scrapping five lines of flesh from the side of his neck. The Organist hit her hard in the face and she fell against the concrete platform. From his pocket he removed the syringe of drugs Cate had stolen from her clinic. He stabbed it into Liza's thigh and depressed the plunger, delivering the full load of strong sedative. She continued to kick at him for a couple of minutes. He held her down until the horse-dose of medicine kicked in, and she became flaccid and unconscious.

The Organist had told the men from Cate's clinic they were getting paid to be in a movie scene. So-called extras. He needed them for thirty minutes, no longer. He would then give each of them cash and enough liquor for a week—or at least a night. He had given Foster a cell phone so he could communicate with the men before he arrived. Foster answered after the first ring.

"Tell them to stand by the columns and keep their places."

A full moon reflected off the Corinthian columns and white cement steps. It cast a pleasant light. Even so, the Organist had given Joey the Flicker a two-million-candle-watt lamp, which sat at the edge of the platform and lit the place like a real movie set.

With Liza draped across his arms, he carried her up the steps to the stage. The men kept their places and watched as he laid Liza on the hard stone floor. He removed a black mask from his pocket and pulled it on his head like a cap. The dog started barking and yanked at its leash, which Foster had secured around one of the columns. The Organist adjusted the lights so that Liza was fully illuminated.

He had given Foster a laptop computer and instructed him to bring it. The Organist located the computer off to the side of the stage and connected the camera cable to it. He typed the web address for SurgCast and its home page appeared. He lifted the shoulder-mounted camera up to Foster's shoulder and made sure he had proper control of it. Then the Organist turned on the camera and manipulated it on Foster's shoulder toward Liza. A quick glance at the laptop screen thrilled him.

Liza's supine body was being broadcast live on the Internet.

CHAPTER SEVENTY-TWO

Eli and Lipsky found the black Trans-Am parked outside the grounds of Elmwood Cemetery, partially hidden behind a group of tall shrubs. Lipsky pulled to a stop behind the sports car and cut the engine.

He had asked for backup and specified no lights, no sirens. So far, no backup at all.

"What's he doing," Lipsky wondered. "Burying her alive?"

If they could trap the killer in the cemetery, they had him. If he got spooked and ran, they might never find him—or Liza. Lipsky and Eli got out of the car, careful not to slam the door.

"He won't take the time to bury her," Eli answered. "He wants to torture her by cutting out her uterus."

"Why a cemetery?" Lipsky asked. "Better yet, why this cemetery?"

"The dissection must be carried out in a public place," Eli whispered. "That was the Vesalius method. The Organist will follow it."

Just outside the stone wall that surrounded the cemetery, they crossed the arching bridge and entered the grounds. Eli thought of the many times he had been here to visit his mother's grave. He never imagined he would come to Elmwood on the trail of a killer.

"Spent a lot of time in cemeteries when I was young," Lipsky said, louder than Eli would have liked.

"Funerals?"

"No, graveyards make a great place to hide when you're running from the police. No one wants to go in them at night."

"And here we are," Eli said.

"Here we are."

They stopped at the end of the bridge. The only sound was the hum of traffic on Interstate 240. Light from a full moon reflected off tomb-stones that dotted the landscape before them. No sign of the Organist or Liza.

"Why Elmwood?" Lipsky asked, this time in a softer, more reverent tone.

Eli began to move quickly along the stone path. "To recreate the scene from Vesalius's title page, he needs five Corinthian columns stand-ing in a semicircle as a backdrop."

"Don't tell me," Lipsky said. "He can find that here."

Eli kept moving. "Follow me."

CHAPTER SEVENTY-THREE

The Organist unbuttoned Liza's blouse.

With her chest bare, Joey the Flicker let out a primal, "Yeah!"

The man continued to undress her.

"Let's see it all," one of the men said, followed by a round of muffled laughter.

The Meatman wasn't laughing. "This ain't right," he said and walked away. "Y'all can have it."

The six men from the clinic who remained stopped laughing. They considered the Meatman their unspoken moral leader, if they had one.

Liza was completely unclothed now and the men stared in silence. The Organist made Foster stand with the camera below Liza's feet so that the image broadcast on the Internet would show him at Liza's side with the motley cast of spectators scattered among the columns behind him. He checked the image on the computer. It was frightfully similar to Vesalius's immortalized scene.

"Perfect."

He pulled the black mask over his face.

Foster asked him what the mask was for, but he received no answer.

Like a symphony conductor, the Organist raised his arms, held them steady, and said, "I need all of you to watch me but don't move from your positions. We're broadcasting live."

From his pocket, he removed a slender leather case and opened it to reveal a scalpel. The spotlight reflected off stainless steel. He admired the surgical tool, held it to the light.

"What do you mean, broadcasting live?" Joey the Flicker asked.

The Organist turned quickly, and Joey cowered near his column.

"I need you to shut up or none of you gets any money."

"Who cares about the money," another extra said. "Just give us the booze."

The Organist sprang toward the man's throat with the scalpel, grabbing him and accidentally knocking Joey into one of the columns. An overlay stone above the column shifted and cracked as though the whole structure might crumble.

Foster stepped forward to help Joey, but the Organist flashed his scalpel and Foster retreated back to his position.

The Organist returned to Liza's right side. He knelt over her, placed the scalpel against the skin of her abdomen, and sliced.

CHAPTER SEVENTY-FOUR

Bright red blood squirted from the fresh incision on Liza's abdomen. The pain cut through even the drugs the Organist had injected. Liza moaned and lashed about on her concrete bed.

The Organist seemed surprised by the sudden flow of blood; all of the other victims had been dead at the time of his cutting. He jabbed one hand into the wound and another against Liza's throat to hold her down.

"Hey, that's real blood," Joey the Flicker said.

The dog lunged against its leash, knocking pebbles loose from the overlay stones with each pull.

Foster left his position. "What the hell are you doing to her?"

The men closed in for a better look. Liza choked and gagged from the grip of the Organist's hand.

"This is all part of the movie," the Organist said. "Get back."

"No, you get back," Foster said.

The men surrounded the Organist.

"This is bullshit."

Rather than leave the scene, the Meatman had hidden behind one of the columns. "Yeah," he said. "Let her go." He grabbed the Organist's shirt and yanked him back. Liza gasped for breath as all six men descended on him, kicking and stomping his body and head.

CHAPTER SEVENTY-FIVE

From a distance Eli could see the lights, as on a movie set. Lipsky trailed him by a few steps as they passed an upright mausoleum. The Corinthian columns came into full view.

"What the hell?" Lipsky said.

Thunder rumbled to the west, followed by a flash of lightning. Neither man noticed.

Eli was stunned by the ingeniousness of it. The Organist had recreated all the key features of Vesalius's title page. The outdoor setting, a background of Corinthian columns, the spectators. His eyes accommodated to the bright light and he saw the dog. Then he saw Liza.

Eli heard Lipsky engage the chamber of his 9-mm Glock. They moved toward the scene, carefully at first. About twenty yards away, they saw the men positioned behind the masked Organist close in around him.

Eli saw the blood on Liza's abdomen. He and Lipsky broke into a sprint, dodging low-lying tombstones.

Before they could reach the platform, the first blow hit the Organist, a single kick to the head. Then another blow, and another, until the overpowering circle of men covered him.

CHAPTER SEVENTY-SIX

"Step away. Now!"

Gun drawn, Lipsky stopped at the edge of the platform.

Liza was bleeding profusely from her abdominal wound. At her side, Eli grabbed her torn blouse and used it to both cover her and stanch the hemorrhage. He held pressure on the wound with his injured hand and wiped blood away with his good hand, relieved to find that the Organist's knife had not penetrated deeply into the abdominal cavity. Her face was bruised, a laceration split her left eyebrow, but her short, raspy breaths gave evidence that she was alive.

The group of men followed Lipsky's order and retreated, their hands raised instinctively. Foster, who up until now had been too shocked to stop filming, dropped the camera and stood there, paralyzed.

Lipsky moved in with his gun pointed at the Organist, who had curled on his side in an attempt to hide his face from the blows. Lipsky punched numbers into his cell phone while he watched the assailant for a few seconds. He jabbed his hip with the tip of his shoe.

Nothing.

"Where's our damn backup?" Lipsky yelled into the phone. "Center of Elmwood Cemetery. And send an ambulance."

Lipsky rolled the Organist's face to him. Blood ran from the man's mouth and his nose. His right ear was mangled, a chunk of cartilage missing.

"Doc, come here a second."

Though the night air was humid, Liza was shivering. She was coming to and trying to open the one eye that wasn't swollen shut. The cloth Eli had placed on her abdomen was soaked but the flow of blood had stopped. He became aware of his shirt plastered to his back, but not from sweat. A steady rain had begun to fall, and he hadn't noticed it.

Lipsky, still bent over the Organist, called to Eli again. Of the men who'd attacked the Organist, only Foster and the Meatman remained. They took a collective step back when Eli stood and walked past them. Joey and the others had fled the scene.

"See if he's alive," Lipsky said, his gun still aimed at the man's head.

Eli knelt and placed two fingers against the Organist's neck. Blood coursed in a thick line down his shoulder and over a prominent tattoo. The artwork was amateurish, and he had not recognized the design the first time he had seen the tattoo. But they were clear now—three weasels, just like in the Vesalian coat of arms.

A police car topped the hill, sirens wailing and headlights flashing through sheets of rain.

"He's alive," Eli said.

Lipsky keyed his phone again. "Make that two ambulances to Elmwood Cemetery." Then to Eli, "Bet paramedics don't get called here very often."

Foster laughed nervously at the detective's joke. He'd inched closer to Liza. Lipsky motioned with his gun for him to step back.

Eli returned to Liza's side. She was trying to talk but her lips were too swollen. He heard static on Lipsky's radio. A clear voice said, "Two ambulances on the way."

CHAPTER SEVENTY-SEVEN

The rain lasted all night. Fresh water droplets now hung from blades of grass and reflected in the morning sun. A mist hovered in the air, slowly reviving a parched earth. Eli imagined the brown grass showing a hint of green.

He drove along Walnut Grove Road, having taken a brief detour through a pleasant residential neighborhood. On the radio, Smokey Robinson sang about the tears of a clown. The song seemed fitting with what he saw from the overnight shower.

The rain had knocked the heat down and the day was actually agreeable. At a four-way stop, Eli waited for an elderly couple to pass in front of him. The man held on to his wife and nodded to Eli in appreciation.

Across the street, three children splashed in water caught by a drainage ditch. What should have been an ordinary sight seemed in every way marvelous. He watched the kids in their newfound pool until the car behind him honked.

A few minutes later, Eli entered Gates Memorial Hospital. He walked through the double glass doors not as hospital faculty, not even as a physician sneaking in to see a patient he had no privileges to treat. He arrived early the first morning after the showdown in Elmwood Cemetery to visit an injured colleague.

Liza French had been taken directly from the cemetery to the operating room, not the usual direction of patient flow. Her abdominal wound was repaired with a relatively simple procedure. Although she lost almost a liter of blood, her laceration did not enter the abdominal cavity. She was expected to make a full physical recovery. Her mental recovery remained in question. She was traumatized by the threat to her life and she did not yet know that portions of the assault had been shown live on a webcast.

Eli found her hospital room on the trauma unit. Two surgery residents bent over her. A medical student ripped open packages of sterile gauze, and tore strips of tape as the young doctors removed Liza's old blood-stained dressing and redressed her abdominal wound. Liza winced from the tape removal. She saw Eli standing in the doorway and stared at him through the pain. The residents recognized him. Like military recruits in the sudden presence of a superior officer, they stopped their procedure.

"Please, continue," Eli said.

The residents went back to work, but the medical student remained distracted. The resident snatched the roll of tape from her hand.

Eli turned to leave. There was nothing that he had to say that couldn't wait until later, if ever. More importantly, he had a meeting to attend this morning—one he hoped would bring closure to the disorder of the last few days. He looked at Liza. Her eyes were wet as she mouthed, "Thank you."

In the lobby, Eli passed small groups of visitors waiting for news of their family members still in the operating room. They held to cups of coffee and open newspapers to pass the time. Even though his stay was brief, Eli felt a sense of relief to be leaving the hospital. He slowed his pace for a young man in a wheelchair trying to exit through the same doors. The boy tried to roll the wheelchair with one hand while pulling an IV pole with the other. Eli noticed a chest tube snaking out the back of his hospital gown to a fluid container hanging on the pole.

Eli stopped as the recognition took hold, flashes of the boy's gunshot wound to his heart, the chaotic scene in the small emergency room in Whitehaven, and Eli's crazy trip to Gates Memorial straddling the boy's chest to keep him from bleeding to death.

The kid was going to make it. He would be showing his scars and boasting to his buddies in a few days.

Eli lifted the IV pole across the carpeted door mat. "You leaving?"

The boy looked back at Eli but did not recognize him. Just another adult getting in his way.

"Need some fresh air, dude."

Just outside the door, the boy grabbed the IV pole from Eli and said, "Thanks," so Eli would leave him alone.

Before entering the parking garage, Eli looked back at the boy. He was hunched forward with cupped hands, lighting a cigarette.

CHAPTER SEVENTY-EIGHT

The driver's license in his wallet identified him as Nathaniel Franklin Canavan.

Nathan Canavan.

The Organist.

While Liza French lay in a heavily guarded room at Gates Memorial Hospital, her face and lips too swollen to talk, Basetti dug into the Canavan family history. Lipsky sent him on this mission while the detective finished up his paperwork on the whole messy incident.

Basetti was quite savvy with this freelance investigation. A little Internet research, a few targeted phone calls to relatives and friends of the Canavan family brought forth some valuable information. In the parking lot of Gates Memorial, Eli found the crime technician sitting in his car and staring at the screen of his cell phone. Basetti spilled all he knew.

Nathan's mother had been a nurse and aspiring artist who received recognition among the local colony of painters, sculptors, and other creative types. His dad had left the family when Nathan was a young boy. His overachieving, could-do-no-wrong sister, Cate, was a fourth-year medical student on the way to an OB-GYN residency, ready to conquer the world. That left Nathan as the one who never quite got it all together.

He was rejected by every medical school to which he applied, his prior transgressions, which included a hit-and-run and a vaguely described assault and battery, proved too great a barrier. To please his mother, he managed to get accepted as an anatomist's assistant, processing bodies for dissection at the medical school. The work seemed to fit him. Though he pissed off the living, the dead didn't seem to mind.

And he was surrounded by the real subjects of his mother's art. The anatomy professor who hired him quickly noticed his familiarity with anatomical structures, the result of hours spent reading his mother's anatomy texts and watching her sketch anatomical subjects.

He began assisting the new medical students with their dissections. He told his mother that although he couldn't get into medical school, he could teach those who did. She was most proud.

But then, fitting to his history, Nathan became overzealous in his job, sneaking into the anatomy lab at night, performing the dissections himself, arranging the bodies in poses to mimic his mother's art. At first his antics were considered a prank by the medical students, a way to cope with the stress of the discipline of anatomy, until the real perpetrator was discovered. Not only was Nathan fired, but a desecrating-the-dead lawsuit was filed against him by the medical school and the families of the deceased. Once again he disappointed his mother, this time in shame.

An anatomy expert from Ole Miss named Salyer was called in and testified in the trial. Ultimately, the prosecution lacked enough evidence to link Nathaniel Canavan to the scene. The suit was dismissed. He bounced around doing various jobs, always supporting his sister, the success of the family. His most recent employment was as a support technician at Renaissance Robotics. His time for recognition would come. And his skills in anatomical dissection would not go to waste. While he couldn't make his mother proud while she was alive, he would prove his worth by exacting revenge for her death.

CHAPTER SEVENTY-NINE

When Eli pulled into the parking lot of the Poplar Avenue Free Clinic, a short line had already formed outside. The front door was closed and it appeared the clinic had not yet opened.

Lipsky had already updated Eli on the status of the assault victim, Cate Canavan. The previous night, Cate had been taken to the emergency room, examined, and found to be uninjured, at least physically. Before releasing her, the police took her statement. She told the police she had never before seen the man who had assaulted her and Liza. She told them she had gone to Dr. French's house to ask for a letter of recommendation in support of her residency application. A man broke into the house and assaulted her and Dr. French. Cate said the man would have killed her had Dr. Branch and the police detective not arrived when they did.

The four men who waited in line for the clinic to open appeared content in the cool morning. Two of them sat crossed-legged on the pavement. Eli joined them, standing at the back of the line. They regarded him with suspicion at first. He asked if they had seen Mr. Norman Felts. They didn't know who this was until he said the name Tobboganhead.

They hadn't seen him. Two more patients arrived and stood behind Eli. He waited a few more minutes and the door of the clinic opened.

Cate stood in the doorway wearing a white coat. Her hair was pulled back, very professional. He understood why the clinic was so popular. The patients looked to Cate as their doctor. The free clinic made a direct impact on the homeless and impoverished. She was doing a good thing.

By the sudden change in Cate's expression, he knew that his presence alarmed her. She approached the line of patients.

"Dr. Branch, I'm so glad you could make it."

Upon hearing that he was a doctor, those in front of Eli turned to face him.

Cate motioned to the door. "Please come in."

CHAPTER EIGHTY

Eli followed Cate inside the clinic.

She shut the door behind them.

"How are you?" Eli asked.

Tears welled in her eyes. She collapsed into a straight-backed chair, hands covering her face.

Eli had a lot of questions for Cate. He decided to let her talk.

"I had to come to the clinic today," she said, removing her hands from her eyes. She kept them cupped over her mouth. "It's the only thing that could get my mind off last night."

Eli nodded. "When I'm in the operating room, that's all there is. Just me and the patient, everything else doesn't matter."

Cate seemed to wait for more words of encouragement from Eli—anything, he guessed, that moved away from the subject of the previous evening.

"What happened last night?"

Cate stood and walked to the window. She was quiet for a moment, watching as more patients walked across the parking lot. "Dr. French has been a good friend to me. More than a friend, really. She's a role model. The reason I chose OB/GYN."

Even though Lipsky had read Cate's police statement to Eli, he wanted to hear it for himself. "Why were you at her house last night?"

"She's writing a letter of recommendation for my fellowship. Dr. French wanted to discuss it with me."

Eli knew this was odd. A letter of recommendation would be discussed in an academic office during regular hours. Not at a faculty member's home at night. He planned to confront her about the intruder. Cate beat him to it.

"That man broke into her house. We didn't hear him coming. He just appeared."

The line outside was getting longer. The patients saw Dr. Cate in the window and started tapping the pane, wanting to come in. When Cate went to the door and explained to the patients that they'd have to wait a few more minutes, Eli went into the break room and unlocked the back door.

Cate returned and continued her story. "I thought it was a joke at first. Dr. French didn't seem alarmed, like maybe she knew him. He started touching her. And she let him do it. Maybe she was scared, I don't know, but I just wanted to get out of there. That's when I saw the gun."

Cate was remarkably calm as she said this, a blank stare past Eli.

He had seen this look on assault and abuse victims in the emergency room. The icy stare as they told of the violence against them.

"He pointed the gun at me and told me to strap Dr. French to the table." Cate described how she'd tried to fight him but he hit her, kept hitting her. "Then, he made us—"

A pulsing screech from Cate's beeper made her jump and stop mid-sentence. She checked the number.

So far, Eli thought, everything checked out. The details were the same as in her statement to the police. Eli wondered what she would have said next, without the interruption.

"I'm sorry, Dr. Branch. I really need to answer this and then see my patients."

She reached for the clinic phone, but Eli pulled out a cell, flipped it open, and presented it to her.

"Please, use this one."

She took the phone, ready to enter the number from the pager, but came face-to-face with her picture on the small screen. It was a little out of focus, the brown clinic building in the background, her in a white coat as the doctor in charge.

Cate looked at Eli, her expression showing that she remembered the picture being taken. Against her steady protest, Mr. Felts—Tobbaganhead—had insisted on it, said he had a new picture phone he wanted to try out. But she wasn't the only person in the photo. It was one of the few days her brother had been at the clinic with her. In the small picture, he was there, behind her, a side shot in profile, but unmistakable.

Cate attempted a smile, as though Dr. Branch might not know of this detail.

Eli wasn't smiling. "This man tried to kill Dr. Liza French. The newspapers call him the Organist. He's your brother, Cate."

Cate looked again at the photo captured on the cell phone. "Our father left us when I was seven. Nathan was a few years older. I barely remember the man, just that he was mean to our mother. She had to work two jobs. Put us in the best schools. Nathan was always smarter than me. Always. But he had a chip on his shoulder, bitter that our father abandoned us. He stayed in trouble, spent six months at a juvenile detention center."

Cate told Eli how her brother had too many incidents from his past for acceptance into medical school. How their mother was disappointed, Nathan felt rejected, and they didn't speak to each other for years.

Patients were knocking on the door now. Gentle taps at first that grew louder. Faces filled the window. The patients were restless and called her name, not understanding why Dr. Cate was ignoring them.

"Just before Mom's operation, she and Nathan came back together. The wounds healed. We were a family again."

Cate looked up at Eli.

"Then she died. In the operating room. Under Dr. French's care."

The patients were shouting now, asking Dr. Cate what she was doing with that new doctor.

"After the shock of it, we both felt incredibly guilty. My brother for the way he detached himself from our mother during the last years of her life. Me, for not being there. I was away on a senior externship at UNC in Chapel Hill. I wanted to fly back for her operation, but I was afraid that leaving during the rotation would affect my grade." Cate lowered her head. "It seems so stupid now.

"Dr. French didn't even come out to tell Nathan our mother had died during the operation. She ran off to meet with her lawyer, trying to save her own butt. One of the nurses came out to tell him. By then he already knew."

Eli had remained quiet, until now, when he felt obligated to say something.

"He already knew?"

"My mother's operation was webcast over the Internet. Some high school kid had a laptop in the waiting room. He was waiting on a family member in surgery, logged onto the Gates Memorial website, and saw the advertisement for the operation. Started watching it. Freaked out when he saw the blood. Everyone ran over to see. That's how my brother found out."

Revenge deaths, Eli thought. The Organist wanted revenge, not only against Liza, but the whole operating room team. Anesthesia, nurses, surgery resident. He killed all of them, except Liza.

Cate became very quiet. Eli wanted her to keep talking.

"My mother died six years ago," he said. "She had cancer. But that didn't kill her. It was the treatment, the chemotherapy." Eli hesitated, measuring his words. "Her doctors miscalculated the dose. Gave her ten times the normal amount. The membranes in her mouth and GI tract peeled off. She died in a pool of spit and blood."

Eli stopped. He made sure Cate was listening to him. She was, intently.

"The doctors never told me about the mistake. They covered it up instead. Two weeks after her funeral, a pharmacist came forward. I knew medical errors occurred. But the fact they lied about it, I . . . I was so mad I wanted to kill them. I filed a lawsuit. But I was a surgery resident then. I had no money, and taking time off from my surgery residency to pursue the lawsuit was not an option. So at the last minute, I withdrew the suit."

While Eli told this, Cate inched closer and closer to him until they stood only a couple of feet apart. "I'm sorry," she said.

Eli chose this moment to strike. "You were there during the most recent operation, when the death occurred."

Cate wasn't expecting this. She took a step back.

"Quite a coincidence, isn't it?" Eli said.

Another step back.

"Or is it?" Eli followed her retreat. "After your mother's death, you went to Dr. French. Became her protégé. Gained her trust. She even mentioned that you could be her partner, after your training. You set it up, made sure you could be there for the next operation after her period of probation was over. That operation was webcast, live, just like your mother's operation. That was *your* revenge, Cate. To shatter the career of Liza French by another operative death."

Cate's chin began to quiver. She clenched her jaw.

"Dr. French taught you about the robotic equipment. You knew which part of the procedure carried the most risk. You could make it appear that it was the robot's fault."

Cate shook her head.

Eli went on.

"During the final moments of the operation there was a distraction. A phone call from a prospective patient's husband. It was all captured in the transcript. The caller was your brother, Cate. No one was watching when you were supposed to remove the instruments, when instead you jammed the trocar into the patient's aorta and killed her."

Cate stared at the picture on the phone.

"But it didn't stop there, did it, Cate? Your brother couldn't stop until every member of the team from your mother's operation was dead."

Eli took the phone from her. He held the screen to her face, visual evidence of Cate's connection to the Organist, her brother.

"And then you both went after Liza."

Cate began to plead. "You know what it's like, Dr. Branch, to have someone you love taken away by doctors who don't even care. It has to stop." She looked again at the phone. "We had to stop it."

Eli waited. He waited for her to realize what she was saying. That killing these five people was somehow justified.

But Cate was defiant.

She pointed at the cell phone. "So what if we're both in this picture, that doesn't mean a damn thing. And besides, you could never prove that I caused the patient's death."

With that statement, Eli knew they had enough evidence. He turned toward the back of the clinic. In the doorway of the break room, Lipsky appeared.

"It proves quite a lot, Ms. Canavan," Lipsky said. The detective walked slowly but purposefully toward her.

Cate stood and announced that she must start seeing her patients. She marched through the front door into those waiting to see her. But she didn't stop. She ripped off her white coat, slung it to the ground, and took off in a dead run across the pavement.

Through a window in the free clinic, Eli and Lipsky saw flashes of sunlight reflected off glass as two police cars lurched forward and stopped Cate at the edge of the parking lot.

CHAPTER EIGHTY-ONE

The police wanted to close the clinic. All the patients had watched as Cate was escorted to the back of a squad car and driven away. But rather than leave, the patients kept their place in line. They knew another doctor waited for them inside.

Lipsky remained at the clinic, said he needed to search the place for evidence.

"Evidence?" Eli said. "What more evidence do you need?"

A second officer stayed behind as well. He looked through drawers and cabinets.

"You never know," Lipsky said. "Anything we find might be important."

Eli watched them. The clinic was so sparsely furnished there weren't many places to hide evidence if you wanted to.

"We have the killer," Eli told Lipsky. "He's in the hospital. He will probably live, but he's not going anywhere. And we have Cate's confession. She was there during the second operating room death, the only member of the operative team, other than French, who survived. She knew all the team members and knew enough about their personal lives so her brother could hunt them down."

The officer found a stethoscope in one of the drawers and was playing doctor, with the prongs in his ears, listening to his own heart.

"Maybe she didn't think it would go this far," Eli said. "Maybe she even tried to stop her brother. Who knows? But five people are dead. Cate confessed the motive—revenge for her mother's death. And we've apprehended both individuals responsible."

Eli waited until Lipsky stopped rummaging through papers and looked at him. "It's over, Lipsky."

The detective returned to the drawer, removed a tangled blood pressure cuff, replaced it. "Maybe it is, maybe it isn't," he said. "We're still going to search the place. So lock the doors and tell those hobos out there to go home."

Through the window, Eli counted eleven people, including a woman who had just arrived and stood at the end of the line. She was holding a baby.

"Search all you want," Eli said. "But these people have been waiting and deserve to be seen. I'm not closing the clinic."

Lipsky and the officer continued their search.

After the night rain's brief respite from the heat, a full sun returned and bore down hard on the people outside the clinic. The newcomer stepped away from the line and Eli could see her more clearly. She was an older than average white woman who carried a black baby.

The woman appeared to be talking nonstop. A man whom Eli recognized immediately stood near them. Tobogganhead reached over to shield the baby's eyes and the woman slapped his hand.

Eli opened the door and motioned for the woman to bring the baby inside. He expected complaints from those at the front of the line, but they were glad to see the clinic open. They made way for the woman, but she yelled at them anyway.

"Get away from my baby, you liquor breaths."

Tobogganhead followed behind. When he saw Eli, a big smile lit up his face.

"Dr. Branch. So good to see you."

Eli shook his hand. "Mr. Felts."

"Norman!" the woman snapped. "I'm talking with the doctor."

Tobagganhead rolled his eyes.

Eli had forgotten his first name. Norman. And they seemed to be a couple. Speaking of odd.

"My baby's sick," the woman said. "Been vomiting all night."

"Come in, please." Eli closed the door behind them. It had been over ten years since he'd treated a newborn. But he was all they had.

"I try to give him milk but he spits it back at me."

Tobagganhead tried to add to the story, but she stopped him each time.

"How old is your baby?" Eli asked.

"About one week," the woman said. Then, for clarification. "He's not our birth baby. We adopted."

"Oh?" Eli said. "I would have never guessed."

They made quite the adoptive parents. The mother with an obvious psychiatric problem. And Norman Felts, the father, with who knows what kind of animal living on his head under his toboggan. How in the world had they become the guardians of this child?

"His birth mother abandoned him," the woman said. "You know, teenage drug addict."

"Yeah, I know." Eli found a thermometer to take the baby's temperature. "How did you adopt so quickly?" he asked.

Tobogganhead tried to answer. "We didn't really adopt, we—"

But the woman cut him off again. "Hush. Let me tell it." She kissed the baby on top of the head, bounced him up and down even though he was already content. Then she placed the infant on a small examining table, reached up, and repositioned the overhead light.

"Mary's a nurse here at the clinic," Tobogganhead said.

Eli tried to hide his surprise. "Oh, really."

"It's all official," Mary said. "The doctor said we could keep it."

Eli held the thermometer steady under the infant's arm. "The doctor?"

"After the drug addict girl delivered, Dr. Canavan and I were taking her home with the baby when she decided she didn't want it. Handed the child to me in the parking lot."

She looked at Tobogganhead and smiled, all of a sudden the loving couple.

"The drug addict mother didn't have any parents. She was a runaway. So we saved this little baby's life. Dr. Canavan said as long as we came to the free clinic for the baby's check-ups and didn't go to any other hospital, we could keep him."

"She did, did she?" The story was so hard to believe that somehow it all made sense. Eli removed the thermometer. The baby's temp was perfectly normal. He was smiling and cooing.

Eli noticed a shriveled nubbin of tissue at the outside tip of the baby's foot. Gently, he flicked the tissue with his finger and watched as it fell off, rolled to the edge of the table, and landed on the floor. The "mother" stepped back and put her hand over her mouth. Eli looked at Tobogganhead. He was grinning at the sight of the mini-amputation procedure. Other than the sixth toe, their child was the healthiest baby Eli had ever seen.

"Wait right here," Eli said and went to the break room.

The officer was searching a cabinet under the sink. Lipsky was reading a memo posted on the wall. It was from the dean of the medical school and addressed to Cate Canavan, medical student director of the free clinic. "Doc. You know all these patients can come here and get free medical care. Completely free. Just like that."

Eli looked through the medical supply closet, removed a round canister with a plastic lid.

"Yeah, I know."

"What you got there?"

Lipsky was obviously bored with his unnecessary search. Eli held up the canister. "Baby formula. Want some?"

"Nah. Ate half a dozen donuts on the way over."

Eli gave the container of formula to Tobogganhead and explained to the mother that baby formula would be tolerated better than cow's milk. She was most grateful.

For the first time in weeks, he felt like a doctor.

Once they had the baby formula and a little reassurance that they were good parents, Tobogganhead and the woman were ready to leave with their baby. But first, Tobogganhead told Eli that after the baby settled down, he would come back to the clinic in a few days and let the doctor fix the sore on his head.

From the break room, Lipsky watched them leave. "What was wrong with that baby?"

"Nothing, really," Eli told him. "New parents."

Lipsky nodded as if he understood. "Say, Doc," Lipsky walked toward Eli, his shoulders pulled back, hands pressed behind him, just above his waist, "while you're at it, my back's been killing me."

Eli opened the clinic door again. A wave of heat rushed in. The typical Memphis summer was back. The rain was over. Not a cloud in sight.

"I'll be glad to take a look at your back," Eli said and pointed. "Just go to the end of the line."

Lipsky returned to the break room. "You doctors, always making people wait."

Outside, an old man sat in a wheelchair, dirty bandages wrapped around both feet.

It wasn't high-tech surgery, Eli thought. Definitely not glamorous. But these people needed a doctor just as much as anyone. And for now, at least, he was that doctor. With undiagnosed illness and late-stage disease, each patient would be a challenge. But the challenge would release his mind from the past days of death that he had been powerless to stop.

To his surprise, Eli noticed a new arrival outside the clinic. A white coat distinguished her from the patients. She leaned beside the man's wheelchair and began unwrapping one of his bandages.

The patients allowed Eli to cut through the line.

Meg looked up at him, kept unwrapping. "So, you're the new clinic doctor now?"

Eli nodded. "Keeps me out of trouble."

Meg let the dirty bandage fall to the ground. "Need any help?"

"Think you can handle an actual live patient?"

Meg stuck out her tongue and then removed a package of gauze and a roll of tape from her coat pocket. She rewrapped the man's foot, tore off a piece of tape with her teeth, and winked at him.

Eli wanted to keep watching her, but Meg rolled the man's wheelchair to him. "Take him inside and see if you can do as well with the other foot."

Pushing the wheelchair, Eli turned to see Meg approach the line and call out, "Who's next?"

ACKNOWLEDGMENTS

I am surrounded by a group of talented individuals at Oceanview Publishing. I thank Mary Adele Bogdon, Frank Troncale, Kylie Fritz, and Susan Hayes. I am grateful for my publicist, Maryglenn McCombs, from day one, and the artisan of covers, George Foster. I extend a special thanks to Bob and Pat Gussin and to Susan Greger for those extra years devoted to publishing.

I cherish Penny Tschantz for her encouragement of my writing life that began during my days at the University of Tennessee. I want to thank Chris Roerden for her insight and I give a hearty thank you to the folks at Davis-Kidd Booksellers.

For their knowledge and assistance with research on Vesalius, I thank Mary Teloh and Jim Thweatt in the History of Medicine Collection of the Eskind Biomedical Library at Vanderbilt University. I especially appreciate the opportunity for a hands-on perusal of a fabulous edition of *De Humani Corporis Fabrica*.

I acknowledge the valuable resource of the following texts in my research and writing on Vesalius: *Andreas Vesalius of Brussels* by Charles D. O'Malley, Berkeley and Los Angeles: University of California Press, 1964; *The Epitome of Andreas Vesalius*, Preface and Introduction by L. R. Lind, Cambridge: The MIT Press, 1949; The Illustrations from *The Works of Andreas Vesalius of Brussels* by J. B. deC. M. Saunders and Charles D. O'Malley, Cleveland and New York: The World Publishing Company, 1993.

I am thankful for my parents, Wilder and Norma Pearson, who gave me my foundation. I appreciate my brother, John, and his family, for preserving and tending the land for the next generation. I thank my wife, Robin, for the opportunity and the inspiration to write, and Will and John for the substance of life.

AUTHOR'S NOTE

In the year 1543, an anatomist from Brussels named Andreas Vesalius published his masterpiece on anatomy, *De Humani Corporis Fabrica*. He was twenty-eight years old. The text challenged the teachings of the ancients, namely Galen, and the anatomical Renaissance began.

The *Fabrica*, written in Latin, is comprised of seven books, each on the detailed anatomy of the seven major human organ systems. Vesalius knew these organs in intimate detail. Unusual for that era, the young anatomist had personally performed the human dissections, often stealing the body from the local gibbet.

The tome is massive and contains over twenty finely wrought, full-page woodcut figures with numerous text illustrations. The original woodcuts were preserved for centuries until they were destroyed by fire in Germany during World War II. In the sixteenth century, Vesalius had the forethought to publish a version with only six books called *The Epitome*, a volume known for its brevity and used by medical students of the day.

Vesalius, an anatomist, surgeon, and philosopher, was appointed court physician to Charles V before moving to Spain as physician to Philip II. In 1564, he took pilgrimage to the Holy Land. Much mystery and speculation surround this departure. One explanation is that during a public anatomy, to the dismay of his audience, he dissected a corpse and found the heart still beating. By taking pilgrimage, he escaped The Inquisition. He died on the Greek island of Zante.

Today, a preserved, first edition copy of *De Humani Corporis Fabrica* is a rarity and is quite valuable. The book is considered the turning point that ushered in the age of modern medicine.

•   •   •

The practice of medicine is at once a fulfilling yet humbling endeavor. The human element in the delivery of medical care is a powerful resource that provides the needed balance to medical sophistication. The addition of robotic-driven techniques to the practice of surgery is a remarkable advance. Many patients have already benefited from this innovation, as will many more.